Born to blossom into an omega, something in Olivia's life went wrong. Instead of having her heats and looking for her own alphas, she is defective. Her body gives her pain, and she wants nothing to do with the thought of a sexual liaison with anyone.

Her sister follows her father's footsteps and keeps her on their property and running the bed and breakfast, which is a boring existence for Olivia until her heat is due and her rule against taking reservations during that time is broken by her greedy sibling. There is an emergency, and they are going to be hosting a guest.

No one said the guest would be an alpha.

What follows is a meeting, a realization, and a rescue that changes not only Olivia's life but that of her pride as well.

Argus is just going to a family wedding rehearsal when he begins hearing the phrase defective omega. He has researched a lot of omegas, and there is no such thing as a defective one. When he realizes that these words are describing the dainty little woman who helped his panthers get settled, he has a quick discussion with his pride mates, and they head off to rescue the omega in question. With any luck, she will choose them. If not, they will have to charm her. Either way, Olivia is theirs.

The characters and events in this book are fictitious. Any similarity to real persons, living or dead, is coincidental and not intended by the author.

No Reservations—Part One
Copyright © 2021 by Viola Grace
ISBN: 978-1-989892-90-9

©Cover art by Angela Waters

Published by Viola Grace

Look for me online at violagrace.com.

No Reservations–Part One
Omega Next Door Book 1

By

Viola Grace

Chapter One

Olly looked at the note on the kitchen counter. "Lara, what the hell is this?"

Her sister came in and said, "Oh, the Henwells called. The hotel for Adra's wedding had a water main break, and every B&B in the area has been contacted."

"Tough. I am not hosting anyone."

Lara chuckled. "Good thing they called me, then. When I told them we were closed for family business, they doubled our rack rates. We only have one guest coming, and he has two pets. I have a list of requirements that he sent on. Raw meat for the animals. He arrives in four hours."

"Well, are you going to shop for them?"

"Of course not. I have to get ready for the party. Call in the order, and it should be here by then."

Olly looked at her. "No. Absolutely not."

"Aw, come on, Olly. You won't even know he is here. He's coming in, going to the party, and staying for the weekend. You will hardly see him."

"Why is he bringing animals?"

"He can't find somewhere to board them. The estate was going to house them, but with the others coming, it isn't considered wise."

Olly muttered, "My heat starts this weekend, sis. There is a reason we were closed. Now you aren't going to be here, and I am going to have to make breakfast for this guy? You are fucking thoughtful."

"Don't pout. The Henwells would have taken him on if they could. They ran out of space."

Olly picked up the phone and called the butcher shop and

ordered the incredible amount of meat that was on the list. Whatever the animals were, they were big.

The delivery would arrive in two hours, and she could turn over the largest room in that time.

Her sister was a smug beta who was technically in charge of the family business. Technically, because Olly did the majority of the work to upkeep the cute and adorable bed and breakfast. "Right. I have to make up the shed, too."

Lara snorted. "Your heat won't start until after he is long gone. You don't need to worry about it."

Olly knew that tone. "You are storing stuff in there, aren't you?"

Lara chuckled. "I have been getting fifty bucks a month for it as a storage shed. It's housing fishing gear from Ander's outfitting company."

"Of course it is. If I need to, I will hide at the main house then."

Lara made a face. "Ew, and get your omega stink on everything? I don't think so."

Olly nodded. "Right. I will figure something else out." Her sister paid for her upkeep, and that was the end of things.

Being stuck as an omega meant she wasn't a person. Not in the true legal sense. Her father had even told folks that he sent her to the Omega Centre, and she came back as a defective, but he had just beaten her every time her pheromones let go until she could hide the signs for everything except two days of her heat. It was not a technique she recommended.

The first surge was about to start, so she quickly got to the building, changed the sheets, fluffed the pillows, and put fresh flowers on the table. It was a guy, and some guys liked flowers.

Olly finished up the room, prepped the keys, and penned a note, leaving it under the keys, just in case he came in late and she wasn't around to show him in. She turned on the exterior lights and went to take care of the rest of the chores around the place. She hauled herself onto the riding mower and started to tidy up the yard and keep her bed and breakfast's picturesque standards. The Victorian home was lovely and took a lot of time to maintain, but she enjoyed it. The ranch house was where her family had lived, and now that her parents were gone, it was where her sister lived. Olly lived in a tiny room off the kitchen in the Victorian.

Working for the family business had been the only thing she was allowed to do. When her omega nature became apparent during her fifteenth year, her family took steps to try and make her appear to be a nice, normal beta . . . with occasional heats that made them lock her in a small space where her scent wouldn't cause them any distress or distaste.

She bit her lip as she finished her two hours of mowing, nodding to the delivery truck as it brought the meat to the back of the B&B. She parked the mower in the shed and walked over to bring the order inside.

Robert waved at her and drove off. She looked at the sections of beef and groaned. She hadn't realized how big they were. Well, waiting wasn't going to get them stored. She hefted the first segment of bone-in meat and walked it to the walk-in fridge. Then, she did it four more times.

When the meat shelf was groaning with the order, she stumbled out and heard the purr of an engine. She looked down and groaned, then peeked out the window, willing Lara to come. No luck.

She pulled on a sweatshirt to absorb a bit of her scent and stayed in the fridge until she heard the bell.

She answered it. Conditioned response. "Good afternoon. You are our emergency guest, I guess."

She came around the corner and was pinned by the brightest green eyes under the slash of dark brows and a sexy mop of midnight hair, decorating caramel skin and delightfully full lips. She caught his scent. "Oohh."

His lips quirked. "Afternoon, Miss. Sorry, I'm early. The roads were better than I thought."

She swallowed when the casual alpha pheromones struck her. She dug her fingers into her palm to stop her reaction and swallowed her whine. "Please, sign the guest register, Mr . . ."

"Denler. Argus Denler."

She nodded, and the name reverberated in her memory. "You are Paul's cousin."

He blinked and smiled. "Yeah. Are you a friend of the family?"

"Um, not really. They are friends with my sister, Lara, though." She smiled brightly.

Argus smiled. "Are these my keys?"

"Yes. The message I got said you have animals?"

"Yes, can I bring them in?"

"Sure. When do they need to be fed?"

"They are nocturnal for the most part, so I can feed them when I am back from the party."

He left, and she waited, expecting large, pampered canines. The two black jaguars that came in at his side were as gorgeous as their owner, and he had a light grip on their leashes.

The two lifted their heads, scenting her, and they pulled him toward her with surprised steps. "Guys. Come on. Don't scare the nice lady."

The large heads scenting her groin and butt were nearly as wide as her hips were and the same weight as an adult beta male.

"Can I pet them?"

Argus blinked in surprise. "Uh, sure."

She dropped her hands near them, she felt the snuffling at her digits, and then, she stroked their heads, and a heavy purr emerged.

Her knees nearly gave way. She clenched and kept her slick from emerging and gave them both light pats. "Pretty. Boys?"

He was looking at her, confused. "Yeah, Romulus and

4

Remus."

"If the party runs long, when should I feed them?"

"Uh, you would do that?"

"Sure. They are well-behaved guys. I think we would get along."

"You have livestock?"

"Yeah, but knowing what these pretty boys are, I will go and mark them, so they won't consider them prey."

He frowned. "How do you know that will work?"

She shrugged. "I am going on instinct, but it's gonna be hard to rub on all the chickens."

He burst out laughing. "Please, tell me you will do that before I leave for the party."

"Oh, definitely not. There is only so much dignity I can lose in a day before it starts to sting."

He chuckled. "Fair enough. They like to sleep during the day, but they will be active at night. Do you have an enclosure for them?"

"I have something, but it won't keep them in. It might give them the idea of where confinement should be, but they have a few sturdy trees to climb. You think that will satisfy them?"

He was looking at her, slightly dazed. "Right. Satisfy them. It should. I will leave you my number. Call me if they get out of hand or anything."

"Sure. Just write it down. I will use it if I have to."

He smiled. "I can just put it in your phone."

"I don't have one. Landline only here." She shrugged helplessly. Lara wouldn't get her a phone. She didn't want her to make friends outside the house.

"Your room is at the top of the stairs. It is a large suite, so there should be room for the boys. You are staying two nights?"

He nodded. "Unless something else needs to be done while I am here. Bailing out the groom might be on the agenda." He laughed, and she saw the sharp teeth that were part of the mark of an alpha. Lara didn't let her near alphas,

5

and if they were all this pretty, she knew why.

He frowned. "If you aren't here and I need something?"

She pointed to her belt. "I have a pager. I come when you call." She clamped her hand over her mouth when she realized what she had said.

His eyes went wide and then heated. "Excellent. Where is the number for that?" He was chuckling.

She pointed to the cards on the desk. "The number for the pager is on there. I am not nocturnal, so it takes me a while to answer after eleven in the evening."

"Fair enough. What is your name?"

"Olly. Uh, Olivia."

"Pleased to meet you, Olivia." He extended his hand in a nice, normal handshake.

She extended her hand and clasped his. He nodded and smiled encouragingly.

"I hope you enjoy your stay."

He grinned and shifted the leash. The large cats left her, and she felt vulnerable when they headed up the stairs. She chuckled as they looked back. "See you later, guys."

Argus turned to her, and there was a smouldering expression.

She blinked, blushed, and bolted. She had chickens to mark.

Chapter Two

Argus stood with his pride members and chatted with other guests. The rehearsal party was going full swing, and when Paul came over, he shook his friend's hand. "Argus, glad you could make it. Where did you end up?"

"A bed and breakfast down the road? Very tidy. Big beds." He chuckled. "The boys are in love with the innkeeper."

"Lara? Really?" Paul shrugged. "That's new."

"No. Olivia."

Paul blinked. "Oh, that makes sense. She's probably near one of those false heats her sister mentioned. That would get their attention."

Ambrose raised his brows. "False heat?"

"Yeah, I mean. Everyone around here knows she isn't a *real* omega. Her family was embarrassed but sent her off to the Omega Centre, and she came back, and they announced she was defective."

Dexter scowled. "Do you have any details of the defect?"

Paul shrugged. "No. Olivia was pulled from school and stayed on the property after that. Not many folks see her, but I hear she makes a mean waffle." He chuckled.

Argus asked, "Were you friends with her?"

"Yeah, she was super smart, very sweet, and good with animals. Her sister is a cast-iron bitch."

Dexter raised his tawny brows. "Alpha?"

"No, just a bitchy beta. Why?"

Argus smiled. "I have some questions about the B&B. Can you point her out?"

Paul turned and pointed to a woman who looked like a washed-out version of Olivia's rich brown hair, full lips, and soft grey eyes. Her figure had been harder to determine, but the lithe athleticism in Lara's body was not the compact softness of her sister.

Argus waited until Lara had consumed two more glasses of champagne.

Dexter asked, "What did you want to ask her?"

"Things about the local wildlife."

Ambrose murmured, "Why are you waiting?"

"I want to make sure she is hydrated." He chuckled grimly.

When she was swaying and yelling about her ungrateful cow of a sister, he and his pride moved around her, and her fuzzy eyes blinked, and she said, "Whoa."

Argus smiled slightly. There weren't many alphas in this county, so he understood her surprise. "You are Lara? From the bed and breakfast?"

She nodded. "I am the owner, the manager, and the maintenance personnel. I can do it all." She looked him up and down then at the others and licked her lips.

He cocked his head. "Ah, I thought that Olivia did maintenance."

She paled. "You met her? Wait. You are an alpha? Huh. Guess the stories are wrong."

He leaned against the bar and got her another drink. "What stories?"

"That an alpha meeting an omega in heat would go crazy. Huh. Lots of fuss for nothing. Good."

"Your sister is in heat?"

She shrugged. "She said it's coming soon, but she will just scream it out like she did the other ones."

Ambrose asked, keeping his voice conversational, "Screaming?"

"Yeah. She screams for two days straight. Dad used to douse her with ice water when it got too loud. It stopped it for a while." She giggled and nearly fell. "Can't do that this time."

Dexter's tone was warm. "Why is that?"

"I filled the soundproofed shed with fishing stuff. She has nowhere to hide now." There was dark smugness in her tone.

Argus nodded, his fist tight. "Thank you. That was very interesting; enjoy the party."

He turned to his pride, and they walked out onto a balcony. "Does anyone else feel like rescuing a damsel in distress?"

"Let's wish the happy couple good luck and then go."

They stalked through the party, and Argus spoke to his mother's cousin Derek Henwell while the other two mentioned having to leave on pride business.

"Do you know a young omega called Olivia?"

Derek nodded, looking at his daughter and fiancé. "Sure. She does the work at the B&B down the road."

"What do you know about her omega status?"

"She has some kind of defect. Her father was mortified that his bloodline had generated an incomplete creature like that."

"So I am gathering. Is there anyplace near here to keep an omega safe?"

"The Winger house is empty. But, I told you, she's defective."

Argus looked at him and spoke clearly. "There. Is. No. Such. Thing. As. A. Defective. Omega. They are either in heat or not. There isn't anything else, and her sister has admitted that the family has confined the omega during heats because they didn't like her screaming."

Derek was shocked. "That . . . that can't be. Russell told me. He prayed with me that god would take the stain of . . . oh god."

"Yeah. We are going to collect her and try and get her to a centre before her heat kicks in."

Dexter brought up his phone. "Nearest centre is two hours north."

Derek spluttered. "You'll miss the wedding!"

Argus gave him a disgusted look. "The other option is that the three of us bring an unmated omega to the wedding and start fucking her when her heat kicks in."

"Why can't you just leave her where she is?"

"Because now that we know, her sister might try to either kill or move her."

"Lara wouldn't . . ." Derek looked over at the very drunk young woman who was flirting with the bartender. "Go and get her. From what I remember, the girl was sweet."

Argus nodded and muttered. "Peaches."

"What?"

He looked the man in the eye. "She smells like fresh peaches, and my cats like her."

Dexter touched his arm. "Let's go."

Ambrose looked at them. "My car?"

Argus shook his head. "My truck. We would be cramped, and she will be in a vehicle with three alphas. She's going to be disoriented, and we don't want to accelerate her heat."

They continued to make plans as they left the party, ignoring the stares as they left.

"So, you didn't notice anything when you met her?" Ambrose asked the logical question.

Argus shook his head. "No, but if she was conditioned to stop her responses or minimize them, and she was in early stages, it might have been subtle." He had another thought. "She also had cold hands. I think she was refrigerating herself before she came out to meet me and mowing the lawn. Damn, I am amazed that I smelled peaches at all."

Dexter grinned. "Peaches, really?"

Ambrose muttered, "I love peaches."

Dexter chuckled. "Me, too. This I have to see . . . smell . . . whatever."

The drive was mercifully short. They got out, and Argus ran inside to check for her in his room. The boys were in distress, and the moment the door opened, they bolted.

Argus knew a giant neon sign when he saw one and whistled sharply for his pride mates to follow him.

They crossed the property and found their target being nudged by the big cats; her hands clawed and dug into the wood of a shed that smelled like fish.

Argus walked up to her and still didn't smell what was setting his buddies off. "Hey, Olivia. We are going to take you someplace safe."

She glanced over her shoulder, her pupils wide and breathing shallow but still no scent. She took in Argus, Ambrose, and Dexter. Her eyes widened, and her mouth opened on a silent scream. Slick coursed down her thighs, and Argus had one thought. "How the fuck could I have missed that?"

He carefully unhooked her bloody fingers from the wood of the shed and picked her up. He wanted to rub against her, stroke her, and let her get used to his scent. She needed the Omega Centre so they could find out why it hurt so bad. Producing slick wasn't supposed to hurt.

"Hey, kitten. Up for a road trip?"

She looked at him in a pain-filled daze. "Where?"

"The Omega Centre. You have been, right? Your dad took you when you were young?"

She shook her head slowly. "No. I was just told to tell people that he did."

One of the men cursed, and she flinched.

"Oh, that's just Dexter. He is normally fun."

One of the men growled. "That is Ambrose, he is not normally fun, but he likes to think he's in charge."

She blinked and looked to Argus as he walked with her. "I fed the boys."

He smiled. "Thank you. That must have been hard, considering."

"It was fine until I let them back into your room and was tidying up." She put her chin on her chest and mumbled something.

"What was that, kitten?"

She whispered as if it was the most shameful thing in the world. "I sniffed your shirt."

He blinked. "And it set you off?"

She nodded and swallowed. "I tried to get into the shed, but she changed the lock."

Ambrose asked, "What's in the shed, baby?"

She blinked. "It's soundproofed. It stops guests from hearing if I am screaming."

The youngest one asked, "Why do you scream?"

"I have to hold the slick in so there isn't a scent; it hurts after a while, and when the pressure forces it out . . ."

Argus kept his voice conversational while he seethed with rage. "And you scream."

She nodded. "I am sorry that I am dripping on you."

If she had said it in a teasing way, he would have described in detail how he wanted to make it worse, but she was genuinely contrite. This omega was in desperate need of therapy.

He opened the back of the king cab and settled her with a blanket around her. He was shocked when the boys bounded in and pressed next to her, purring. They were doing what he couldn't.

The other two piled into the truck. "We'll take turns driving," Ambrose commented.

They buckled up; he put the truck into gear while he went as fast as the law allowed and a little bit more.

The boys took good care of Olivia, purring and nudging her to keep her awake. Dexter called the centre and explained the situation, handing the phone over to Olivia when she needed to talk. She answered all the questions frankly, and Argus really wanted to kill a dead man. Every omega instinct had been quashed or turned into pain. Beatings stalled her sex drive and any emission of scent. They knew how he dealt with her heats.

She spoke in low tones and said, "Three of them. No.

Nothing. No touch aside for carrying me to the truck. Mean? I mean . . . some country music, but they changed the station."

Argus grinned at that.

"Uh. Two big cats. Yeah. They are purring and in contact. It's nice. I am not supposed to touch people."

Argus's grin died. Omegas were incredibly tactile. They loved to touch things, people. They liked soft things, warm things, fuzzy things . . . geez. The boys were a walking nest for her.

She handed the phone back to Dexter. "They want to talk to you."

"No, we don't have a pack alpha. We have the feline aspect. Right. Miracle we all get along." Dexter chuckled. "Uh, I don't know. We just found her. She has a bit of work ahead of her."

Ambrose held his hand out. "This is Ambrose Wells. Yes, that is understood. We would like to be presented when it comes time to choose. Yes, we are registered. Can she be transferred to a centre closer to us? We would like to visit."

Argus heard her voice, thin and sleepy. "Can the boys visit?"

"It might be too far for me to bring them to you, kitten."

"Oh. Okay."

Her simple acceptance at being denied something that soothed her set Argus's teeth on edge. "I will try, but we don't know how long you will be there."

Olivia nodded. "Right. They have to find out what is wrong with me."

Ambrose nodded. "Yeah, baby. When you feel better, if you want, we will come and take you home with us. You can cuddle with the boys and us."

She perked up. "I can touch you?"

Dexter chuckled, and it was a strained sound. "Yes, please. Your scent is . . . very nice."

Olivia buried her face in Remus's neck, and she mumbled,

"It isn't disgusting?"

The entire truck groaned. Argus muttered, "No, kitten. It's the nicest thing we have smelled in a very long time."

Dexter nodded. "Like . . . ever."

Ambrose looked back at her. "We are just trying very hard not to show you how much we like it because we don't want to scare you."

"Oh. Well, that's nice then."

They chuckled, and she buried her face in the big cats.

Chapter Three

The drive hurt. She kept her face buried against the cats, but it was self-preservation. The men smelled really good, but every time her body reacted, there was pain. She kept herself silent, and when Argus finally said, "We're here," she looked up.

There were people waiting for her. For them.

The alphas got out of the truck and walked around. Argus spoke to the people who were waiting. The people waiting looked nervous when he spoke to them, but the woman in the front lifted her chin and made a gesture for him to proceed.

Ambrose nodded, and he opened the door next to Olivia. He smiled. "Come on out, precious. These people are going to take care of you until we can."

She nudged Romulus, and he huffed but got up and left the truck. Remus pressed down with his head, and he grumbled. She stroked his large head, and she pressed her forehead to his. "I am sure it will be fine. Maybe Argus can bring you to visit me."

Olly carefully moved out from under the grumpy cat and eased onto the cement, walking with her two buddies next to her. The woman in the centre of the waiting group had a comfortable-looking suit. She was also a solid beta.

"Miss Olivia Haven?"

Olly nodded. "That's me."

"I am Margot. I am here to help you. How long have you been active as an omega?"

"Uh, twelve years? The heats started seven years ago."

"You experience pain?"

Olly didn't know how to explain it. "Yes."

"Can we examine you?"

She frowned. "I suppose you would have to."

Argus chuckled, and she looked at him, catching a wave of his scent, and her body tried to respond. She fell to her knees, and the cats nuzzled her, purring hard to help her as her body spasmed and pain rolled through her in waves.

Argus was at her side, which wasn't helping. "Olivia, what can we do to help?"

She whimpered. "You smell too good."

He blinked. "My scent is causing you pain?"

"No, it is making my body react, and that is causing pain."

Margot stepped toward her and said, "Olivia, please, take my hand. We will see what the problem is."

Olly looked at her earnestly concerned face. She let go of the cats and got to her feet. She didn't look at the men. She couldn't.

Ambrose watched the woman walk into the building with the phalanx of betas. "What do you want to do now?"

Argus looked toward the building. "I want to know that she's okay."

"Then, we will wait."

They had turned back to the truck when a beta came out and said, "She wants you to wait."

"Who does?"

"The omega. They are taking her in for a medical exam, and if she is *defective,* she wanted you to know, so you don't waste your time waiting."

Ambrose frowned. "She doesn't want us to waste our time?"

Dexter blinked. "What is going through her head?"

Argus answered. "Pain."

They took the boys and brought them inside. They were put in an alpha waiting area where those who were there for interviews could meet omegas in a safe environment.

They were there for twenty minutes when a grey Margot came into the room, and she said, "Oh my god. That poor girl."

Argus got to his feet, and he was vibrating with tension. "What?"

Margot was shuddering with horror. "The source of the pain . . . they stitched her."

Dexter frowned. "What?"

Ambrose put his hand on Dexter's arm. "It was an anti-omega method of making them betas again. They stitch through the muscle and tissue and slick gland. When their heat hits or they scent an alpha they want, the tissue flexes and . . ."

Dexter paused then ran to the garbage can in the corner and vomited.

Margot nodded. "There is a lot of that going on. A med team is working on her right now, but she is fully sedated."

Argus asked, "Will she recover?"

"We don't know. I have never seen a case like this. There were pamphlets that the pure beta movement was circulating with photos of this procedure, and I hate to say it, but the particular stitching matches those images. I think she was the test case." Margot asked, "So you know who did it?"

Argus growled. "Her father had it done. He told the family he was taking her to the Omega Centre and that she was returned to them as defective."

Margot grimaced. "Where is he?"

"Dead."

"Damnit." Margot took out her phone. "I need every detail of her home, and I need it before they can hide the evidence."

Argus pulled out the card for the Haven Bed and Breakfast. "This is where she lives. The family has a bungalow on the property. If you could make arrangements for the animals to be seized and given to animal rescues, that would be ideal. I can help with that a bit, but I don't normally re-home farm animals."

Margot paused. "Right. Are you waiting until she is out of surgery?"

Ambrose looked at Argus and Dexter. "We are."

"She is going to need a *lot* of therapy. Based on what you told me and what she confirmed, she's been kept as a tortured servant and denied access to modern technology. She has to learn from about a six-year-old level of tech and work upward. She needs life skills, healing, and to learn what her body should actually feel like."

Argus nodded. "You took pictures of the stitching?"

"Yeah. Every layer."

Ambrose asked, "How many layers?"

"Eight. The entire knot band was included. Her heat would have been agony for days, and scenting an alpha would be pure torture. As she is combining both situations, I am amazed that she was conscious."

Argus smiled. "She's surprisingly strong, and the boys kept her calm and blocked our scents in the truck."

The jaguars were flopped out on their sides, looking pleased with themselves.

"They probably saved her a lot of pain. Geezus. I just . . . fucking monsters." Margot teared up. "That poor girl."

Argus tightened his jaw. "We want to know how she is doing. Will you keep us updated?"

"I will need her authorization, but if she says yes, then yes."

Ambrose asked, "Can we see her when she is out of surgery?"

"Only for a moment. No physical contact. It will be about an hour. Can we get you some water or coffee?"

They answered as one. "Coffee."

She smiled slightly and nodded. "Coming up. Oh, and gentlemen?"

Ambrose looked at her. "Yes?"

"Thank you for bringing her in." She smiled weakly. "As

you might guess, other packs might have tried to keep her for themselves. You did the right thing."

Argus nodded. "Thank you. Please, take care of her."

Margot nodded. "It's what we do."

Dexter looked up from his seat on the floor next to the waste bin. "So . . . every time she scents an alpha . . ."

Ambrose finished. "Her body tore itself apart. The slick built up until it could open her skin enough to escape."

"Fuck." Dexter frowned. "How would you even begin to treat that?"

Ambrose guessed. "Let the body heal then start to stretch the tissue. She might not ever be able to take a knot, but she would be close to a beta." He nodded. "There shouldn't be pain. It's soft tissue, so it has a better chance of healing without scarring and healing quickly. There could be nerve damage, but if she was still in such pain after years of it, she heals, and the nerves aren't damaged."

Argus ran a hand through his hair, and Romulus butted at the back of his knees. He leaned down and scratched behind his ears. "Yeah, I am worried, too."

Their group waited until a beta male in medical garb came in, and he was shaking. "We got it all out after documenting it. She's doing . . . surprisingly well. They sewed her cervix shut as well, but we managed to get an IUD into her since she was already out. She doesn't need to end up pregnant unexpectedly. She should really have a few normal heats before a breeding is attempted."

Ambrose smiled. They were being addressed like she was theirs already. "You might be telling us too much. She has not chosen yet."

He snorted. "Yeah, fuck that. She has been demanding to bring in her guys and her boys. You are the guys."

Argus pointed at the jaguars. "These are the boys."

"Well, she is awake and in recovery. She will still need to be here for months until she can be educated for the modern age, but her pain is already dissipating. Margot will have a list of things you need to do before you can take custody of her." He sighed. "First things first. Come this way, keep the big cats close."

He opened the door, and the boys shot past him. Argus chuckled. "She's that way."

There were startled cries from down the hall. Ambrose chuckled. "Over there."

Dexter heard a female shout. "We should probably hurry."

They walked quickly with the doctor through the medical area and to the clean and sanitized room that held Olivia.

Olivia was sitting up, and the boys were lying on her bed, one to each side of her.

She waved slightly. "Hi, guys. Um, thanks for bringing me here. I don't hurt anymore. Of course, that could be the drugs."

Argus looked at her, and Ambrose watched him lean over the bed. "How are you feeling, Olly?"

"Um, horrified with what they found, but now, the pain makes sense." Her hands clenched, and she rubbed them on her thighs. Ambrose could see that she wanted to grab Argus.

Dexter walked toward the bed, and he sighed. "I am so sorry that was done to you."

She nodded. "So am I. I didn't even remember it. I just know that it hurt, and trying to touch myself got me a beating." She smiled brightly. "He's dead now."

Ambrose watched her hands move. "Peaches, you can touch Argus if you want."

She jumped, winced, and turned crimson. Her eyes turned to Argus, and he extended his hand to her. He smiled. "I am all yours, kitten."

Chapter Four

Olly wasn't quite sure. She was aching, but it wasn't pain. The doctors said that the wounds were closing and time would see to the scars.

She stared at Argus's hand, and then, she gave up the most profound statement. "Aw, fuck it."

She put her hand in his, and his fingers closed around hers. Her skin got hot from head to toe, and she inhaled sharply, and his scent heated and filled her nostrils.

"Ohhhh." Pine trees and cold wind. She felt the clench and the slick, but it just ached. There wasn't any pain. She took his hand in her bandaged fingers and turned it over in her hands. She licked his palm before either of them knew what she was doing. The purr came as a shock, and for a moment, Olly thought it was her, but Argus was purring. The boys looked at him, and they joined him in the deep rumbling rattle.

Her body relaxed, and she kissed his fingers, licking his thumb and taking his index finger into her mouth next. She swirled her tongue around, and she felt another spasm, but it wasn't agony; it was . . . something else.

She rubbed her face against his hand, and he stood there, purring for her. "You smell good."

He swallowed, and his purr faded. "You, too, kitten. How are you feeling?"

"Hot, achy, swollen." She couldn't help the look up through her lashes. "Empty."

He crouched next to the bed. "You know why you have to stay here?"

She nodded. "The world went by without me, and I

21

have . . . issues that need to be addressed."

"They will take care of you, and if you choose us when you are ready, we would be happy to have you as our omega, kitten. But . . . that being said. There is no pressure. Well, there is pressure, but that is for my zipper to deal with."

She turned hot pink again. She glanced over to Dexter and Ambrose. "Can I get your scents, too?"

They looked surprised, and they both stepped forward, extending their hands, fingers down. She took Dexter's hand first, inhaling and rubbing her cheek on him, pumpkin spice . She licked his skin, and Dexter's mid-range purr sounded. She took his finger into her mouth and sucked, but she smiled slightly when his purr stuttered.

She reached for Ambrose and inhaled him, blinking in surprise.

He frowned. "Don't you like my scent?"

She kissed his palm and murmured, "You smell like breakfast. Hot cinnamon rolls. I didn't want to bite you."

He chuckled. "Bite if you like. If you choose us, I will be returning the favour."

She nipped his thumb, and he slid it between her lips. His eyes locked with hers, and she stroked him with her tongue, sucking softly. The look in his eyes said that this was the only time she would get to pick what went into her mouth, and she wanted to cross her arms over her breasts because her nipples were scraping at the hospital gown. He stroked her cheek with his finger and smiled. "Good, kitten."

He pulled his thumb out of her mouth, and she rubbed her cheek against his hand.

Dexter asked, "What do I smell like to you?"

She bit her lower lip, and they all winced. "Pumpkin spice."

Argus smiled. "Pine trees?"

"And a cold wind that makes me want to curl up somewhere warm."

His eyes widened, and he grinned. "I like the way your

senses process me."

She swallowed. "So do I." Another wave of slick came out of her with all three of them so close, and they were all purring.

Margot came in. "What the fuck! Guys, out! Fucking alphas trying to press an advantage. Out! Go home."

Olly smiled. "You can go. They will take care of me. Oh, and Argus?"

He had turned to leave. "Yeah?"

"I got every fucking chicken."

He blinked and then laughed, beckoning to the boys. They moved reluctantly, but they followed him into the hall. Ambrose and Dexter smiled gently at her, and they left.

Margot huffed and pressed a button on the wall. The scents that the guys had been sharing with her dissipated.

Olly looked at Margot. "Hello again."

"You are doing well. Much pain?"

"No. It just aches, but the drugs might be helping."

Margot smiled. "You aren't on painkillers. Your body started healing itself the moment the stitches were out. That's good. So, you are set on the pride?"

Olly murmured, "Don't tell them, but yes."

There was a masculine whoop and laughter from far down a hallway.

"Well, I am glad *I* didn't tell them." Margot smiled. "They seem kind, and I checked their application, and they have enough resources to keep you comfortable if that is your wish."

"Um. I just got my lady parts back. I don't have a job lined up, nor do I have a high school diploma. I need to learn a ton of things and find a carer for my animals."

"The pride is already working to re-home your animals at shelters and petting zoos."

Olly sat there, and she squeaked. "Really?"

"Really. Apparently, your sister can be violent, and they wanted to act before she knew you were gone."

"Aw, they are so sweet."

"Well, your slick production is up. How are you feeling about that?"

"The first one sort of stung, but the other waves were actually quite pleasant."

"Uh, your bloodwork says you are in a full heat. How are you feeling?"

"Fine. Heat without the pain is actually fine. I wish the guys were here, but I am not quite sure why, so I think I need an alpha-omega sex-ed course stat."

"Before you get your GED?"

"Yeah. I don't want to do something stupid just because a guy smells edible." Olly looked at Margot.

The woman blinked, and then, she nodded. "Right. I think you actually will need *less* self-control for that. And . . . this is an awkward question, but would you consider speaking on omega abuse once you have gone through therapy and have caught up on your education? People don't understand that this is going on."

"Are more women being tortured like this?"

"A few pop up, but yours is the worst case that I have seen."

"Why are you asking me now?"

"Because when the omega hormones take over, you are going to have trouble thinking during your heat. I wanted to have a conversation while you are clear-headed."

"Uh, I don't *give in* to my hormones. I was beaten when I did, so this is pretty much the me you are going to get unless my guys are in the room."

"Why did you attach to them so soon? They told me that until they came to get you, they hadn't even scented you."

Olly smiled. "The boys. The jaguars. He has the leashes for appearances, but he doesn't need to use them. The boys follow his orders with calm words and light gestures. He alphas by trust, not force. And the boys are super friendly, which indicates solid socialization."

Margot nodded in understanding. "So you got to see him in action, so to speak."

"Yeah. And whatever the part of my brain is that purred when they watched him take care of his animals set her sights on him. I feel calm and relaxed around him, and that is a rare feeling."

"What about the other two?"

"Dexter, indulgent, and Ambrose, nervous."

Margot nodded. "Good assessments."

"How long am I stuck in bed?"

"They will assess you in the morning, and we will move you into an apartment here at the centre. You will get a schedule, and then, you can catch up with the rest of the world, and you will learn what it is to be an omega."

Olly smiled. "How long is this going to take?"

"Weeks? Months? It depends on you. I think you will probably be out of here in ten weeks."

Olly thought about her guys and her boys. "I am going to try and do it in four. You might want to warn them that they are going to have to put me somewhere."

Margot made a note on her clipboard. "Noted. Now, get some rest."

Olly nodded. "I think I can do that."

"Then, that is one more hurdle crossed."

"Good. Now, I just have to figure out what the guys are going to look like naked, and I can start figuring out how to make a sex fantasy." She wrinkled her brow.

Margot sighed. "Typical omega."

Olly smiled. "I am glad that you think so. It's the first time I have heard anyone say that."

"Good night, Olivia."

"Good night, Margot." Olivia set her bed flat and wished for a large warm body that she could wrap her arms around that would purr for her. Four-footed or two-footed, she wasn't picky.

She slowly rolled to her side and curled up in a ball with

tears tracking down her cheeks while she wished to not be alone for just one night in her life.

Even as a typical omega, she was alone.

A wry assistant gave them a stack of pamphlets on the care and maintenance of an omega.

Ambrose looked to Argus. "You start reading, I'll drive. We might make it to the wedding after all."

Dexter snorted. "You can't be serious."

Argus nodded. "Actually, that is a good idea. Time to see if we can dislodge some local information, but Ambrose, I am grabbing my bag and staying with you."

"Fair enough. We will stop back there and grab your stuff. We don't want you in the way when the Omega Centre investigators arrive."

Argus looked at the stack of pamphlets. "You want me to read them out loud?"

Dexter chuckled. "Beats country music."

The boys hopped into the back seat, as did Dexter, and Argus sat in the passenger seat while Ambrose drove. "*Your omega will need a private space to feel secure. It should be snug with low ceilings and large enough to host only one or two alphas at a time.*"

Ambrose nodded. "Right. So, we can build a separate quiet space in the nest. How much time do you think we have?"

"They said ten weeks, but having met Olly, I think she is going to push the timing forward. We should be ready any time from a month from now."

Dexter was nearly spinning. "I still can't believe she picked us. She doesn't even know us."

Ambrose smiled. "Smell the hand she touched."

"Holy . . . peaches. I couldn't smell anything at the centre."

He chuckled. "They have scent scrubbers to keep the omegas calm, but also, she has practice subduing her scent. I look forward to the day that her scent cuts loose. I want to be balls deep in her with her squeezing my knot and the air filled with peaches."

Argus shuddered. "That . . . sounds amazing. I just want to start by making her cum with my mouth and hearing her moan."

Dexter sat quietly. "I want to hold her after we are all sweaty and sticky and listen to her breathing with the air around us full of our combined scent."

Argus waited a moment. "I like that one. I am changing my answer."

Ambrose chuckled. "Me too. Now, read another pamphlet."

"When your omega goes into heat."

Dexter agreed from the back. "Yeah, read that one."

"An omega approaching heat may be irritable, weepy, or gaining in sexual aggression. You need to watch for the signals and monitor their scent so that you are ready when your omega is. Supplies should be arranged to see your omega and you through their heat. Do not forget to hydrate."

He continued to read each of the handouts, and they discussed a few points, like who would like to go first and what if she tipped them into rut in an order different from what they had chosen. Inevitably it would be her decision, and they would have to abide by who she chose. All they could do was make themselves agreeable.

They grabbed his bag from the bed and breakfast and sorted things with Ambrose's host. The boys went for a quick run and settled in the room while he and Ambrose changed for the wedding. He stroked Romulus's head. "I am pretty sure that you are the reason she picked us, so you guys are going to have to look so nice on the day she comes with us. We are going to have to sort some kind of formal wear for you."

The big cat rumbled and looked smug.

Argus chuckled. Tense but happy. He smelled his hand,

and the heady scent of peaches struck him. He wanted the scent all over him, mixing with his own. He didn't know what the cold wind smelled like, but her nipples had been erect and scraping at her shirt while she licked and kissed at him. He was delighted by her shy enthusiasm. Given her situation and the firm expectation of pain, she had still started coaxing herself to arousal, taking the chance on pleasure instead of agony.

He got up, fixed his bowtie, and slipped on his tux jacket. They may look sleep-deprived, but they were all excited for what had started for them last night. They had an omega. The potential of a mate, and she wanted them.

No one was going to threaten their little kitten again.

Chapter Five

Derek and Paul were relieved that they had made it to the wedding. Argus watched his cousin Adra walk down the aisle, and she beamed at him.

It was a nice beta wedding filled with nice betas and a handful of alphas. Argus's uncle Derek was one of two betas in his family. The other two siblings were alphas. Argus was representing the alpha side of the family. He was the only one who had been friends with the family since childhood. His siblings had other interests.

Olivia's sister was in the crowd, looking none the worse for wear after her binge the night before.

When it came to Lara, he kept his mind blank. He didn't want to disrupt the wedding by clawing her up.

The pictures after the ceremony were strange, but he didn't know why the betas would want pictures of their triad without any other family; it was very possibly for their exotic nature. Feline alphas were not commonly seen and certainly not in a group.

The reception started, and they moved together to their table. Paul and his fiancé were sitting with them, as well as some elderly relatives. The fiancé, Emily, smiled at Argus. "So, what is the difference between feline alphas and the other kind."

Ambrose leaned over and said, "We don't bark, and our hands are the most obvious difference."

Emily blinked.

Ambrose took Dexter's hand, kissed the back of it, flexed the tip of his index fingers, and the sharp, hooked claws emerged, previously invisible. "Like that."

Dexter smiled and tapped his forehead to Ambrose's. "I need my hand back."

Argus looked back at Emily. "Is that enough of an explanation?"

Emily nodded. "So, you are romantically involved?"

Argus wanted to laugh. It was the head boop between the other two that had got her thinking. Possibly the kiss to the hand. What Emily couldn't know was that Dexter's hand still wore Olivia's scent. Ambrose was paying homage to their omega. The scent would wear off soon, but today, she was with them.

Argus shrugged. "It isn't particularly romantic, but we fuck when we want to."

Paul laughed, and Emily blushed.

Ambrose chuckled.

Paul said, "Any luck finding a poor little omega to take you on?"

Argus smiled slowly, his hand near enough to waft traces of Olivia toward him. "Funny you should mention that."

"Really? Congratulations!"

"Don't congratulate us yet. There is a long road to go. She is recovering from abuse and heinous torture. The Omega Centre has never seen a case so involved or long-running."

Paul frowned in concern. "That sounds serious. If she is that bad, how did they let you meet her?"

Dexter answered. "We brought her in."

Paul scowled. "When?"

Ambrose got an email and checked his phone. He chuckled. "We are going to have to send her some worn clothing, guys. She broke into where they keep the binders and found our scent cards. She's now gone feral over them."

Argus snickered at the idea of their little kitten going feral, but he supposed she was a lot scarier to a beta. "We will courier something today. Everyone ready to sacrifice a shirt?"

Dexter murmured, "Boxers. Hell. Both."

There was a second chime. "And can we send her something to keep her mouth busy."

Argus groaned, and he wanted to get back in the truck and give her something to wrap her tongue around. Years of repressed sexuality were hitting her at once, and they couldn't even watch.

Ambrose and Dexter groaned as well.

Dexter smiled. "We should send courting gifts."

Emily asked. "Courting gifts?"

Argus answered, "Gifts that make sure she is thinking of us."

Paul frowned. "You didn't mention her yesterday."

Ambrose murmured. "We didn't have her yesterday. We are hers now."

Argus waited for Paul to make the connection.

"Wait . . . not Olivia. She's defective."

Argus sighed. "No, she had been surgically damaged so that most omega impulses caused her agony and conditioned to hide the benign signs. She was never taken to the Omega Centre. She was taken to a Beta First surgeon, and he mutilated her."

Paul grew pale. "Oh. God."

Emily was concerned. "Olivia? Lara's sister? She's so funny and sweet."

Argus nodded. "She is, and she's ours."

Paul scowled. "If she is as bad off as you say, how can you claim her?"

Ambrose chuckled. "She claimed us. I think she is just in it for Argus's big cats, but I will take it." He put his hand near his face and inhaled deeply, his lids going heavy.

If Argus had thought that he would rather happily sit and inhale a scent off one hand rather than spend an evening out, he would have considered himself insane. But now, it seemed like the most natural impulse in the world.

Dexter filled in a detail. "After she got out of surgery last night, they said that her recovery would be slow, but we can wait. We met her, and she chose us and then confirmed it to the centre. They are going to take care of her and catch her education up as well as teach her what she should already have been taught about being an omega."

Paul blinked. "You are telling me that her father did that to her? The screaming that Lara always talks about."

Argus nodded. "They had layers of stitching to connect her muscles and glands together. When they flexed for heat, she was tearing herself apart. The agony lasted as long as the heat did. Lara liked the sound of her screaming. She put a new lock on the soundproofed shed, which is where we found her with her fingertips dug into the wood, blood everywhere."

Emily had her hand over her mouth.

Argus apologized. "I am sorry. This is not a conversation for a wedding."

Emily looked grey, but she shook her head. "No. It's fine. I am training to work with omegas in my practice and was going to ask Olivia if she could give me insight. Now, I wish I had done it sooner. I might have noticed."

Paul narrowed his eyes. "If she is an actual omega, how did you miss her scent when you got to the bed and breakfast."

"Well, she doesn't give up much of it. And she had just mown grass and gotten out of a walk-in fridge. She smelled pleasant, but her scent is similar to a food item, and it was easy to dismiss. She is more mature than an untethered omega has any right to be, so it was easy to look past what my senses were telling me. It was only when she rubbed up against the boys that I started to get a clue. They were sensing what she was hiding."

Emily frowned. "The boys?"

Ambrose chuckled. "Jaguars. He works for an exotic pet rescue, and these two bonded to him, so he takes them around and educates folks on why keeping them as pets is wrong. Wait. Argus, what was it she said about chickens?"

Argus grinned. "When she offered to let the boys run at night, she said she would mark all of her animals so that the boys knew they were hers and that she was going to have to scent mark the entire flock of chickens. There was something about the idea of her rubbing all those fluffy bodies against hers that captured my imagination."

Ambrose blinked. "Wow. That is something. Shit. We don't even know what her body looks like."

Paul frowned. "Do you need to?"

Argus chuckled. "Eventually, yes."

Emily smiled. "Wait a minute. There is something from a school website from when she was on the swim team. She was really fast."

She flicked through sites on her phone and snagged a photo, enlarging it. "This might be inappropriate, but it was when she was fourteen, and she had just won gold for the school."

Argus nodded. "We are interested in her now, not her then; we just need a reference for scale."

Ambrose looked at his phone and said, "I am just going to ask for measurements so we can work on her wardrobe."

Dinner arrived, and Argus copied the reference of the school site so he could find the image again. She had been grinning, head high, proud, and holding a gold medal while other girls had their arms around her. That would have been her omega manifesting. The gaze in the girls' eyes were slightly unfocused and worshipful.

Emily's face was right there next to Olivia.

"Emily, were you friends with her?"

Emily took her phone back. "I was. When her father started beating her, I tried to tell our church and the sheriff, but they wouldn't help. That is when I first learned of the Beta First movement around here. She couldn't run away, they had taken all of her resources, and when she came back after that *visit*, she wasn't the same. She was nervous all the time, moved slowly, would stop, and breathe deeply at random times. If they had done some kind of FGM, that would make sense. It is horrifying but would make sense."

Dexter scowled. "FGM?"

Ambrose answered, "Female genital mutilation. By removing part of the female anatomy, they remove pleasure and, therefore, the urge to sin."

Paul sighed. "Yeah, they had a pretty strong presence here about ten years ago. An omega born in their midst must have been a tremendous blessing as far as they were concerned. They could use her to prove their asinine theories."

The meal could have ceased to exist as Argus asked Emily about his new favourite topic . . . Olivia. He found out what she had liked, disliked, favourite colours, and that she purred easily when smug.

Emily grinned. "And she loves jerky, spicy pepperoni sticks, that kind of thing. We used to have friendship bracelets of woven threads as well."

Ambrose got another email; he frowned. "Wow. Okay. Our little kitten has quite the rack." He laughed. "And she fought them on the measurements until she was told they were for us, and even then, the betas that were around her were hypnotized by her scent. Her heat isn't waning, but she's healing well."

Argus shuddered. "Better we are here then. I don't want to be near her until she isn't in pain."

Ambrose got another picture, and he dropped his phone like it was hot. He whispered, "I asked how her sexual response was doing, and Margot took this."

Argus looked at the image, and his claws flexed out. Dexter saw it and groaned. Olivia was on her knees, bent back with her thighs wide, the front of her smock was torn, and her breasts were fighting to spill out the tear. Slick covered her thighs, and her hands were cupping one breast and clutching at her inner thigh.

Argus nodded; his voice was thick with a growl. "She seems . . . better."

The air around them was thick with alpha pheromones. Emily blinked. "Uh, what's in the picture."

Ambrose clutched the image to his chest. "Olivia is doing better."

Argus muttered, "Send me that picture."

Dexter murmured, "Me too."

Argus looked at an amused Paul and a concerned Emily. "There was nothing overtly lewd in the image, but she is getting in touch with her omega biology, and since she has chosen us, we want nothing but to be with her through this. But she is healing, so we can't."

The speeches were made, the toasts were made, and the dancing started. After the requisite dances, Argus's cousin Adra came over. She beamed. "Daddy said you might miss it. Gah, that is strong! Are you in rut or something?"

He smiled at his cousin. "No. Not yet, but probably soon. We found an omega."

Adra hugged him, despite the pheromones. "Congratulations. Damn, I wish you guys had weddings or something when you did that."

"We don't. But once we settle, we may have a party."

"That would be excellent. Come on, let's dance."

He smiled and danced formally with her. He waited, and then, he heard, "Well, who is she?"

"You may know her, but the details can wait for another day. We are hopeful that it is a good match." He smiled. "Today is your day, and you should not have to think about unpleasant things." He glanced over and frowned. "Shit."

Lara Haven was being arrested on the dance floor. The officers of the Omega Centre and the federal representatives were there, leading her out. "Lara Haven, you are being arrested under the Omega Abuse Act. Anything you say can and will be held against you at a binding tribunal."

Argus blinked. "I wasn't expecting it to happen that quickly."

Adra blinked. "Lara? So . . . the jokes she made about

Olivia screaming and her dad slapping her to shut her up . . ."

"All true. Her dad had a surgeon lock her up, and whenever things flexed during heat... Pain."

"Oh, god. That is . . . oh, god. I laughed at her."

"When?"

"When she came back from the Omega Centre and said she didn't feel good. I called her a wannabe and a defective and . . . I was horrible."

"She never went to the Omega Centre. She's not registered—well, she is now—but she had no protections, and her sister wouldn't let her leave the property or have a phone."

"Oh, god."

"Don't cry now. Don't mess your makeup. But do know that once she recovers, if you invite me and the pride to any events, she comes along."

"Oh, of course. I am just reeling. So, she's really a proper omega?"

Argus thought to the image now saved in three places on his phone. "Oh, yeah. Definitely."

"Does your father's pack know?"

He chuckled. "You were the first after Paul and Emily."

Adra was serious. "Do the boys like her?"

"The cats? Love her. Ambrose and Dexter want to lose themselves in her the same way I do. Well, not the same way as I don't want them in the room for the first time, but that is weeks and weeks away. I believe we will be insane by then."

Adra laughed. "Olivia is very sweet, but she has issues."

"I know. She is in therapy, or she will be within a few days."

"On the plus side, she is adventurous and patient, so you are going to have a fun time of it."

Argus grinned. "I am looking forward to it."

Chapter Six

Every time someone tried to take the cards she carefully kept in the sealed bag, she hissed. It was her precious tie to her alphas, and she wasn't parting with it. A relieved Margot came into her apartment on Monday afternoon with a huge box. "Here. Presents from your pride. Keep them in the room, so you don't set off any other omegas; they have also included some snacks for you and toys."

She perked up. Toys? Olly scrambled for the box, her shorts loose, and she opened the box that had been tacked shut again.

"Why did they send me stuff?"

"Because if you are going feral over old scent cards, you need your alphas to keep calm. So, since you can't have them, you can have their scent. This is quite the variety."

"Ohmygod. The boys!" She pulled out two jaguar stuffed toys that smelled like the boys.

Margot watched and chuckled as she discovered a box of lollipops, a case of spicy jerky, and hot pepperoni, bags that had fabric in them, and her fingers shook as she let a tiny bit of air out, and she smiled. "Dexter." The next bag, "Ambrose." The third bag she inhaled deeply as the calming cool wind washed through her. "Argus." Her purr was thick and heavy.

Margot stared at her. "That is impressive for someone who couldn't do it three days ago."

Olly beamed at the bag full of boxer briefs, and she looked at Margot. "I will save those for later."

"Thanks for that."

She blinked at the box of graduated sex toys. "Oh. Right. I

should be working on capacity."

Margot shook her head. "You are an odd thing. We also have toys here for you."

"Yeah, but I am starting at pencil and trying to work up to garlic sausage, so I need to get to work."

"Keep looking in the box. There's more."

She grinned and found underwear that was pretty and lacy and, shockingly, in her size. "Wow. They must have really looked."

The object at the bottom, nearly as large as her hand, was sitting, waiting, and had a slow blinking light.

"Is that a . . ."

"It's a phone, Olly. All yours. You can use it for data, texting, or even talking to your guys. If you want to video chat, you can do that, too, but I would wait until you are a little further along in that dildo collection for that because we don't want those guys on our doorstep in rut."

Olly looked at her and asked, "How does it work?"

Margot sat next to her at the table and explained how to use the phone, how to dial, how to hang up, how to do hands-free. Video chatting. They practised it all, and then, Margot showed her how to view her contacts and make calls to the three pre-programmed people in the phone.

She had spent the morning and most of the afternoon with medical and taking baseline tests on her education. If she was good enough, they would let her get her GED that week. Then, she needed things like driver's training and testing. She drove vehicles around the farm all day, but she didn't have a license.

Her penchant for reading would probably let her pass high school equivalence, but she didn't want to go to her pride at a standardized disadvantage. She didn't know what their occupations were; she did know that she wasn't suited to one without the degrees and categories that she needed. She was trying to catch up to ten years of deprivation in one month. It was a good thing they had sent her the scent packs; they would help her concentrate or, at least, make her feel secure.

It was the first thing they taught an omega. Your alpha would make you feel calmer with scent alone. She had three, so that meant if one was injured or dead, it was unlikely that the shock would kill her. Well, she didn't have three yet, but she wanted to. The high whine surprised her.

Margot looked at her and smiled. "Well, it seems that your instincts are intact. Are you going to eat in the general area today?"

She shook her head. "No, I want to . . . hey, if I want to send them something. Can you forward it to them?"

Margot nodded. "I can. Do we need a scent-locking bag?"

Olly pursed her lips. "I would really recommend it. It isn't for the faint of heart. Three small bags and one large . . . to keep it in."

"Fine. Courier?"

"Yes, please. I want to thank them properly for the gift."

Margot laughed and ruffled her hair. "I doubt there will be anything proper about it."

"And I will send down for an extra sheet and a set of scissors. I have an arts and crafts project in mind."

"Right. I will let you go and make some calls."

"I am gonna flip the lock, just in case."

Margot laughed. "Thank you, but don't forget dinner. Even in heat, you still need to eat."

Olly chuckled. "You rhymed."

"Right. Go make those calls. I am sure they know we have received the package by now."

Olly walked behind her and closed the door, locking the deadbolt before she dove to the box of toys and lay back on the bed to try the smallest. She blinked. Oh, that was easy.

She bit her lip and skipped to the third size out of ten. This one nudged at her as she slid it inside. Still no pain. She could grip it though, that felt fun.

She skipped to number six and lay back with her feet on the mattress and her thighs wide as she slid it in. She moaned at the feeling of being filled and slid the faux shaft in and out of her to places that hadn't been touched before. Something hot and urgent started in her, and she blindly pressed the phone to call one of the guys.

A low, smooth voice answered, "Hello, precious. You got our present?"

She gasped and whispered, "Yes, it's very nice; thank you, Ambrose."

His voice had a hint of tension. "Precious, are you using one of them now?"

"Um, yes?" She gasped and moaned. "Sorry."

His voice changed tone. "Which one are you on, Precious?"

"Um, six is a good starter."

He cursed, and there were groans in the background. "Is it inside you now, precious?"

"Yes." Her voice was breathy. Her slow movements were increasing that itch of urgency in her body.

"Aw, honey, are you sliding it in and out really slow?"

"Uh-huh." She kept the deliberate motion up, but it was getting harder.

"What are you feeling?"

"Hot, itchy pressure under my skin. It wants me to go faster, but I want to make it last. First times shouldn't be rushed."

"Oh, god, precious. You are so right there. Do you know how to put the phone on speaker?"

"Uh-huh. Margot thought I would need to."

"Ohhh, she's a smart lady. Can you reach one of our scent packs? The one with the boxers in it?"

She flailed around and found it. "I have it."

"I want you to stop using number six and to take number eight and tease your opening with it. Let me know if you can do that for us."

"Us?" She pulled the toy out and whimpered.

"Us. We are all here with you, precious."

Argus growled, "We are with you, kitten."

Dexter growled. "Just waiting on you to be ready, kitten."

She blindly grabbed for the box, and her hand came out with a thicker, longer specimen.

Olly circled her opening with the wide head, and she clutched the bag of scent. "Okay, I am ready."

Ambrose murmured, "Good girl, precious. Now, open the bag, inhale and go as fast or slow as you want. We will be here until you finish and tell us you are okay."

She nodded and opened the bag, inhaling deeply, and she felt a roar of slick leave her. She lifted the toy and used it on herself, sliding it in and groaning as it pushed at her opening, the walls, and deep inside.

Argus murmured, "Fuck yourself, kitten."

She moved the toy faster and faster. The width stretched her, and she felt her clit swell, so she patted it to calm it, and her scream went on and on until she fell back to her bed, the toy still inside her.

She panted, whimpered, stopped seeing stars behind her eyes, and took stock of the items around her. She was sweaty, her thighs were coated in slick, there was a wonderful ache deep inside, and the box of toys looked wrong. "Uh-oh."

Ambrose was there in an instant. "What is it, Olivia? Did you tear?"

"No. I grabbed the wrong toy."

He exhaled in relief. "You can work up to ten; it isn't a problem."

There was an amused tone to Argus's voice. "Which one did you grab?"

"Uh . . . ten?" She licked her lips. "It is a really good fit and feels so nice. Thanks for the present."

She listened to their low voices and groans, as well as the sound of skin on skin. "If you guys are jerking off to me, let me know."

Dexter chuckled. "Just finishing up. We were with you all the way, and now, we are rock-paper-scissoring for cleanup.

It's a cum-splattered mess in here."

She groaned, and her hip rolled.

Ambrose said, "Precious, is it still inside you?"

"Yeah. It feels good."

He chuckled. "Glad to hear it. Can you touch around where it is inside you and feel how deep it is?"

She blinked. "Oh, you want to know if the knot is in."

"Yes, baby."

"Oh, yeah. I am right up to the hand grip."

A chorus of groans.

"Precious, it doesn't hurt?"

"No, there is an ache, but it's nice. After I hang up with you, I will try it again. I haven't figured out what the clit does, but patting it seems to work."

"We will help you with that when you are with us, precious. Now, start to fuck yourself again and tell us what your favourite foods are."

She moaned as her hand started to move the toy and her body provide the slick. "Anything I don't have to cook myself. Next question."

She moved her phone to her belly, so she could speak more easily, and while bending forward, she grazed her nipple with one hand; she bent her head and licked at the nipple, holding her breast and continuing to move the toy as her hips rolled with it.

"Precious, what is that wet sound?"

"Um, I am licking?"

"What?"

"My nipples? I can just reach them. It feels super nice."

He groaned, and the others were with him. "We are not going to let you out of bed until we are all exhausted and sticky, and even then, we may crawl back in."

"Aw . . . that is weeks away. I don't want to be alone when I cum. Can I call you guys if I need to do what I am doing now?"

"Masturbate?" Dexter supplied helpfully.

"If it isn't an evening, Dexter has the most flexible schedule. He can talk you through it. After five, we are all yours."

She chuckled the moaned. "What about mornings between five and seven?"

Ambrose chuckled. "I have got you there, precious."

Argus sighed. "I will just have to settle for waiting for you, kitten, and listening to you."

She let out a throaty moan. "Fine. I will reserve video chatting for Argus."

He let out a hoot of triumph. "I will definitely take that, kitten. Just you and me, and when we're both exhausted, the boys can come and say hi in the chat."

Ambrose growled. "You meant the guys, right?"

She laughed and got the scent bag. "He meant the boys. They came for me first."

She opened the bag fully and was surrounded by the scent of all three of them, and this wasn't a casual scent; this was sweat, cum, and the musk from their cock. She moaned, thrashed the cock inside her, and whined for contact with another being. She held one of the stuffed jaguars, and she was in a frenzy of licking, moaning, and thrashing before she let out a keening cry, and she dropped to the mattress, landing on the folded sheet she had created for that very day.

"I think that was a good start. If I go off again, I won't bother you."

Ambrose's voice was steel. "You will call us, precious. No matter what time, day or night. It will be our pleasure to be with you."

She looked down and blinked. "Oh, I got stuffy Romulus all sweaty."

Argus asked, "You needed something to touch?"

"Yeah."

"Hug the stuffing out of them. They are there because we can't be."

She was suddenly shy as she pulled the toy out. There

were some flecks of blood around the knot, but she had been using it aggressively, so it was unsurprising.

"What do you see, precious?"

"I got a little overly enthused with the knot, and there is a bit of blood."

"Does it hurt?"

"No, just a deep ache that makes me want to do it again. Heats are frustrating." She chucked low in her throat. "Maybe you guys can be around for the next one."

They chuckled. "Oh, kitten, if you think we aren't going to be there, you had better get your head examined."

She grinned. "Are you calling me crazy?"

Dexter smiled. "He is calling you ours. Have a good evening, Olivia. I hope we get a call later tonight."

Ambrose sighed. "Keep to eight or lower. Now that you have gotten all worked up, you are a little swollen, and it will feel tighter."

"Yes, sir."

He chuckled. "You have delightful instincts. Good night, Olivia."

She blinked and was going to have to look that up later. He responded to the word *sir*. She was rather glad that he was there, and she was here.

"Good night, Olivia." His tone was stern.

She whispered. "Good night, Ambrose, Dexter, Argus."

They murmured a final good night, and the call was over.

Olivia groaned and slumped back to the bed. As tests of her recovering biology, it had been wildly successful. It had gotten her in touch with her pride, and they wanted to touch her, so the deep ache from lack of contact would be satisfied. She just had to catch up with her education, go to therapy, and pretend to be normal. She could do that. Well, she could if she figured out what normal was. There didn't seem to actually be a linear path to what folks considered acceptable. She was currently humping a piece of silicone, and folks considered it normal, so it was obviously a sliding scale.

She bit her lip and inhaled the scent of them mixed with the scent of her. That stimulation was one-sided, and she had a plan to change that.

Three days and eight sex-filled calls later, Ambrose went to the door of his office, and his assistant handed him a box. The faint scent of peaches clung to the box, and he smiled slowly at the return address of the Omega Centre.

He called Argus, and the sound of a worksite was in the background. "Hey, Argus, what time will you be home tonight?"

"Normal day, should be home around five. Why?"

"We just got a parcel from the Omega Centre. It smells like peaches."

He groaned. "What time is it?"

"Eleven."

"You sick bastard."

"Didn't want you to make other plans." Ambrose chuckled.

"Fine. I will be home promptly. Are you going to torture Dexter next?"

"Of course. His parents are already confused by him working peaches into every design he does. They will be relieved to find that it is a woman and not your pert butt."

Argus laughed. "Probably. Have fun, Ambrose."

Ambrose called, and Dexter picked up. He sounded frazzled, and Ambrose grinned. "Are you going to be home by five?"

"Yeah, of course. Why?"

"We got a parcel from the Omega Centre. It smells like peaches."

"You fucking bastard."

"Did you want me to wait to tell you?"

"No. Damn. This is not going to make my parents happy."

Ambrose snickered. "They built the company around your

designs, so this year, the theme will be peaches. When they meet Olly, they will understand."

"They will be so relieved. I have been jumping for the phone so much lately, I think they think it's one of you." Dexter chuckled. "They still want me to find a nice beta and settle down. I haven't told them about Olly yet."

"When she's with us, it will make more sense." Ambrose chuckled.

Dexter's tone was tortured. "When will that be?"

"She's going as fast as she can . . . for us. You know that. She is going to need a lot more therapy, and we will need to help her continue her education in any direction she wants to take it. She missed out on a lot of options."

Dexter sighed. "I know. I have been designing items for her all day. My parents are in despair, and I can't say shit until she's with us."

"Yeah, but if the box contains what I think it does, it will make it harder and easier at the same time." Ambrose chuckled. "See you tonight."

"Fucking hell. Yeah. See you tonight."

Ambrose hung up. So, their little kitten liked to play. It was good to know. She also defaulted to calling him *sir* when they were on private calls, and that was encouraging. He suspected that she had been doing some research, but it was something he wanted to ask in person. He wanted to watch her eyes get wide, and her thighs clench together.

It was going to be so much fun having her around. He wondered what she wanted to take up as a hobby when they were done spending every waking moment between her thighs, rutting deep.

He shook himself and put the parcel near his jacket. He now had to get back to the home he was working on and maybe put some more peach trees to the side. He snorted as he worked, their little omega was sending shockwaves through their lives, but until they had her with them, things were uncertain. He wanted that certainty, and they wanted

Olivia.

Chapter Seven

She waited in the outer room and paced. She bit her nail and fidgeted while her exam was marked. Her perfume was broadcasting her distress, but her guys weren't here, and no one else gave a rat's ass.

The invigilator came out and smiled. "Olivia Haven, ninety-six percent. Well done."

She sighed and nodded. "Yay. Thanks. So, it's a GED?"

"No, it is a high school diploma. We would classify you with a GED if you were in the sixty to seventy percent range. Well done, Olivia."

"Wait. So, you can just classify me with a high school diploma? From what high school?"

He grinned. "Omega Tech. To be frank, you aren't allowed to work in the majority of occupations without being supervised by your alphas, but this at least lets you pursue education without limit."

She blinked and nodded. "Okay. Thank you. Can I get something printed out? I am talking to my pride tonight, and I want to show them."

Margot appeared behind her. "Why don't you just tell them in person? You are ready for your handoff, you little twit."

She paused while the air went out of the room, and then, she said, "Fucking excellent."

Margot chuckled. "We will be taking you to them tomorrow."

"Do they know?"

"They do. They are getting their house ready for you. They went a little crazy for a moment when we told them. I would recommend you avoid phone sex tonight. Pack your things, and we take you tomorrow morning. It's a four-hour drive, so you are going to need to get rest tonight because the odds of you resting tomorrow night are slim to none. I will say, they have been rather well-behaved for alphas."

Olivia smiled brightly while her skin tingled in anticipation. "They are ambush predators. They can wait."

"You are still going to call them and tell them you passed?"

"Yes, but I am not going to tell them my score."

Margot took her out of the waiting area and walked her down the hall. "They have arranged a therapist for you, set up a nest, and gotten you a wardrobe. They will bring you to any depositions you need to attend regarding the original matter that brought you here. We have your video testimony, and sixteen investigations have been launched from the data we found at your family home. You might save some lives with your honesty."

"If I can stop one woman from getting that done to her, it is all worth the exposure."

"And we are happy that your alphas feel the same." Margot smiled. "They are bringing you to one of the fundraisers later in the year. If there is anyone who exemplifies what we are supposed to be doing . . . it's you."

"I can't argue there. Everyone has taken good care of me and been very professional while I worked my way through my heat."

"Ah, about that. I will warn your alphas, but you are rapidly cycling into another heat. We did the bloodwork this morning."

"Oh, that is what the command to medical was about."

"Yeah, we need to make sure that everything is right before we let you out into the world." Margot chuckled. "You are in excellent health, your body has recovered now that we have gotten the last of the stitches out, and your IUD is in place, so you won't need to worry about pregnancy for the next two years."

They were walking back to her room, and Olly wrinkled her nose. "I am on lockdown?"

"Until we come get you tomorrow morning. Early. Four in the morning early. Call your guys. Tell them that you will see them in the morning. Weirdly, not one of them minded that we were dropping you off on a Friday morning."

Olly smiled. "Yeah, that doesn't surprise me. They have been very attentive with their schedules, and yes . . . I know that it won't last. It is nice for now."

Margot smiled. "You never know. They are all from good families who are still together. It's a good sign that they have seen and know how to execute a solid family."

"I haven't asked them about their families yet. We are going to ease into that."

"Oh, good to have some conversational gambits." Margot snickered. "You want to work up to that."

Olly grinned. "Are you referring to my virtual sexual exploits?"

"I would never mention whatever it takes to get you out and enjoying your life, Olivia."

"Thank you, Margot. Your help and support have really meant a lot."

Margot paused outside her door. "Having you up, whole, and ready to leave under your own power to the men of your own choice is our goal. Still stuck on your alphas?"

"Oh. Yeah. For the boys if not for the guys. There is nothing like cuddling with a big cat and feeling that purr take the day away." She smiled. "Can I give you a hug?"

"Yes, but no rubbing."

"Yes, Ma'am." Olly went in for a hug, and Margot held her, squeezing her tight.

"I am very proud of you, Olivia. You are going to do great things."

"If I do anything, I will call it a win." She rubbed her cheek against Margot. "Oops."

Margot sighed. "Now I am going to smell like you until I dry clean this jacket."

"Sorry. I can pay for the cleaning." She blinked and leaned back. "Eventually. I just realized that it is a throwaway phrase I can't back up." Olivia couldn't help it. Her chin wobbled.

"Oh, hey now. Your guys have to set you up with accounts as well. It's part of the care agreement. It might not be much, but it will be enough to get your scent out of strangers and friends." Margot booped her nose with a finger.

Olly chuckled weakly and let Margot go. "Thanks for the hug. Sorry about the jacket."

"It's fine. We have nullifying spray in the office. Password is *bring me to the boys*."

Olly nodded and headed into her room. She was upset at a realization that she should have had earlier. She needed money in the normal world. She wasn't a prisoner anymore, and she was going to need money to be able to buy ice cream and coffee like a normal person. Damn. She wanted normal with everything in her.

She got changed into her comfort clothes. Argus's shirt on her, Dexter's shirt around her main pillow, and Ambrose's shirt around another pillow. The stuffed animals were at her back, and she felt safe. She checked the time and video called Argus.

He smiled, and he looked sweaty and rumpled. She started purring.

"Hey, kitten."

"Hey, Argus. So, I just heard I will be seeing you tomorrow."

He grinned wide. "Yeah. We have been waiting patiently for you." He ran a hand through his hair, and she caught the greying white against his tanned skin.

"Uh, Argus, are you wearing the scent band I sent you?"

"The third one out of the set of twelve. You make a sturdy product, kitten." He brought it to his nose and inhaled, then shuddered.

She hugged the Ambrose pillow to her nose and nuzzled it. "You look like a junkie."

"And you look adorable. Is that your nest?"

She looked around and nodded. "Yeah."

"So, your head is on a pillow wrapped in a shirt. Whose?"

"Um, you want the tour?"

"Please." He sat back and smiled.

"Um, Dexter is my sleeping pillow, Ambrose is my body pillow, the boys are at my back . . ."

He gave her a slow grin. "Where I am?"

"I am wearing you. I save this for when I am nervous or upset." She put her head down and rubbed against Dexter's scent.

He frowned. "Nervous about tomorrow?"

She shook her head. "No. I forgot something important on the way to normal, and now, I feel like an idiot. Such a basic thing."

"You forgot about money." Argus sighed. "I figured that one out a while ago. You have only ever worked for family, and they didn't pay you, so the bare necessities were always just covered. Don't worry. You have an account, cards, cash, whatever you need is waiting."

She peeped at him from behind Ambrose's pillow. "I still feel stupid."

"You will feel less stupid tomorrow when you are in our arms. Do you wanna talk to me while you pack?"

"You look sweaty. You should take a shower."

He chuckled. "I busted my butt to get stuff done today so I could spend all day with you, kitten. And all weekend. And possibly part of next week. Can I take you with me into the shower?"

She blinked. "Will you keep the camera above the equator?"

"Yes."

She sighed. "Darn."

"I shower, you pack. We sent you some luggage. Did you get it?"

"Yes. I got it." It was hard-sided, hot-rod red, and when she had looked it up, it cost a lot. That made her nervous.

She set the phone on its stand and carried it to where her meagre closet was. She set it on a dresser and started to pack.

"First, pick out tomorrow's outfit, kitten. Make sure it's comfortable. You are going to be in that car for a while."

She nodded and picked out underwear that she liked. There was a heavy purr, and she blushed when she realized he was going to be seeing it in person fairly soon. She picked some strappy sandals, and that was her outfit sorted. "What will the weather be like tomorrow?"

"It's going to rain."

"I will ask for an umbrella. I don't have a raincoat."

"Okay." He stripped off his shirt and set the phone down on what seemed to be a ledge in the shower. He carefully removed the small wristband embedded with the scent from that first time, and he peeled off the rest of his clothing. She heard it and quickly turned to packing when he started the water. She was packed when he said, "Since you don't have a lot of stuff, is it okay that we bought you some?"

She chuckled. "It is either that, or I run around the house naked to save wear and tear on the outfits I do have."

He groaned. "Oh, promise me you will do that at least once."

She snickered. "As long as I don't have to make breakfast. Nudity and bacon should never be combined."

He shampooed and said, "I can't believe it is tomorrow. You worked so hard to get to us, kitten."

"Get to you, get out of here. It all blurs together."

"That is going to earn you a teasing smack on the backside. Are you going to call for a group event tonight?"

"Um, no. I am under orders to go to bed early and be ready to leave at four."

"Yeah. We offered to come meet you, but they said they didn't want the transfer recorded as a highway incident when we pulled over to fuck you."

Her body clenched, and she nearly folded over. She whispered hoarsely, "That wouldn't look good for the centre."

"No, so they are taking you before dawn. You will be with us for a late brunch. Ambrose is already planning it. Come hungry."

She nodded. "I will text you when I am on the way. You guys can jerk off a few times, so you don't maul me."

He chuckled and rinsed off. "Oh, kitten. We are going to maul you anyway. The boys are excited. They treat those chew toys you made like they are baby dolls."

She sighed. "They are supposed to rip them to bits. I filled them with jerky and everything."

"Yeah, kitten, but they smell like you, so they are going to be cherished whether you like it or not."

She sighed. "Nice tile. Glazed porcelain?"

He paused and looked into the camera. "Yeah. How did you know?"

"I did all the renovations at the B&B by hand. I made up materials lists and got my sister to pick up the orders."

"You did all the work yourself?"

"We hired guys to help with the demo and disposal, but I wasn't in heat, and they were betas, so it was fine."

"Wait, so you decorated the rooms?"

"Yeah, all of them. Why?"

He chuckled and rinsed the shampoo out of his hair. "Just trying to think of income streams for you. You might want to look for interior design distance-learning courses. Just in case."

"Oh, uh . . . why?"

"Sometimes I do a build, and the owner has financing issues for the last instalment. Sometimes I just want to build a house, but in both cases, I need it decorated and designed.

I can give you a budget, and you design an interior on the computer. Ambrose can help, and if I like it, you can pick up the occasional job."

She smiled. "And if you don't like it?"

"You can either try again or be lightly punished for not doing your best."

"What is a light punishment?" She bit her lip.

"Aw, kitten, I don't want to spoil the surprise."

She felt her chest tighten, and she whispered, "I really don't need a surprise that ends in punishment."

He blinked and looked at her. "Ah, right. A light punishment would just be an open hand applied to the delightful curve of your ass. A heavy one would be using an implement that left hot stripes on your skin."

She blinked. "Oh. No broken bones? No punching?"

He looked horrified. "No, of course not. Kitten, we aren't going to hurt you."

She wobbled a little, blinking tears from her eyes. "Okay. I will see you tomorrow."

He didn't look happy, but he cut off the call with a, "See you tomorrow, kitten."

She closed her suitcase and crawled back into her nest. Dawn was going to show up after she had left. She set her alarm for three and tried to sleep. It was only by taking deep drags of Argus's scent that she was able to rest.

Chapter Eight

She had texted Argus and the guys when she left, and to her shock, they all answered back. They were going to be with her every mile, and now that she had physically left the building, they could text her at will.

Her toys, clothes, scent items, and shoes were all in the small suitcase. She was sitting next to Margot, answering texts and keeping her phone on the charging pack. This day, she didn't want to be out of communication.

One of the guys would check in every hour, and she answered, getting nervous as the signs indicated that they were nearing their location. She swallowed and rubbed her hands on her thighs.

Margot smiled. "You have gone from a peach jelly to peach nectar to peach bellini for a moment. Now you are just plain peach."

"At least I haven't gone lemon or apple."

She bit her lip and watched the buildings go by. There was a ping, and she found a cross street to text them about.

She read the next text with a hitch in her breathing, *You are five minutes away, kitten.*

She wanted to lean over and hyperventilate, but Margot rubbed her back. "Easy, Olivia. Things will be fine. Your guys are solid and haven't wavered once. They learned what happened to you, and it didn't matter. Your past is in the past, but your future is theirs. That is what matters. You are going to make a future, Olivia. Today is the day you start."

She smiled at that. The past was the past. She would leave things there. Her future was four minutes away.

She looked at the house. It was pretty big. It looked deep, too. Georgian style. Three stories.

Olly held her breath as the SUV she was in pulled in through the tree-lined drive. The door to the house opened, and her guys stood there, watching the vehicle come to a halt. She shivered as Margot got out and went to speak to them, she handed them a clipboard, and they signed for her like she was a delivery.

Olly waited, and the driver came around and got her luggage, bringing it to Dexter, who put it inside the house. He opened the door for Olly next, and she stepped out nervously and then slowly walked toward Ambrose. She walked up to him and bowed her neck. "Alpha, I put myself into your care."

He caressed her cheek, and she looked up. "I accept the joy of your keeping."

The kiss was a surprise, but her body sang at the contact.

When Ambrose released her, she turned to Dexter. He straightened as if it was a serious business. "Alpha, I put myself into your care."

Dexter nuzzled her cheek. "I accept the joy of your keeping."

She licked her lips and went to Argus. She did the same as for the others. "Alpha, I put myself into your care."

Argus gripped her arms. "I accept the joy of your keeping."

She blinked as she was pressed against him. He pressed his lips to hers savagely until she opened her lips and whined in distress. He slowed, gentled, flicked his tongue into her mouth, and stroked her back.

She settled against him, and his tongue flicked and teased with hers until she responded. Short jolts of lightning started to rip through her. Olly slid her hands up his chest and gripped his shoulders as the exchange and slide of tongues made her hotter and hotter. Slick emerged when he started to purr. The small hot wave made her blush, but suddenly, other hands were at her back, smoothing down her hips, and mouths were at her neck, licking and sucking.

Purring surrounded her in a wall, and she caught her scent swirling wild and hot while they touched her. Perfume. In an omega, it was perfume. She had to remember this stuff.

The purring rattled through all her lonely places and told her that she wasn't alone anymore. Her channel started to flex with her excitement, and her clit throbbed. She clutched at Argus as her orgasm hit from being surrounded by her pride. Hers. Tears started to streak down her cheeks. She slowed and softened the kiss, pulling away and resting her head against his chest while she took Ambrose's and Dexter's hands.

"Kitten, why are you crying?"

Margot spoke from the sidewalk. "She has worked very hard to be here, and it was stressful. None of us could offer her comfort, so she has had to soothe herself for the last five weeks, knowing that you would if you could. So, now take her to her nest, help her get comfortable, and when she has rested from the drive, you can check on her progress with you."

Olly looked at her assigned officer and smiled. "Thank you for getting me this far, Margot."

"It's my job, and in your case, my pleasure. We will be checking in on her over the next year to make sure she is well and to smooth over any issues that arise." Margot said, "Call me if you need me, Olivia."

In a minute, the vehicle was gone, and they were alone.

Olivia looked up at Argus, and his smile had a glittering gleam in his eyes. "Do you want to see your nest, kitten?"

She looked at Dexter and then the very intense Ambrose and nodded. "I need to know where it's safe."

That word acted on them like a bucket of water. They went from predators to caretakers in an instant. Dexter smiled. "I will show you, Olivia."

She was pretty sure he was younger than she was, but he was serious, and he wove his fingers with hers as he tugged her away from the other two.

Once inside the building, he didn't let her look around all the warm wood and stone; he coaxed her up the steps and down the hall. "We have a few smaller nests around the house that are big enough for you and the boys. To let one of us in, you have to kick them out or move around, so you are lying on top of us." He chuckled. "We tried a few combinations to see what would work."

"Wow. That seems like a lot of effort."

Dexter squeezed her hand. "We want you to be safe, happy, and comfortable. After that happens, we can work on what else you want to be."

Olivia smiled. "That is very thoughtful."

"Thanks. We are trying not to freak you out, and we know you don't have a lot of tactile experience, so we will start with the nest, and you can come out and find us when you are ready." Dexter's cheeks warmed. "Have you given any thought to which one of us you want first?"

"Argus. I think he will let me learn, Ambrose will want to teach, and you will get really enthusiastic, and I don't want to freeze up on any of you."

Dexter chuckled. "I can be last. I am good with that."

"No, you're second after Argus. Ambrose has patience. He can wait."

He pulled her to him and kissed her softly. "You have thought this through."

"It has taken up a fair bit of my focus." She licked softly at his mouth, and their kiss deepened.

Her senses were filled with pumpkin spice, and she moved her head against his as she crowded close to him, her hands flat on his chest.

He groaned, and they stood there for minutes, slowly kissing, and she got a hit of her perfume wrapping around him. His eyes were narrow, his pupils wide, turning the dark blue nearly black.

She shivered, and she could feel her body responding like

an omega's was supposed to do. She swallowed and asked hoarsely, "The nest?"

He grinned. "Right. You need a safe space."

He took her to the room with an antiqued bronze handle; the others all had worn silver. She walked into fairy land.

A soft light had a slider on the wall. The closet was easy to move around in and would double as a sleeping space if she felt overwhelmed. There was even a bedroll and bolster pillow in the corner. The clothing was all very pretty but practical in one section. Elegant, graceful, and silky in another section, and then there were the playtime outfits. She blushed. There was a tower with different styles of shoes and a bureau with nothing but lingerie. Workout clothing was in a separate section. No jeans anywhere.

She frowned. "I am going to need jeans and t-shirts."

Dexter smiled. "They are in here."

She blinked and walked to the wall, feeling nothing until she pressed a panel, and it popped out, a selection of jeans and tees neatly arranged. The sneakers were at the bottom of the hidden cupboard.

He whispered, "Ambrose doesn't like them, but we explained that if you accompany him or Argus to a jobsite, you might need to wear something more practical with steel toes."

She was crouching and saw something behind the shoes. It was a hardhat with the word, *Kitten* emblazoned on it. "Oh boy."

He chuckled. "I work from home, so I might need you to come and model something for me so I can make sure I get the scale right."

"Um, I don't know what you do."

"I design jewellery for my parents' company, Ambrose is a residential and commercial architect, and Argus is a contractor." He smiled and helped her to her feet. They closed the jeans cupboard, and he led her out of the closet.

"Ambrose and Argus met eight years ago at a jobsite. They

had a helluva fight and decided to start a pride that day. I met Ambrose four years ago when he came into my family's jewellery store to buy something nice for his mom. He knew what I was, so we met for coffee with Argus a few times, and I moved in a year later. My parents think I am having a relationship with Argus because he is so pretty."

She chuckled. "He is. But he is also nice and intelligent, and I like his personality. And his scent. It makes me want to curl up against him."

He led her to the bathroom, and she blinked at the size of the tub. "That's huge."

"Just in case, Olivia. We tried to plan for any eventuality."

They left the bathroom, and she looked at the curtained area, drawing the curtain back. A nest full of pillows was there, and the scents of her guys were all around it. She reached down, kicked off her shoes, and dove into the pile, rolling and murmuring as she twisted and rubbed herself in scents and softness. She made a pile, and Dexter pulled the drape closed, leaving her in softly illuminated darkness.

She rolled around in the pillows, and when she heard the soft click of the door, she shucked out of her clothing and rolled around a bit before settling in a space where she was surrounded on all sides by the scents of her pride. She hugged the pillows to her, and she slept.

Argus got an alert from his phone that she had settled and motion ceased. He growled at the image of her silky limbs wrapped around the pillow with her hair loose and flowing down her back. She wasn't sobbing or fidgeting, so he would remove the camera that he had mounted in her nest.

Ambrose asked, "How is she?"

"Asleep. She's smiling, so she can't be too stressed." Argus sighed in relief.

"How long are you going to leave the camera there?" Dexter scowled. He had been against the break in privacy.

"Until she is bonded to at least one of us, and we don't need to guess if she is upset."

Ambrose raised his brows. "You still want her to choose when the binding happens?"

"Yeah. She hasn't had much choice in the rest of it, so choosing when is her prerogative. Of course, we still get to choose where."

Dexter grinned. He had his spot picked, and it wasn't traditional, but it would look good at some of the parties they had to attend. Ambrose was taking the back of the neck, Argus was biting her wrist, and Dexter was getting the inner curve of her hip where her waist was narrowest. He fucking loved that curve.

Dexter rocked on his feet. "What do we do now?"

Argus chuckled. "We wait. But we can make brunch for her. She's going to be hungry when she gets up, and if not, we want her to keep her strength up."

They got to work.

Chapter Nine

The scent of bacon got her up, and she sat bolt upright, pawing her hair from her face. She was hungry.

She untangled herself from the pillows and got a change of clothing. The stuff she had arrived in was all sweaty and rumpled.

She put on a slip and a sundress made of a silky fabric with buttons down the front. She undid a few of the buttons, ran her fingers through her hair, and went in search of bacon.

She stopped to brush her teeth, just in case more kissing was on the menu before she ate.

Argus's heart nearly stopped in his chest when Olivia came around the corner. His growl and deep purr rumbled the cutlery on the table.

She was wearing a soft blue dress that hung to mid-calf. Tiny buttons marched up the entire thing, but she had left the top six open, showing the white slip she had under it, and by the sway of her breasts, it was all she had on. Her nipples poked at the fabric as he watched. The scent of peaches filled the large kitchen.

Ambrose paused and turned. Dexter put the bacon on a warming tray and looked up. "Holy . . . Olivia, you look beautiful."

She blushed hot pink, and her grey eyes smiled before she looked away. She bit her lip. "Um, is there a chance of coffee?"

Ambrose nodded. "Of course, but first, house rule. No

matter how pissed you are at us, a kiss when you see us first and a kiss before bed, unless we aren't home, in which case, we have to find you before we sleep."

She nodded, stiffened her shoulders, and approached them like she was going into battle.

Ambrose got to her first, and he cupped her head in his hands. The brush of his lips against hers and the deep rumble that he was putting out must have worked on her nervousness because she went up on her toes and pressed her hands against his chest when he leaned back. She slid a hand up his chest and pulled his lips to hers with a hand around his neck. Her own purr rumbled free as Ambrose took his time with her.

Argus watched as Ambrose pulled their omega close until she was plastered against him. She squeaked a little as he lifted her, but when she pulled back, he let her slide down his body.

Dexter made sure nothing was on the oven as he walked around, and when Olivia stepped away from Ambrose, Dexter held out his hand, and she went to him. Dexter's kiss started slow and picked up intensity as Olivia responded. She was wrapping herself around him when he slowed the kiss and backed away.

Olivia was panting, and her pupils were wide as she turned to Argus. Her small bare feet carried her toward him, and she paused a few inches away. She looked up at him with her grey eyes windows to her arousal. "Hey, Argus."

"Hello, Olivia. Do you feel settled in?"

"Um, getting there. Do I have to ask for a kiss?" She looked up at him, hypnotized. "They told me at the centre that consent was important."

He quirked a grin, gripped her waist, and turned to put her butt on the counter. "That is absolutely correct. If we do something you don't like, let us know. Once we know, we can do more of the things you like."

She inhaled sharply as he stepped between her knees and

put his hands next to her on the counter. Their faces were on the same level. He leaned forward and rubbed his cheek along hers, and her purr broke free again. Argus smiled and leaned in. "You never have to ask. We are yours for the taking."

Her breathing came faster as he leaned in, and when he made contact, she let out a little mewl. He brushed his lips against hers, backing up each time until she followed him. She scooted forward, and it put her hips against his erection. She paused for a moment and then continued the kiss, undulating against him, her hips rolling against his cock through his jeans until she was trembling and her rhythm broke. He leaned toward her, his hands gripping her thighs and pulling her into him, rocking against the slick-coated fabric of her dress. Their rocking together got violent, and then, she let out a wail against his lips, and he continued to rock against her as the aftershocks ran through her. Her hands were clutching at his shirt, and she whimpered at every slow roll of his hips.

She gasped and blushed as she licked his lower lip and pulled her mouth away. Argus glanced over, and Ambrose had a wry expression, and Dexter looked stunned. "Can we do that?"

Ambrose chuckled. "You can if she consents."

He clapped his hands together. "Ohh boy. Brunch is served."

Olivia chuckled and pressed her forehead against Argus's shirt. "I need to change my dress."

"No need, kitten. You can just sit on my lap." Argus chuckled. "I am already covered."

She blushed hot pink. She opened her mouth, and he kissed her and tapped her lips. "Don't apologize. I am delighted that we could arouse you to this degree."

Ambrose added. "It was a group effort."

Dexter grinned. "I will happily take some credit."

She looked down and up at Argus. "Um, so this is

normal?"

He stroked her cheek. "I certainly hope so."

She was slick and sticky at the same time. Olivia swallowed and tried to hide the flex of aftershock as she let Argus set her on her feet again. Internally she felt a flutter, and she wanted to cuddle against him again.

Argus led her to the table, and she held the skirt away from her skin. He sat down and patted his thighs. She sighed and climbed onto his lap.

"You have to get used to us, Olivia, and we would like it to be sooner rather than later."

He wrapped his arms around her, and she breathed him in. She leaned against his chest, and Ambrose prepared a plate for her. "What's for breakfast?"

"Brunch. They said they would feed you." Ambrose scowled.

"Oh, uh . . . I was too nervous to be hungry." Her stomach snarled, casting its vote for food.

Argus sighed. "Well, we need to fill you up then."

She gasped, and the others grinned. She pushed away the mental images and hid against Argus.

She was lifted and moved to another lap. "No letting Argus have all the fun, Olivia. We are all yours, and we will take care of you. It is our joy and our pleasure."

She smelled cinnamon buns with vanilla. She looked up at Ambrose and smiled. "That sounds really weighty."

Dexter got her a cup of coffee and handed it to her. "We had to do research to get authorization to get an omega. There was study, psychological evaluations, and bloodwork. We are all disease-free if it matters."

"Uh, yeah. It matters. So, thanks for checking."

Ambrose chuckled and murmured in her ear, "Breakfast is poached eggs, hollandaise, bacon, toast, and fruit salad."

She perked up. "Hollandaise?"

He pulled a plate toward her, and there was the most desirable eggs benedict she had seen in her life because she didn't have to make it for someone else. Someone had made it specifically for her.

She turned, but he held her in place. "Um, I am not going to be able to cut it at this angle."

"I will feed you." He reached around her and sliced the food into small wedges. He picked up the first piece. "Open."

She looked at Ambrose, and his expression was kind with heat in his gaze. She opened her mouth, and he put in a wedge of food that exploded on her tongue. She moaned happily, chewed, and swallowed before she grabbed Ambrose's hand and sucked the sauce off his fingers.

"Good girl."

She sucked on his thumb, and she felt his erection swell against her hip. She rolled her eyes to meet his as she released him. "That was really good."

He smiled. "Back at yah. Now, we can save the play for later; now, I want you to eat."

"Yes, Sir."

She ate, and Dexter and Argus did as well. She paused and sipped some coffee. "You aren't eating?"

Ambrose said, "After you have yours, you will feed me mine."

"Yes, Sir." The reference wasn't lost on her. Everything they said was going to revolve around sex until they actually had it. So, the references would probably stop by that afternoon.

She was full when the second piece of toast was finished. She looked at Ambrose, and he licked his thumb and forefinger. She looked around the table. "Um, where is your plate."

He chuckled. "Who said I was going to need a plate?"

He wrapped his arm around her and got to his feet, setting her on the countertop. He eased her skirt up, and she watched him in shock. "What are you doing?"

He ran his hands along the inside of her thighs. "What does it look like?"

"Um . . . I have no idea." His fingers were tracing around in the slick that she had slowly been leaking during him feeding her.

"Allow me to demonstrate. I fed you; now, you are returning the favour." His nostrils flared as he bent his golden head.

He flipped her dress and slip back, exposing her to the bright light of the kitchen, and she flinched and ducked her head.

"Oh. Lovely, Olivia. So slick and pink and wanting."

To her shock, he pulled up a bar stool, settled on it between her thighs, and he feasted.

At first, with his tongue, she registered warmth. Then, she took in the slightly rough texture of his tongue, and when he licked her folds in one long swipe, she jerked and whined, unable to balance and grip his hair when he pulled her feet up to splay her thighs wide on either side of her hips. His hands kneaded her ass as he pulled her to his mouth, and he dove in, tongue swirling as she whined and tried to find something to grab hold of.

Pumpkin spice filled her senses, and Dexter gripped her hands, giving her an anchor point as her hips rolled and rocked against Ambrose's mouth.

Dexter kissed her softly, and she returned the delicate touch with a frenzy. She moaned, and her tongue licked and danced with Dexter's in a disorganized panic. Ambrose's tongue was circling her clit. Slick was coming out of her in rivulets, and he lapped it all up. Dexter took her hands and pinned them over her head while caressing her breasts with his fingers through the fabric of her dress. Her small cries became frantic, and she pulled and twisted under their touch and tongue, and then, she shattered apart into a million bright pieces. She shrieked, and Ambrose kept thrusting his tongue into her, feeling her fluttering spasms inside. He let her go on and on until she lay back with a moan, and Dexter smiled against her lips. The kiss softened, and he took her lower lip between his, plucking it softly as he raised his head. Ambrose kept going until the soft flutters led her to a sob, and after one last kiss and suck to her clit, he lifted his head. He rested his chin on her mound and said, "I could get used to breakfast like that."

She was sweaty, gasping, and exposed to the bright light of morning from the waist down. She stared up at the ceiling and shook her head.

Dexter stroked her cheek. "What are you thinking about?"

She murmured, "Honestly?"

All three said, "Yes."

She sat up with Dexter's help. Ambrose's mouth and cheeks were still shining, and she stroked his face, wiping herself off. "I am thinking about the nutritional value of slick."

They laughed, and she chuckled, trying to close her thighs. Her perfume filled the kitchen.

Dexter and Argus each leaned in for a lick in turn, and she had her hand over her mouth. On the phone, they had told her they wanted to lick her pussy; she just thought it was something guys said. Apparently, they did it as well.

Ambrose pulled her toward him, and she landed with a thud on his lap. He murmured, "Do you want more?"

She blinked and then caught on. She nodded. "Yes."

"Then, pick one. It doesn't matter which. Today is your choice."

She looked around and turned to Argus. She held out her arms, and he lifted her up, setting her on her feet. He smiled. "You want to be with me first?"

"Yes. You, then Dexter, then Ambrose."

Ambrose chuckled. "Why me last?"

"Because you like things to go a certain way, and you have more patience. You can wait."

Ambrose chuckled. "True, but I will be thinking of ways to

make you regret making me wait, precious."

She shivered. "It is a risk I am willing to take."

Argus swung her into his arms and carried her to his room.

His space was blue and brown, with black dotted around the room. His bed was a king, and he set her down next to it while he pulled off his clothing while she scrunched her toes against the thick carpet.

She looked at his sculpted body and stifled the giggle at his divided tan. He was bronze to the hips and then a pale gold down his legs. His chest was broad and his pecs rock hard, the rippled muscles of his abdomen demanded that she reach for him, and his cock had something at the top, under the band of his knot. She frowned. "What's that?"

He chuckled. "It's the mating spines. They cause inflammation after we withdraw, having the effect of causing your body to tighten and hold in the cum. They have evolved into this form in feline alphas and are usually the first thing we notice when we go through puberty. Mine aren't very abrasive, but it's a good thing that Ambrose is going last."

She shivered. "Will they hurt?"

He beckoned her closer. "Touch them. See for yourself."

She stepped toward him and reached out, stroking over him with her fingertips. The slightly rough skin was fine if she stroked down his cock, but when she stroked up it, they had some resistance. She looked up at him. "How does it feel to you?"

He inhaled slowly. "It feels amazing, but you could hit my dick with a brick, and I would think it felt awesome."

She chuckled. "That is some biased cognition."

His eyes burned with delight. "Those are some fancy words."

"I got a hundred percent on my English exams. I know a lot of really fun words."

She knelt and stroked him. "Beautiful. Smooth." She leaned forward and lapped at him. "Salty. Musky." She licked off a thick pearl of precum. "Creamy."

He groaned. "I am supposed to be seducing you."

She wrapped her lips around his head and sucked lightly. "You are doing an amazing job. Can't you tell?"

Her perfume thickened the air and wrapped around them as she moved her head to take him deeper. Practising on a toy had nothing on sucking him into her mouth and feeling the pulse, tasting the dribble of precum and enjoying the heat as she moved her head. She took him nearly to the band of short spikes, and he stroked her cheek. "Time to stop playing, Olivia."

Chapter Ten

She let him slip from her lips, and she got to her feet. He bent and lifted her dress and slip up and over her head in one move.

Olivia didn't cover up. She let him look like he had let her look. When he stroked his hands over her breasts, she exhaled softly, when he wrapped his hands around her waist, she smiled, and when he lifted her and set her on the bed, splaying her thighs wide, she blushed.

"Aw, Olivia, you are lovely, and your slick shines in the light."

She heard the whine from her lips before she could stop herself.

He grinned. "I am also so happy that you can let yourself react now without injury to yourself." As he said it, he slid two fingers in, and she arched.

She wanted to pretend that her body hadn't been waiting for him, but the light touch going deep made her arch, and she cried out as she came at the careful contact. A surge of slick covered his fingers, and she moaned as she fluttered around him.

"Beautiful, Olivia. That was lovely." He slid a third finger into her, which continued the tension and pulses around him. He flexed his hand and widened her. Olivia squeaked.

Argus bent forward and nuzzled her breasts, sucking one and then the other. She felt like her face was on fire as his fingers were lubed with every thrust. She had learned over the last few weeks that her breasts alone could bring her to orgasm if she was determined.

He seemed very determined.

She twisted her hips against him and sobbed. She shook, and her whispered begging came to her ears. "Please, Argus. Please fuck me. I'll be good, please, please."

He murmured against her breasts. "You are very, very good, Olivia. I just want to make sure you remember your first time."

"I already will; now, I want it to blur with a thousand other times."

He chuckled and moved, so his head was above hers. "A thousand?"

She stroked his cheek and murmured, "I would have gone for a million, but I didn't want to pressure you. Please!"

He nuzzled her neck and murmured, "We have planned out your marks, but today isn't the day."

She was disappointed. "It's not? Oh."

He kissed her. "Soon. Very soon. We just want you to know us without the marks and with the marks, so there is a basis for comparison. We have plans for you."

She shivered and whined, her hips rolling against his hand. She gripped his shoulders and stroked her hands over his back. Olly touched warm skin over hard muscle wherever her hands roamed, and as his kisses got intense, she met him stroke for stroke, trying to get him to put her out of her anticipatory misery.

When he pulled his fingers away, she was on the edge of another wave, and as he looked into her eyes, his cock was nudging at her. She clutched at him, pulling at him, the desperate whine still rolling through her.

He nuzzled at her neck and murmured, "Olivia."

She was arching against him and trying to get him to move inside her. Her body was giving off waves of scent, and she squirmed under him.

"Olivia." He kissed her and nipped her lip.

She blinked and looked into his green eyes. "Argus?"

He thrust into her, and she gasped, arching, and her release licked through her with lightning in her veins. She opened her mouth in shock as she tightened around the first half of his length but moaned and rocked against him as he went deeper with every slow slide.

He undulated against her, working into her bit by bit until she could feel the edge of his knot. Argus kissed her, a slow, licking kiss that urged her to lean up and meet him, motion for motion.

Argus kept her sheltered between his arms as he thrust into her, and her whines and thrusting hips matched him as he kept slow and deliberate moves, drawing out and sliding in.

The wet sounds between them she had gotten used to, but she was still blushing as she raised her legs and angled her hips to take him deeper.

She grabbed his head and licked and sucked frantically at his mouth as she got closer. She panted, whined, and finally hid her head against his chest as she shook. He slowed, but he didn't stop. His hips stroked slowly until her aftershocks had stilled to a light, occasional flutter, and then, he started again, stroking faster, deeper, and bringing her back to her frenzied state.

She was clinging to him in a hurricane of senses. Her body was hot, wet, aching, and needing more, and she knew he would give it to her. His thrusts thudded against her, and when she was on the edge again, he locked.

She whined and twisted, but she was pinned, panting.

He kept control and rocked against her, moving his hips and stroking her from the inside out. He brought his fingers down and stroked her clit, and she went off, twitching and clutching at him as her body found what it wanted and then demanded more.

She rolled her hips against him, her eyes narrowing at the tug, and then, she pressed a hand to his chest, focused, and began to contract around his knot with tight pulses.

Olivia watched, and his eyes went wide, narrowed, and then he rutted against her with hard thrusts that moved her on the bed. She screamed as her concentration shattered and pleasure rushed in. He kept going.

Dexter listened to the moaning, growling, and screaming coming from upstairs. "How long do you think he is going to take?"

Ambrose chuckled. "Well, I know that when I have her, it is going to be hours before you see either of us again. When we start doing marks, each of us with have a full evening, with her curling up with her bond mates to sleep." Ambrose chuckled. "I am the first mark."

Dexter looked at his pride mate nervously. "So, I will have an entire night with her?"

"Until you settle into sleep. Then, I will join you."

"Wait, so Argus goes last?"

Ambrose shrugged. "He chose the most protective marking. He has to wait."

"Is that how it works?"

"You marking her won't interfere with my mark, nor mine with yours if you take her from behind, but Argus's is too easy to mess with on the first day. No way to keep it clear."

"But . . . he knew that."

Ambrose nodded. "He chose it for its alert value. If anyone grabs her, we are going to know about it."

Dexter frowned. "Is that an actual thing?"

The older alpha sighed and rubbed his neck. "On the black market, an omega like Olivia could bring in millions. Her ability to hide her designation makes her incredibly valuable, and she's stunning. In the right light, you would mistake her for a supermodel. Well, the right light and if she lets us get her nails done. This year's award season is going to be a lot of fun."

Dexter's felt his eyes light up. "So, I won't just be running around with you two to all my family stuff, and the advertising shoots and . . . wow. I hadn't considered that."

Ambrose smiled. "I have been looking forward to the design award ceremonies and having her sit close enough that I can get a hand under her skirt to see if she can hold it in until the dinner is over."

Dexter chuckled. "It's quiet. What do you think is going on?"

"Well, his knot is in, and now, they wait."

Olivia shuddered as his tongue made long strokes up her neck, tasting the sweat and leaving her shaking. "I feel like I just exploded." She moaned.

"You did. A few times. It's a good start." Argus continued calmly licking at her. He chuckled. "I wish I could spend all day with you, but the others need to gain your confidence as well."

She sighed and blushed. "It is going to be a mess when the knot gives way."

He smiled. "Good. I want the mess; I want your scent all over my sheets. The boys are coming back to the house tomorrow. We wanted today without you being molested by them."

"Do they sleep with you?"

He nodded. "Usually. The other guys have their felines that like them more than other people. You will meet them, too."

"Where are the other ones?"

"Out back. This place is a registered big cat sanctuary. There is an office and everything in the back. We have staff who feed and care for the animals."

"Wow. Wait, this wasn't you. Was it . . ."

"Ambrose. He designed this place decades ago, and when he and I met on a job, it was time for him to get it built, so I built it."

"You two get along?"

"More or less. Until now, we have all dated outside the

pride, but our differences to most alphas throw people off." He started purring as his knot finished pumping her full.

She squeaked at the feel of the rush of fluid that was coming out of her. It couldn't have been more than a few tablespoons, but it felt like litres.

She moaned as he left her and trembled at the emptiness.

He stroked her neck. "Good girl, excellently done, Olivia. Now I know you, and you know me."

She nodded and tried to huddle underneath him.

He wrapped her in his arms and rolled to the side, stroking her back. His deep purr calling to her own. She relaxed and calmed down from the nervousness of being fucked but not bonded. She would deal with that.

Her bond would come soon. She just hoped it was before her heat, or things would get tricky.

"Argus, if I go into heat again, do you take time off work or do you have somewhere I can hide?"

He blinked. "Oh, sweetie, we will all take the time off work. You won't be alone."

"I have been alone during heats all my life; I am just trying to figure out the rules."

"Once we have bonded, delaying contact during a heat will hurt us as much as it hurts you. We will feel your stress and tension, and we will do what we can to alleviate it as quickly as possible." He stroked her hair. "Don't worry. We are going to be there for you."

She chuckled and ducked her head. "That is almost as scary. I don't know how to deal with that either. I guess I will learn."

He kissed her forehead. "You will learn. Now, do you want to go to Dexter and traumatize him?"

She chuckled. "He is both eager and timid. It is a fun combination. I am horny and ignorant, so things are going to get awkward."

Argus stroked her forehead. "If you have a doubt, let him lead."

She nodded. "Do I go like this?"

"I think Ambrose might blow if you did, so . . . wear the slip from breakfast."

She nodded and sat up, stretching and hauling her hair over her shoulders.

Argus toyed with a nipple and smiled. "Have fun."

She got up, put on the slip, and kissed him before heading downstairs. It was time to get familiar with her youngest mate.

Chapter Eleven

Dexter heard the soft footfalls on the stairs, and he looked toward the door, his body vibrating with tension. Olivia stepped around the corner, and she paused in the doorway. The light behind her cut through the slip that she was wearing, and she twisted one toe on the floor. He swallowed. She was cute, curvy, and she smelled like sex and Argus.

"Um, hi, Dexter."

He followed what Ambrose had drummed into his head, and he swallowed and held his hand out to her. "Hi, Olivia."

She walked forward and took his hand. He pulled her close, and she cuddled up against him. She was so small and dainty, and she smelled like peaches. He filled his lungs with her scent and ignored the throbbing of his cock. This was a moment he didn't want to fuck up. His first encounter with his omega was going to be second only to the bonding night in his memory, so he had to get it right.

He ran his fingers through her hair and pressed soft kisses to her head and her temples before tilting her head back and brushing his lips across hers. He gave her tiny, light kisses until she was up on her toes to keep contact with him. Her body was squirming against his, and Dexter fought his grin. When they broke the kiss, she looked at him, and her eyes were sparkling with laughter. "Feeling smug?"

"Oh, very." He pressed his forehead to hers. "Can I take you to my room and explore the smugness?"

She nodded shyly, and he flipped her over his shoulder. She laughed as he carried her, and it was when he slid his hand up her thigh and stroked the soft skin near her sex that she stopped laughing and whined softly.

He chuckled and entered his room. "Sorry about the heavy scenting, but it has been a stressful few days."

She murmured. "What? Ohhh."

Dexter eased her off his shoulder and held her against him, her feet off the floor. He rubbed his head against her, adding his scent to Argus's and her own.

He stood her on his bed and slid her slip up and off. He took a look at her, and his purr rumbled out. She was perfect. There were some pink marks that had obviously been left behind by Argus. Her nipples were pink and erect, the scent of peach was thickening into a nectar scent, and her lips were full. The rest of her was all curves and valleys, and he couldn't wait anymore.

He kept himself calm, and he murmured, "Lie down."

She flopped onto the bed, and he snorted with laughter. Her breasts jiggled, and her thighs shook as she came to a slow stop. "Good mattress, alpha."

Precum started leaking from him at her husky words. He fought the urge to tell her that his mother had picked it out.

He stripped off his shirt and climbed onto the bed. "I am glad you like it, omega. I am going to keep my trousers on until I am going to be inside you."

She looked at him through heavy-lidded eyes. "Stick to the underwear. It will be faster... later. For me, fine coordination goes right out the window when I am trying to cum."

He snorted. "Good point."

He unbuttoned, unzipped, and stepped out of his trousers, taking off his socks for good measure. She grinned, looking at him. "Good call."

He moved over her and parted her thighs wide, lying along her body and realizing how small she was compared to him. She groaned, and she bent her legs to either side of his hips, pulling him down to press against her. The soft slide of her skin against his nearly undid him, and he understood Ambrose's warning.

He kissed her softly, and she tried to take charge, but he growled softly, and she whimpered and leaned back.

He lifted his head in remorse. "I am sorry, I didn't mean to. I don't usually growl."

She blinked and looked at him with a soft twist to her lips. "And I usually don't stop when I have something I want in front of me. I am still getting used to this. I am not used to folks trying not to upset me. If I tick you off, feel free to growl. I might cringe, but I will get over it."

Her little speech was so sweet, and he could see that she was trying to be brave.

He purred for her, and she relaxed instantly. Her hands moved up and down his back, and he had trouble concentrating. She leaned up and sucked at his lip before licking and humming happily.

Dexter began a slow kiss, rolling his hips into the sprawl of hers, and the heavy scent of peaches filled the air. He smiled as his senses focused on the pounding of her heart, the temperature of her body and the silk of her skin. He kept the slow roll of his hips against hers until she was whimpering and clawing at him, and when she wailed softly, he continued to torture himself until she wound down to a soft whimper.

He purred deep, and she jerked in surprise as his cock pressed against her carried through with the vibration. He moved his hips against her again, and she moaned, "Dexter, can you be inside me, please?"

He grinned. "You are very polite."

"Never an excuse to be rude."

She ran her hands across his back, and to his shock, she used her nails and brought her fingers from his shoulders down to his ass in a pair of long scratches.

His mind went blank, he shoved his underwear out of the way, and lined up to bury himself inside her. She gasped and moaned but gripped his back and rolled her hips in time with his.

Dexter focused on the heat of the tight fist of flesh around him and not on the urge to rut away until he was knot-deep and she was squealing with every deep tug.

He frowned and carefully moved inside her while she went wild around him. He wanted to give in, wanted to flip her over and drive into her from behind until they were fused together and she couldn't get away, but this was for her. She needed to know that pleasure was the end game at their hands.

He thrust slowly and evenly, but she wasn't going for it. She rocked her hips upward with increasing ferocity, and then, she took his knot, and he paused. It took to the count of two before his control shattered again, and he thrust against her with his knot squeezed for the first time in his life.

Olivia had been desperate, but he had been in a weird Zen state, so she thrust upward and took his knot. He had worked through his shock and then started pounding into her, growling and purring in equal measure as she squeezed him, and her second orgasm swept through her, a weird shivery sort of thing.

She clasped him as his steady pace built her lust and frenzy again. She clawed at him, whimpered, and he continued to rut her until she screamed and he roared again. He dropped onto her, and she licked and kissed at his chest and neck while they waited for his knot to recede in girth.

Reading about it, practising with toys, hadn't prepared her for the variety of length and width that she was running into.

Dexter asked, "Are you okay?"

She blinked up at him, panting. She smiled. "Yes. Pretty sure. How are you doing?"

The bright beam of happiness shone from his expression. "Amazing. You feel . . ."

She clenched on him, and he purred deep, which made her tighten around his knot again.

He kissed her and murmured, "You feel like heaven."

Her mind froze at the mention of heaven. She had been beaten often enough with god behind the fist that heaven and hell weren't something she sought out.

His brows snapped together. "What just happened?"

She blinked, and tears welled in her eyes. "It doesn't matter."

He stroked her cheeks and feathered kisses across her lips. "It matters. Now, what did I say?"

She took a deep breath. *"There is no place in heaven for a broken bitch like you. Heaven doesn't take omega sluts, and certainly, the defective cows like you won't get in."*

He gasped. "You . . . they told you that?"

She looked up at him. "It came with fists. I don't believe it, but I can't stop the memory."

He sighed. "What can I say to undo that?"

She rolled her hips and shuddered.

"Aw, fuck."

She gave him a shy smile. "That sounds better. Compliments are not really something I am good at. I don't have any experience with them when it comes to me." She stroked his cheek. "I am in therapy. I am working on it."

He kissed her palm. "I am glad because you are a thousand shades of beautiful, and I want to be able to tell you about all of them."

She smiled softly. "I look forward to hearing about it. For now, I am happy, my body is humming, and I think my soul is panting with exhaustion, but I want to keep going."

Dexter groaned, his ginger-kissed hair and black brows giving him a delightfully serious expression. The golden-green of his eyes was hot when he looked at her.

He was an adult, but he was still filling out. He would have massive shoulders when he finished maturing, and she really wanted to be here for that. Right now, he had the build of an athletic beta, but it was pretty obvious that he wasn't done yet.

He smiled. "I wish that tonight I could tangle around you until you could accept how you make me feel, but today was so that we could learn what you tasted and smelled like and felt like. We needed to learn you." He nuzzled her cheek. "Argus was the only one who had even had physical contact with you before the Omega Centre."

She blinked and vaguely remembered scent marking their hands. She blushed. "I don't remember much about that."

He growled. "You were in heat, so it is no wonder you don't, but you weren't reacting like any heat I have ever heard of. We got instructions on how your reactions might be unexpected, but we will try and work with you during your next one. They said it would start soon . . ."

He raised his brows hopefully.

She giggled. "That is what my bloodwork says. As you stated, I don't give off the regular signs, and you don't know me well enough yet to read the other signs."

He kissed her temple and her cheek. "What other signs?"

"I eat an obnoxious amount of fruit, I clean obsessively to get ready for the lockdown, and I hide when I am tired instead of trying to find someone to touch."

He blinked. "Oh, that is good information."

She smiled. "You asked. Secrets won't do me any good in the long run if I bond to someone."

He frowned. "If? You are our bond mate; we just don't want to rush you."

She sighed softly, wanting to ask him how he would feel about pulling someone hanging off a cliff edge when they didn't feel rushed. She didn't want to be rushed; she wanted to feel safe. Everything else would grow from that.

His knot was finally milked to satiation, and their combined fluids slipped out and dripped onto her body and then his bed.

Dexter sighed and kissed her softly. "I don't want to leave you."

She teared up and blinked. "I don't want to go."

To her surprise, the door opened, and Ambrose came in with a kind smile.

Dexter sighed. "He has a sixth sense for sex."

Ambrose chuckled and said, "Dexter, hold onto her and roll over to your back."

Olivia blinked as Dexter tucked his arms around her and obediently rolled.

She settled her legs to either side of his hips, and she was firmly down to his base. Dexter started swelling inside her again, and she blinked in surprise.

Ambrose chuckled. "Don't be surprised, Olivia. We will constantly be as aroused as you during your heat. A few minutes between us will be the norm."

He peeled off his clothes, and her eyes went wide. She jolted on Dexter, but he flexed his fingers around her waist and soothed her. "It's fine. Ambrose is our alpha, by age if nothing else."

Ambrose knelt behind her, and he touched her cheek, turning her head to his. "Let me know if you don't like something. Right?"

He kissed her sweetly. "I am waiting for verbal confirmation."

She took a deep breath. "Right. But no anal on the first date."

He grinned. "Noted."

He cupped her breasts and smoothed his hands over her skin; she exhaled and let the feel of his hands on her and the hard cock inside her take her away. They didn't cover this in the brochures.

Chapter Twelve

Ambrose did know what he was doing. Small kisses down her spine followed with licks and thick swirls of his tongue. He paid attention to where she relaxed, where she tensed, and where she vibrated with energy. Dexter's gasps when she tightened were also an excellent indicator.

Olivia was a picture-perfect omega; she just needed some help loosening the bonds created by pain, humiliation, and rejection. Ambrose and the others were willing to devote their lives to the project. An omega of their own had seemed unattainable for a fringe set of alphas. Feline manifestations were not common. The bark and knot were still there, but retractable claws and needle-sharp canines came along for the ride with growls, hisses, and a purr that could rattle concrete. He grinned and pressed against Olivia from behind and started to purr.

Olivia's eyes went wide at the deep rumble that ran through her. When Dexter joined in and his pitch was deeper and slightly off tempo, her body felt like it was being stroked by a thousand tapping fingers. "Ohhh." She leaned back on Ambrose, and he chuckled but kept purring.

She gripped his thighs as he stroked her breasts, and she rocked against Dexter as he fucked up into her. The purring got intense, and then, she screamed, fire blazing along her nerves and pleasure pulsing from her skin inward.

Dexter was knotted inside her, and she had no idea when that happened. She twitched and shivered in Ambrose's arms. Dexter's hands were on her hips, and he was panting as his cock bucked inside her.

She panted and leaned back, feeling the slicked erection behind her. Dexter grinned. "That was . . . you were . . . I liked that."

Something in his words caught her attention, and she blinked. "Dexter, how much sex have you had with other people in the room?"

Ambrose chuckled.

Dexter blushed. "Your phone calls were the start of it. I hadn't found anyone I wanted to be with before."

Ambrose smoothed Olivia's hair, "And Argus was your first so that you and Dexter wouldn't create a private lock over this. Losing virginity together can get weird if folks have a sentimental nature, and both of you do."

Olivia blushed. "Is that a bad thing?"

"No, but we are in a group, and while it is good to have things that are special, locking the others out is not a good idea, and when we are bonded, you will know how we are feeling, but if you have a private bubble before you start, it might be an issue. Felines do not normally create a pride with only one female, so balancing us will be awkward, even for us." Ambrose murmured.

"What?"

Dexter sighed. "We are jealous and solitary, but we got together because we got along, and then, a female is dropped into our midst, and we go from being a cooperative to a family. It will be an adjustment."

She squeezed around him, and she felt him spurt again. He was hotter than she was, and so was his cum.

"I don't want to be any trouble." She whimpered. "The Omega Centre said there were other packs that were looking for an omega, and a few said they would provide me with the therapy and stuff I needed."

Both of their hands tightened on her. Ambrose murmured in her ear. "Don't even joke about it. You are ours, Olivia. This is day one. So far, we are doing well. We have a gym, so we take care of our aggression there. We will never turn it on you."

"You get aggressive with each other?"

Dexter chuckled. "We are cats. Beating the hell out of each other at random is part of our charm."

She blinked. "Oh."

The knot eased, and the rush made Dexter groan. Ambrose moved swiftly. "And off with you before the cub starts again."

The arm around her waist lifted her free.

Ambrose murmured, "Do you mind if he watches?"

Olivia blinked. "Um, no?"

Dexter grinned. "Seriously? Best day for my bed ever."

Ambrose smiled. "Excellent. Do you mind if he touches you?"

"No. It's fine." She blushed. "He has clever hands."

Dexter beamed, and Ambrose chuckled. "He is going to put that on a needlepoint above his bed."

Dexter snorted. "T-shirt at the very least."

Ambrose eased her to her belly, and she brought her hands up to clutch the sheets. He stroked her hands. "Relax, Olivia. All you have to do is relax."

She tried to relax, but he started purring, and she knew that no big cat should have a purr like that. When he pressed his lips to her neck, she arched into the slight caress. He gnawed gently at the base of her neck and continued the deep purr down her spine.

His purr felt like fingers moving inside her and hitting her g-spot while fingers drummed along her skin. She moaned, and he spoke to Dexter while the sound of his purr filled her consciousness.

Dexter moved to her side, and he lay on his stomach to kiss her; she whimpered and clutched at him as slow fire was building inside her. His tongue duelled with hers.

Ambrose's voice murmured, "When she tenses, move away."

She whined as Dexter leaned back.

Ambrose's large hands smoothed over her ass and thighs. "Relax, Olivia. Relax or the touching stops."

She focused on relaxing, and it must have worked because he brought his mouth back to her as he kissed his way down the muscles of her shoulder blades to the curve of her hips.

Ambrose murmured, "I have never seen a female omega with this much muscle. You really did physical activities. Your ass is incredible."

She pushed her face into the sheets. The steady rumble of his purr continued, and it was arousing, but it took contact with both of them to make the pitch that took her over.

He stroked two fingers into her and a third immediately after. "Aw, did the cub's knot stretch you out?"

She whined as his deliberate caresses took her higher. He coaxed her knees up so her legs were bent and her ass was lifted for him. She felt him at her entrance, and he thrust inward, and she let out a shuddering groan as she took him in a slow slide that stretched her wide, right to the edge of the knot.

Olivia could feel the surge of slick around him to ease the fucking that was about to occur.

Ambrose laughed. "Oh, that is delightful. Good girl, Olivia."

She shuddered and kept herself burrowed in the sheets. He lay over her from butt to shoulders, wrapping around her. "No embarrassment in this; you are wonderfully responsive to us, Olivia."

She shook her head and turned to say. "Not embarrassed. I don't know what to do."

"Aw, honey." Ambrose chuckled. "That will be remedied with practice, and we are going to practice a lot. Every chance we get."

She shuddered.

"As for what happens next, it starts with this." He pulled out and then thrust in hard and fast. His thighs slapped into hers, and his knot nudged her clit. He got into a heavy rhythm, and she moaned, groaned, and her hips rocked to take him deep.

"That's my girl. Then comes this." His hips rocked forward, and she cried out as his knot pushed into her and locked.

She whined and panted. He reached under her and cupped her breasts, kneading the mounds and flicking her nipples.

She squirmed in his grip, and he started the rocking rut that took him to the end of her and pulled at her entry point. She whined and arched her head, rubbing it along his while he pumped into her and made a chuffing exhalation. He nodded to Dexter, and she yelped when warm fingers moved around her clit, and she started to shake as Ambrose took her to the edge of release. She whined again, confused and unsure. It was too much, too intense, and then, her control shattered with her scream.

Her body went limp around Ambrose, and he roared; there was no other word for it. He slowly came down on top of her, and he licked at her neck and ear. When he reached her cheek, he paused. "Olivia, are you crying?"

She ducked her head and kept her face down. She didn't answer. Not answering wasn't a lie.

Ambrose was still stuck, so he bent down and said, "Soon, you will be our bonded mate, and you can feel what we feel, and we can feel what you feel. You panicked a little? Scared? Nothing to hold on to?"

She nodded.

He sighed. "Well, you have had all of us now, so you know how we smell, taste, and feel."

She peeped at him through her hair.

"Nothing to be afraid of. We are all here for you."

She nodded.

He was able to ease out of her a few minutes later, and she closed her legs as he stroked her back.

She whispered, "Can I go now?"

Ambrose looked at her, and a frown formed between his brows. "Yes, of course."

She moved on shaking legs, grabbed her slip, and she ran back to her room, grabbing a pillow and a blanket and heading into the darkest corner of her closet.

She wailed into the pillow and panicked and dealt with the new instinct that had just unfolded. She felt more alone than she had ever felt in her life. They were going to wait to bond to her. She was going to be catatonic by then.

Argus checked the nest cam, and he frowned. "Ambrose, I thought you said she went to her room."

Ambrose had a pair of shorts on. "She did."

"Was there something wrong?"

"Well, she was panicked and was crying when we finished. She didn't feel like there was a connection."

Argus thought back to those pamphlets they had gotten from the Omega Centre. He dug them out of his bookshelf, and he found the one he was looking for that involved bonding. "Aw, shit."

He slammed the pamphlet into Ambrose's hands as he headed upstairs, and then, he heard behind him, "Dexter, Olivia's room. Now."

Argus got to her room, saw the cum-stained slip huddled on the floor, and followed their scents to the closet. Their scents. Hers had disappeared.

He opened the closet and looked around before he saw a small foot poking out of a rack of dresses.

"Olivia?"

The foot jerked into the shadows.

He crouched nearby and said, "Olivia, we forgot something important. You need one of us to bond you today. We won't have sex again today if you don't want us to, but one of us needs to anchor you to us, or your instincts will tell you that you don't belong. Nothing could be further from the truth. Just tell us which mark you want, and we will give it to you."

He saw a grey eye in the darkness.

The whispered word caught him by surprise. "Ambrose."

Argus blinked, and the other two were surprised. "What? Why?"

Her hoarse voice whispered, "He pushes me, so he needs to know when he went too far. I need the bond so I can punch him in the nuts . . . so to speak."

Argus blinked and chuckled. "Yes, Ma'am. Ambrose it is."

Ambrose chuckled. "I confess I hadn't thought of that aspect. If anyone could deliberately lash out through the link, it would be you, Olivia."

The grey eye crinkled in a smile. Ambrose reached out, and she pulled him forward. "In here."

He chuckled. "Can we compromise, and I will bond you in your nest?"

She paused and then nodded. "Okay."

He got up and pulled her out of the shadows, and her skin was shining with sweat and oils from the morning's activities.

Argus watched as they left the closet, and he exhaled in relief. He was disappointed that he wasn't first, but she had chosen based on logic and need. If she was asserting herself, it was an excellent start. They were all single-minded in this pride; she needed to know she had the right and responsibility to demand what she needed.

Argus patted a bemused Dexter, and they headed for the door. "Stay!"

She was settling in her pillows, her body still gloriously naked. "I want you two to stay."

Ambrose sighed. "I thought bonding was private."

She looked at him with narrowed eyes. "You had your chance to bond me in private. You wanted to play with Dexter."

Dexter grinned, and Argus raised his brows, then laughed. Well, it looked like Dexter's family was worried about fascination with the wrong pride mate.

Ambrose sighed. "I can't do this without touching you, Olivia."

She nodded. "That's fine."

Dexter's face lit up. "Group hug."

Ambrose looked up, and Dexter started purring. Ambrose's eyes lit up.

Ambrose took Olivia's hand and got her to her feet.

Dexter leaned toward Argus. "When she is between us, purr like you are trying to make her tits jiggle. She really likes it."

Argus was skeptical, but when a bemused Olivia stood between them, the guys crowded her toward him, and the purring started. He started his up, looking at her, and as the vibrations increased in pitch and tempo, her pupils widened until they were blown, she was gasping, and as he reached down to cup her sex, she cried out, and her knees buckled. He caught her and looked at the other two. From zero to orgasm around his fingertips . . . twenty seconds. They were all covered in peach perfume as well.

She blinked. "Oh, for the love of Pete."

Dexter laughed. "Argus, with you here, it worked even better."

Ambrose chuckled. "Oh, yeah, *Group hug* is definitely a pride thing."

Olivia mumbled against Argus's shoulder. "Fucking hell."

"After agreeing to go find you, this is the first thing we have done together." He stroked a hand down her back. "Let's try that again. Knowing the outcome, I thought we could beat our previous time."

Ambrose grinned. "I am in."

Dexter nodded. "Me too."

Olivia yelped, "Wait . . . hey . . . come on . . . aahhh!"

Argus started to purr with two fingers curved inside her.

The other two joined in, and they turned up the vibration.

Fifteen seconds later, she had thickened the air with her scent. They had found the key to unlocking their princess . . . it was a group effort and a sound no beta or other alphas could make. Nothing purred like felines.

Olivia slumped in their arms. They carried her to her nest, and she settled her dazed self in the pillows. Ambrose rested across her back as she floated in her warm haze. He pressed soft kisses across her shoulders and the base of her neck.

She shivered and squirmed against the soft, wet caresses. When he licked the base of her neck, she slumped with her eyes half shut. The bite that came a second later was followed by a purr that rendered her boneless. Her soul was pulled, thinned, and connected. She felt a wave of lust and heavy satisfaction that she couldn't figure out the motivation for. Ambrose let her go and licked the punctures.

There was smugness in the thread that bound her now. She fed irritation, and Ambrose chuckled. His licking was slow and thorough.

Argus asked, "Did it work?"

Ambrose nodded. "Yup. She is irritated with me. I get the feeling it will be a fairly constant state."

She hmphed. "He is really smug."

She could feel his smile, and he kept licking, his slightly abrasive tongue encouraging her body to heal the bite. Slick was forming and emerging as she took in his scent. The cinnamon bun-vanilla was surrounding her, and she remained relaxed in his embrace. He started to move his hands over her and nuzzled at her neck. The lust she noticed earlier was banked, but when he kissed her, it flared on her end of the connection as well.

Her pussy throbbed, which was normal, considering her activities that day. Ambrose turned her and came down on top of her with a thigh between hers. He cupped the back of her neck, and she gasped at the sensation. She knew what this was. This was a cheat code. She whimpered and twisted against him while he sucked hard at her nipples and squeezed her breasts. She arched as the wet suction threatened to pull another orgasm out of her. She threaded her fingers through his hair, and he purred again. She shrieked as his fingers slipped and slid around her sex, caressing her clit and delving inside her.

Wet. Hot... *omygodwhatishetouchingnow?* She came hard and clenched around the fingers that had been rubbing a spot inside her.

His pleased surprise was ringing in her mind, and smugness came immediately after, followed by a roar of lust as he tackled her to the soft bedding, and he thrust into her.

She came again when he bottomed out, and it continued when his thrusts lodged his knot and locked them together. Her feeling of being swelled, overfull, and aching for more ran through their link. His knot throbbed, his cock jerked, and she felt how tight she was around him and felt every time she squeezed.

He gasped and pressed his forehead to hers. "You... Precious..." He moaned and kissed her. He wrapped a hand behind her, and her new bond mark set her nerves to zinging.

The panic that had filled her during her first encounters was gone. Ambrose was her sex-obsessed anchor. She arched against him as waves of pleasure broke through her again.

She was feeling something she hadn't felt yet. Fatigue.

"Aw, precious, just wait. You are almost done with me."

She looked up into his dark amber eyes. "I am just getting started." She leaned up and licked his jaw. Her hips rolled, and his eyes widened as she massaged his knot, and he groaned, and she felt the hot jets inside her again.

She purred at him and stroked his hair. "Good kitty."

He burst out laughing, and they giggled together as he slowly released from her, and he slid out. She stretched and smelled popcorn.

Argus and Dexter were sitting in the corner of her nest . . . and they were sharing a bucket of popcorn.

She looked at them and burst out laughing. They grinned, unrepentant. Ambrose kissed her shoulder and licked the mark again.

He held her close. "We are going to nap for a bit. She's already started healing, so give her about twelve hours, and she can pick the next bond."

She chuckled. "Argus."

Dexter sighed. "Aw . . ."

Ambrose murmured, "After experiencing this with her, she's not wrong. We are going to need to hold you down, Dexter, or you are going to pounce on her."

Argus grinned, and he set his watch. "Twelve hours, and you are mine, kitten."

She shivered and whined, reaching for him.

Ambrose pulled her back into his arms. "Maybe you should take the viewing party outside. I don't want her crawling over Argus and trying to force a bite. Trust me on this . . . she can do it."

She purred and snuggled back against Ambrose. "Twelve hours of freedom, Argus. You might want to do some light stretching."

Ambrose laughed and covered her mouth with his hand. "Ignore her. She's high. You will figure that out as well."

The guys escaped, and Olivia was pulled into a nap with her first alpha. She snuggled against Ambrose, wished wistfully it had been Argus but knew that it had to be Ambrose. He had control, and she liked control, so their controls now meshed together.

Chapter Thirteen

Olivia was warm, comfortable, sweaty, and she smelled cinnamon buns. She looked at Ambrose, and he kissed her softly. "Good afternoon, Olly."

She wiggled happily at the name she liked. Then, she paused and sighed. "Did I just wiggle?"

He chuckled. "You did. Don't worry. Omegas are supposed to be bundles of excited emotion. It is part of your attraction."

She stroked the thick column of his neck. "So, what was my initial attraction?"

He was honest. "Omega in heat. Followed by woman in distress. Followed by omega who wanted us, not just one, but all of us."

"So, you guys get hit on a lot?"

"Sure. Women. Men. Other packs. We are pretty and talented, so they consider us assets to their unions."

She looked at him and cocked her head. He was pretty. Stunning. Golden-toned skin, golden eyes, and thick golden hair that didn't come out no matter how hard she had pulled. "So, you wanted your own pride?"

"Yes. Argus and I are from pack families; Dexter's parents are an alpha and beta."

"Oh. Does everyone live nearby?"

He stroked a hand down her back and caressed the bond mark. "Within two hours. Argus's father is his link to your area. His father and Derek are brothers. He spent every summer over at Henwell House."

She blinked, and a memory surface from before she had manifested. She had been ten and was doing swim trials with the other kids at the lake. She had been swimming with Paul and the older boys, cutting past them easily through the water. She had loved swimming.

That day she had been getting out of the water when a hand reached down and pulled her out by the left wrist, just lifting her out as if she weighed nothing. Paul muttered, "This is my cousin."

She had stared up at the man with black hair and icy green eyes.

He smiled. "You kicked his ass. Well done, little miss."

"Olly."

He nodded. "Olly." He turned around and walked off with the older kids and young adults.

Ambrose chuckled. "You met him?"

She looked at her wrist. "Sort of. He fished me out when I was waiting to climb the dock once. It was sixteen years ago, and he was already grown."

"He was eighteen. You were ten. He has a photo from that summer with you and the younger kids in a cluster in the corner. You were adorable. Do you want kids?"

"Um. Probably? I haven't had a chance to even think about it yet. They put in birth control during that first surgery just to keep my body from going haywire."

"I understand, but it is an option. Dexter's family would have a heart attack, but I think Argus's would be delighted."

"What about yours?"

"They would worship the ground you walked on." He smiled. "You're hungry. Some lunch?"

She nodded. "Yes, please."

He paused. "You know that I want to play with you, right?"

She smiled and patted his cheek. "And I think it is unfair that a guy with dark urges like you should have the scent of vanilla. There should be some chili pepper or dark chocolate in there or something . . . as a warning."

He grinned and helped her up.

She looked down and blinked. "Did you bathe me?"

"Wiped you down a little."

She blushed. "I need to get dressed."

"Fine. It's ten hours until Argus, by the way."

Her thighs were gleaming in a few seconds. "That was mean."

"But funny." Ambrose smiled. "You like him, huh?"

"He was sweet and funny, and he let me take care of his cats." She sighed. "It had been quite a while since someone offered me trust and flirted with me. The flirting was funny. I looked like hell. Wait. Maybe I was flirting with him. Oh . . ."

Her shoulders drooped.

Ambrose hugged her. "What is it?"

"I was flirting with him. He wasn't flirting with me. So . . . I am like one of those people chasing you guys. I suck."

"Aw, Olly. When he heard about you and got your sister drunk to get the truth of your situation out of her, you weren't there. Not even in the room, but you were on his mind. It could have been the way the boys went to you. They normally avoid strangers and stick to Argus."

She swallowed. "Oh."

"And you were the first thing he talked to us about when we got together at the party."

"Did you guys make the wedding?"

"Yeah. Don't you remember?"

She blinked. "Um, I don't remember much from my heats. It is better that way."

"Ah, well, I hope this next one is memorable."

Olivia chuckled. "Wait. What happens if it is on a workday? Or week?"

"We take it off. We know your heat is coming, so we are already moving things around and making sure that an hour of work per day will let us keep up with our obligations to you and our jobs." He hugged her. "Mainly to you. There are all kinds of regulations to allow alphas to be with their omegas. It is considered a medical emergency."

She exhaled. "Well, that is a relief."

She tried to get out of his grip, but he lightly purred and inhaled their combined scents for a few moments longer. When he helped her pick out another dress, he graciously allowed her a bra and some panties that were more a theory than a practical item.

"What is the purpose of panties made like this? I mean, seriously, I nearly tore them putting them on."

He growled. "But it is so much fun tearing them off."

She gasped. "They look frigging expensive."

He grinned and shrugged. "Spoiling an omega is the privilege of her alphas. We have enough saved to carry us through retirement and have decades more worth of working time ahead of us."

"I want to get a job."

He scowled. "Precious, you don't need to work."

"I have worked every day since I was fifteen. I can't just stop that urge to work because you guys want me to look soft and pretty."

He blinked. "What do you want to do?"

"I dun no yet, but I am going to figure it out, and you guys are going to have to support me or just catch me when I crash and give me a hug." She had no idea where the confidence was coming from, but she had a hint that it was the same source that was now feeding her wary encouragement.

She grinned. It seemed you could teach an older cat new tricks.

They walked into the kitchen, and an array of sandwiches, chips, dips, and vegetables were waiting.

She blinked. "Where did that come from?"

Dexter chuckled. "Takeout. Since you two were napping, we decided that we needed a half-decent break when you emerged. So, Argus, are you going to let me watch?"

Argus got him in a headlock, and they grunted and

wrestled, dropping to the floor with a thud as Argus got him in a hold and pinned him down. Argus growled, "You have to ask the lady. You are the performer; she's the stage."

Dexter huffed and nodded, relaxing. When he was relaxed, Argus stepped off him, and he smiled at her. "That is only going to last for six months more. He's in his final growth spurt."

Olivia looked at Dexter and looked up and up. "How much bigger is he gonna get?"

He smiled. "My dad is six-six. He stopped growing at twenty-four."

She nodded weakly. "Oh, good. Are any other parts of you going to get bigger because it was a pretty snug fit?"

He blushed and reached out to hug her. "I will never do anything that hurts you, but you are an omega, so you are super stretchy. It will be fine, Olivia."

She grinned and pulled his head down to kiss him. "I am sure it will be. It's just like seeing one of the giant sundaes on television and then seeing one in person, knowing that you are supposed to eat it because you ordered it. Good thing for you, I have a serious appetite."

She squealed as he picked her up, and when he cupped her neck to kiss her, he pressed the new bond mark. Lust shot through her, and Ambrose jolted and cursed. The air was heavy with her scent in seconds.

His eyes were wide when he lifted his head. "That was what the marks do?"

"Yeah. I believe modern parlance is either a hot key or a cheat code. Also, touching me there sends a signal to Ambrose, so unless you want him in your ass, be careful where you are touching."

Dexter didn't jerk his hand away as fast as Olivia would have thought, and Ambrose snorted. Argus laughed.

There was a lot of sex in the air, and it would have been weird if Dexter hadn't been curious.

She looked at the food. "Can I eat?"

Argus walked up to her and wrapped his arms around her. "Most omegas don't ask. They assume that everything is for them, including any other alphas who don't have pack affiliations."

She frowned. "Like . . . predators or bait?" She grabbed a sandwich and put veggies and chips on her plate, kneeling on a chair so that she wouldn't get the skirt messed up from the slick that had shown up.

Argus asked, "Why are you sitting like that, kitten?"

"So that the slick that just showed up doesn't mess up another dress before I finish eating. That mark thing is cheating."

Argus leaned over and tongued the mark.

Ambrose hissed and took a few steps toward them before he stopped. Olivia sent him a *sit down and eat* message. He blinked in surprise. "Did you just tell me to sit down and shut up?"

She chuckled. "Close enough." She opened her mouth wide and took a huge bite of the sub. She was halfway through the mouthful when she looked at them staring at her. "If you watch me every time I eat, you are going to have a part-time job of it."

Ambrose smiled. "You have mayo on your cheek, and it looks like cum."

"Oh, geez. Considering my morning, I am lucky it isn't all over me."

"Naw, baby, you took it all inside you and held it like a good girl." Argus kissed the top of her head.

She elbowed backward, nearly missing his groin.

He hissed. "I am going to need that in precisely nine hours and forty-two minutes."

"I am pretty sure that *I* am going to need it in nine hours and forty-two minutes."

He threaded his fingers in her hair and tipped her head back, kissing her soundly.

She looked at him and said in a firm voice, "Yes, Dexter.

You can do that."

He laughed. Argus grinned, and Ambrose ate his first sandwich.

They sat and ate, threw the occasional carrot stick, and then Argus said the magic words. "Did you want to go out and meet the boys?"

Olivia perked up. "Yes!"

Ambrose chuckled. "You can meet Caesar."

Dexter mumbled around his mouthful. "And Hector."

"More cats?"

Argus grinned. "Yeah."

They finished their meal, put the leftovers in the fridge for after the event, nine hours and fifteen minutes from then.

They took her out the back, and she saw an open yard that was acres of green space with sparse trees.

There was a jeep waiting near the back door, and they got in, driving down a path and around the corner. Argus was driving, and he filled in, "We started a big cat sanctuary on the property but realized that living too close made the neighbours nervous, so we bought the property nearest the lake and connected them. Technically two lots, but one is commercial, and one is residential." As they got closer, she could hear growling and roaring. The buildings and large cages became visible, and she smiled softly. Big kitties.

She remained calm when Argus came around to lift her out of the jeep, but she started to perfume as he slid her down his body. Ambrose chuffed and pulled her to him, walking her along the large enclosures and showing her Caesar.

She smiled. "Oh, who's a big friendly boy."

The cat walked to her and was rubbing against the heavy chain fencing. Argus was talking to three people who were staring in her direction.

Ambrose smiled. "Did you want to meet him?"

"Yes, please."

He smiled and went to the front of the cage, stepping in

and meeting with the chest-high cat who looked like he was greeting his best friend.

When Ambrose beckoned to her, she stepped in, closing the gate behind her. She walked up to Caesar and Ambrose, standing still and letting the big guy come to her. She was snuffled from head to toe and had a lot of interest around her groin. Ambrose grinned, and then, the huge head pressed against her, and she started to scratch everything she could reach. The thick fur was coarse, but he seemed to enjoy the scratching. There was a lot of chuffing, and then, Caesar pushed her toward Ambrose.

She grinned and then cuddled with Ambrose. "Is this what he was after?"

"Yeah. He was rescued as an adolescent from a breeder. They were planning on having him make more cats, but he has a sperm motility issue. An injury when he was little." He reached out and rubbed at Caesar's magnificent mane. "So, he looks amazing, but he doesn't make cubs. The rescue went in and grabbed the cats marked for death, and he was one of them. They called us when they couldn't place him. It took a while for him to warm to us, but now, we are buddies."

Caesar snuffled over her again and then dropped to his belly.

"What is he doing?"

He was trying to keep a straight face. "He wants you to get on his back."

"You are kidding."

"No. Not kidding. It's his way of flirting with pretty girls."

"Has he gotten any takers?"

He shook his head. "Not yet."

"Well, I do love a trier."

She walked up to Caesar and massaged his fur. The huge head turned, and he seriously nudged her toward his back. She sighed and hiked up her skirt, climbing onto the back of the lion. Her hair swung forward, and she settled with her legs bent, and her full weight was on the big cat. When he stood up, she yelped, and Ambrose laughed. Caesar walked toward the back of the enclosure, and when he reached the open space, he started running.

Cats were not made for riding. They were too wiggly and slippery.

She buried her fists in his mane, and Caesar bolted to the top of a pile of rocks where she was going to get off the lion when a tiger bounded up to them. When the boys came streaking toward her, she smiled and was going to step toward them. Caesar growled at the others, and she tugged on his mane. "Smarten up."

He stopped growling and lowered his head. The three human figures paused as she reached out to offer her knuckles to the jaguars, and she held still for the tiger to examine her.

She spoke to the lion. "Caesar. Bring me back to Ambrose, please."

She didn't know if it was the tone or the word Ambrose, but he walked down the rocky hill and then paced to Ambrose. Olivia got off and walked into his arms. "You were right; he wanted me on his back."

The other cats were gathered around and sniffed the spot she had been sitting on. She covered her mouth. "Oh god."

Ambrose was laughing, and Argus came up to them. "Yeah, the same thing that won the boys' devotion was sensed by Caesar."

She looked at him with wide eyes.

"They know a spectacular pussy when they smell it."

She punched him. "Rude."

The tiger was looking at her and was getting flirty. "Hector, I presume?"

Dexter grinned. "Yeah. She's amazing."

"Hector's a girl?"

Dexter shrugged. "I liked the name. She looks like a Hector."

The tiger walked around the other cats and came toward

Olivia. Dexter put himself between them, but the tiger pushed him away. She snuffled over Olivia.

Olivia looked at the tiger, and she smiled, extending her hand, but it wasn't necessary. Hector went straight for her groin.

"She's just about mature, right?"

Dexter blinked. "Yeah, how did you know?"

She grinned and stroked Hector's face. "Girl talk is universal."

Olivia could feel a few things. The primary thing was that Hector was about to go into heat; the next was that she had a thing for Caesar. Olivia looked at her and then asked permission. She was pushed to the back of the tiger, and Olivia extended her hand to Ambrose. "Kiss."

He kissed her and stroked his fingers across his mark. When it had the desired effect, Olivia dismounted.

The other cats gathered around Hector, and Caesar was obviously aroused. Olivia headed back toward the pens, and the boys came with her. "Guys, it is going to get loud and messy, and she isn't going to like it."

Dexter was shocked. "They are going to have sex. Wait, why isn't she going to like it?"

"You know the sandpaper near your knot? He has barbs. When he goes in, he doesn't come out without a fight."

The roaring was starting.

Ambrose asked, "So, what did you do?"

"He has a possessive interest in me via your scent, so when I slicked down her back, it triggered the right impulses in him."

Dexter frowned. "Why are we leaving?"

"Because if he isn't fast enough, she is going to beat the shit out of him. He can't have it if he doesn't earn it." She made it out of the enclosure with the boys and her guys.

The enclosure was carefully closed, and she exhaled. "So, that was fun."

She knelt near the boys, and they pushed their big heads

against her. "How are my brave babies? Screaming woman in heat didn't even phase you."

They rubbed against her, and she petted them, scratching under the chin and behind the ears.

The three staff in khakis were standing nearby. Argus smiled. "Den, Jerry, Harry, this is our omega, Olivia."

She got up and walked toward them. "Hi. This place is great, and the animals seem so happy."

Jerry, a brunette with soft green eyes, smiled. "Hello. Are you really an omega? I thought they were all soft and helpless, and you rode Caesar like a champ."

She chuckled. "I have very recent experience in clinging to aggressive blondes for dear life."

Ambrose growled and slid his hand over the mark. She yelped and looked up at him with an annoyingly fascinated expression. She could feel it.

The other guys laughed.

Den grinned. "Can I show you the rest of the animals? We have a hospital, a recovery centre, and also, we do educational shows and interviews. Well, Argus does most of the interviews with Romulus and Remus. They are the most well-behaved."

"I would love to see them. Argus, the time?"

"Eight hours and twenty minutes, kitten."

She smiled brightly. "Den, lead the way."

Den and the other two were betas, but they were strong, calm, and confident. Den took her through the displays, and Dexter loomed around. She extended her hand to him, and he moved to her side, wrapping his hand around her waist. He purred, and she leaned against him.

Den paused. "Wait. So you are an omega? I didn't smell anything before, but now, I smell . . . peaches?"

She wrinkled her nose. "Yeah, that is how I manifest. Dexter smells like pumpkin spice to me. When we fuck, it smells like thanksgiving dessert."

Den barked a laugh.

Dexter looked at her and kissed her slowly, lots of soft licking with his tongue and no care for the audience.

Den wasn't laughing a moment later. "Dexter, do your parents know you guys have an omega?"

"No. We didn't want to say anything until it was a done deal. The Omega Centre could have pulled her anytime."

"Uh, they are going to know right away. They are coming through the gates."

Dexter hissed and held Olivia close.

Ambrose and Argus joined them, and they faced the first social hurdle. Parents.

Chapter Fourteen

Dexter kept his body tight to Olivia's, and the others protected them. "Hey, Mom. Hey, Dad. What's up?"

His father was, indeed, six and a half feet tall and looked half as broad. His ginger hair was neatly styled, and his green-gold eyes were familiar. He looked at their gathering, his nostrils flared, and he touched his wife's shoulder. "We should go, sweetie."

The woman with black hair and dark blue eyes sighed. "You know I need to talk to him."

"After the weekend, Mira. He's busy." The alpha was wary of the pride facing off against him.

"Dad, Mom, this is Olivia."

Mira looked at her dismissively. It was no wonder. Olivia was squashing her scent with a practised move. Dexter sighed and looked down at her. "Shy?"

Ambrose murmured, "I think she doesn't want to upset your parents."

Dexter nodded. "Right. Let's get that over with."

She didn't know what he was planning, but she didn't have to guess when he lifted her against him, and he kissed her, touching Ambrose's mark. She whimpered and rocked her hips against his. Dexter's mother gasped, and his father chuckled.

"Wait. Do I smell peach pie?" The woman's voice was stunned.

Dexter grinned against her lips, and they giggled. She kissed him again, and he wrapped his arms tightly around her.

Ambrose ignored the necking couple and looked to Thomas. "So, our omega finally arrived. We have been marking the calendars for weeks."

Thomas blinked. "The peaches?"

"Yeah." He chuckled. "We have no issue smelling like dessert."

"Why didn't her scent come out earlier?"

"She has issues with letting it out, but as you can tell, with us, she has no difficulty. We've started the bonding, so Dexter won't be leaving today."

Olivia was kissing Dexter slowly, neither of them in a hurry, and Olivia's scent wrapping around them.

Mira looked at her little boy, and when Dexter slid his hand under Olivia's skirt and stroked her ass, she made a distressed sound.

Thomas wrapped his arm around Mira. "I will get her out of here. So, she's actually an omega?"

The perfumed slick started to emerge, and Thomas's pupil's dilated. "Right. Got it. Come on, Mira. Let him have his day off, and he might consider talking to us again in a week or so."

Ambrose grinned, and Thomas looked shocked. He looked at Argus and smiled slowly. "You look . . . relaxed and happy."

Argus nodded. "We have our mate. We have been worrying and waiting, but she's here now, and we are getting used to each other. Olivia's scrappy and has her hang-ups, but we all do. So, it was nice seeing you, Mira, but Dexter is not going to be chatting with you this weekend. Or probably for a good chunk of next week. She's about to go into heat, and it will be all hands on deck."

Thomas grinned. "Is sex with an omega all it's cracked up to be?"

Olivia squeaked on cue and then started whining as Ambrose guessed that Dexter's fingers slid into her. She was right. The panties weren't a barrier. Her perfume thickened, and Dexter purred.

Ambrose watched Thomas's startled expression, and Mira looked a little irritated. "Why is he doing that?"

Thomas sighed. "He's letting his omega know that he's happy and she's safe. Her response is going to be pretty immediate."

The delicate, happy purr that tinkled like glass bubbles on crystal sounded, and there was a lot more licking and kissing going on until Olivia gasped and squeaked against him. Shaking in his arms.

Ambrose could feel her bright orgasm in his side of the bond. His erection was going to be a familiar friend by the time they were bonded, but seeing the look in Mira's eyes as her little boy made Olivia cum with his fingers and a purr was priceless.

Thomas started laughing. Ambrose looked at him.

"Peaches. All of the designs for the last month have been peaches."

Mira looked at her husband and opened and closed her mouth with a snap. "She's the one?"

Thomas looked at his wife, and he laughed. "Yeah, I am pretty sure she is. Instead of frowning, try and think about how we can include her in the family business. Bye, Dexter. Have fun bonding to that nice young lady."

Mira's eyes were wide as her husband steered her back toward the entrance to the rescue centre. "But my boy . . ."

"Hasn't been a boy for years. Let him and his pride enjoy their omega. Think of things that she can do with the company. She's adorable with a sense of humour in her eyes. I think he is going to be designing for her for a while. Just let him, or he will break with the company, and we will be screwed."

Ambrose listened to Mira asking why Olivia was so special and Thomas's answer. "Because she's theirs."

That was what summed it up. She was theirs.

Ambrose felt the urge to continue bonding, and he walked to Dexter and held his arms out. Olivia was in his grasp a moment later, and Dexter licked and sucked his fingers, and they walked back to the jeep with Argus bringing the boys along.

Olivia twisted in Ambrose's arms, and they kissed slowly, tongues soft and raspy during the drive back. The boys grumbled a bit, but that was just because Olivia was in his arms and not Argus's.

She was relaxing into his arms easily now, her mouth tangling with his, and her thighs rubbed together. Ambrose growled and clutched her to him; the urge to take her again was overwhelming.

She blinked slowly, pulled herself up to straddle his lap, and he unzipped and unbuttoned, his erection thick in her fingers as she guided him in. Once he was inside her dripping heat, he gripped her hips and pulled her down with a firm stroke as his hips thrust upward.

He had no idea if it was the bond working, but she felt hotter, wetter, tighter as he began to move her over him. He opened the top of her dress and pulled the cups of her bra down, forcing her breasts up and out. She gasped at the first touch of his tongue, and he felt the surge of slick around him. He moved her with his hands and sucked at one breast and then the other in turn while she squeaked, whined, and moaned.

They were behind the house, and they continued to fuck slowly as Argus parked the jeep. Ambrose looked up and watched as she arched, threw her head back, and moaned as his teeth teased her nipples before his mouth dove in, and he worked her breasts in a frenzy. She tasted like peaches, smelled like peaches, and they were his new favourite fruit. Tangy, sweet, and feminine, her breasts carried a different scent than her belly, and her pussy was the well of all the variations. Right now, she was fresh peaches and peach syrup with an overlay of Dexter's spices.

Ambrose smiled. "You smell like pie."

She groaned and tugged at his hair. "You smell like a cinnamon bun with vanilla icing. Are we comparing scents now?"

He thrust deep, and his knot was desperate to lock into her. He lifted her up and pulled her down fast. She stretched around him, let out a cry, and his knot locked in place, and a growl crawled from his throat as the stranglehold on his knot squeeze him until he shouted, and his cock spilled ropes of cum into her belly.

Her cunt was fluttering around him in hard squeezes, and he grinned that taking the knot had brought on her orgasm.

She whimpered and rolled her hips against his, the undulation squeezed his knot in a slow wave, and his cock could still feel the clasp and squeeze of her channel. He lasted longer than he thought he would, and his knot pulsed waves of fluid into her before they were able to rest.

Olivia pressed her forehead to his. He stroked his mark, and she moaned, squirming against him.

She shuddered, and her internal clasping resumed.

They sat in the jeep for ten minutes. There was no way he could walk with her on him. He would have started over again. He chuckled and licked her cheek. "How are you feeling, precious?"

She gasped, and when the hot fluid bathed his cock, he chuckled. Her strangled, "Fine," made him laugh.

She muttered against his mouth, "Have you guys been saving up or something because this is ridiculous."

"A quarter is my cum, a quarter is knot fluid, and the rest is you, precious." He tapped her nose.

She blushed. "I'm gonna dehydrate."

He laughed, and they left the vehicle after he righted his trousers.

He held her hand, and it felt completely normal though he had never had a giggling lady at his side in his life. His normal impulses did not elicit laughter, but with Olivia, it was joy that she shared through their link, and he loved it. The power of the bond was knocking him on his ass, and it hadn't even been half a day yet. He didn't regret a thing.

Argus went through Olivia's wallet and cards, including her license that had been transferred to their address by the Omega Centre. He explained what they were, how to use them, and what their limits were.

She blinked and edged away from them. "That's too much."

Ambrose raised his brows. "It really isn't. I am sure we forgot to pick up certain things for you, and this way, if you see them, you can pick them up for yourself."

There was distress coming through the link. "What's wrong?"

He took her hands and rubbed her knuckles. "What's the problem, precious?"

She looked at him with huge eyes, and he could see her freaking out behind those eyes. "I am . . . not used to having money. I work for it, but I never get it, so I don't know what I am supposed to do or how I pay the bill if I don't earn money."

Ahh. The other two looked surprised. They were used to omegas and their adorably narcissistic ways. Olivia hadn't even met another omega, let alone seen one in action. They might want to arrange that once they were firmly bonded. She needed to see the difference between her and other omegas. He rubbed her knuckles; it was quite a difference.

He smiled. "You read the terms of our taking you in with our pride. We have to supply you with everything you need. The money is what you need. That way, you won't feel pressured to comply with us. You have funds to go out and have fun when you make friends."

That snapped her brows together in a scowl. "Why would I want to go out with other people who aren't you guys?"

Argus leaned forward. "Kitten, you used to have friends,

used to laugh, go to the beach, you swam like a shark. These are things that we want you to do again."

She blinked. "So, we did meet when I was little."

"Littler. Yeah. You are still teeny. Paul was pissed when you beat him, and I had to hold in my laughter."

She sighed. "You were very pretty then."

Ambrose snorted, and Dexter chuckled. Argus raised his brow. "I *was* very pretty."

She nodded. "Now you are stunning, but I think you know that."

Ambrose stared as Argus turned beet red. "Wow. That's . . . not a look I have seen on him."

Ambrose reached for his wallet and took out a five. "This is for making his face do that."

She giggled and put the money back in his hand. "First one's free."

She was still fretting, but it was subdued.

"You have time to figure out what you want to do." Ambrose tapped her nose. "What do you already know how to do?"

"I can run a guesthouse . . . but that's about it."

Argus perked up. "We can help with that. I have been debating putting one in at the rescue. Letting folks learn how the animals live and how the rescue works is something we want to do."

She frowned at him. It was so cute Ambrose wanted to fuck her again, right there. She looked like an angry kitten.

"Don't you dare just make a bullshit job for me to keep me from wandering around."

Dexter looked at her and cocked his head. "You could model jewellery for the family company. I have some pieces that I have designed in the last day that would suit you. I just need to get them down in a digital render."

"Uh, I don't think that your mom would like that."

"Yeah, but my dad owns the company. It would be fine. We use a male omega for some of the stuff, but I think you and Ford would get along. He would also show you how to do things as an omega."

The other two groaned. "Only after we have all bonded to her. Ford has a tremendous draw, and while he isn't a threat to the pride, he is a persistent flirt."

She blinked. "A male omega? There were two or three at the centre, but they kept us apart."

The guys looked at each other and snorted. Dexter explained. "Ford never met a set of legs he didn't want to split, male or female. If you met him, one of us would be there as chaperone."

Olivia scowled. "Why? I have defended myself from gropers before."

Ambrose smiled slightly. "He wouldn't grope . . . well, he would, but he is excellent at seduction, or so the betas around him say."

"Wait. I am allowed to seduce betas?" She blinked in surprise. That wasn't in the brochures.

"No!"

Olivia's lip trembled after they all shouted at her. It was a sudden roar, and it startled her hard-won calm. Tears welled in her eyes, and Argus lunged to her and pulled her onto his lap. The seating area was comfy, and she was better able to cuddle against them.

"Olly. Kitten. We would prefer that you didn't run around attracting random attention. We are private people, and sharing you with betas would be rough. Plus, they might only be using you as a stepping stone to us. We don't want you hurt."

She blinked. "Then why introduce me to a horny omega?"

He chuckled. "Ford means well. He is in my age bracket. He had a pack, never bonded, and they went their separate ways. No bonds, no ties. Now, he has bodyguards that he uses for relief, and he invites other alphas in to ride through his heats."

She was relaxing against him, and he purred for her.

There had never been anything as satisfying as her body relaxing into him because she trusted him. That trust was something that she gave, and he was going to keep earning it as their time together spun on.

She rested her head against his shoulder and stroked his chest. The tiny caress made him want more, and he checked his watch. Four hours to go. He groaned.

Ambrose chuckled. "Do you want me to take her?"

Argus growled. "I am fine. She's fine."

"How is her mark?"

Argus sighed and checked. It was red, but it had been getting a lot of action. "You need to take care of it."

"Hand her over?" Ambrose chuckled.

"Do it while I hold her."

"Fine. Scoot over."

Argus made room for him, and Ambrose slid in next to him, stroking the hair away from her nape and licking it slowly.

She gave a hiccupping little purr, and Argus cuddled her close, stroking her back and holding her tight. Ambrose reached for her, and they curled into a small ball with her at the centre. Dexter didn't want to be left out, and he curled on Argus's right with his head in Olivia's lap. Argus cursed himself for not thinking of it first.

They remained curled up until Olivia's stomach snarled angrily.

He chuckled, and he pressed a kiss to her forehead. "Time for a hot dinner."

She blinked. "We have subs in the fridge."

"You have had a rough day. You need a proper meal; plus, it will keep us distracted."

She peeped up at him through her thick lashes. "Okay."

Dexter unravelled himself, Ambrose got to his feet, and Argus carried her into the kitchen. He set her on the kitchen island and kissed the tip of her nose. "Now, let's get something hot into you."

She wrinkled her nose. "That is why I was trying to burrow through your chest. I have had something hot in me at strange intervals today."

Dexter and Ambrose laughed.

Argus tapped her nose, and then, they went and put together a mountain of fajitas.

The air was thick with the grilled vegetables and steak. Dexter took care of the flatbread, and Ambrose picked her up and set her at the table on one of the chairs.

Argus set the platter of grilled stuff down on the table, and he put a fajita together for Olivia.

He watched as she picked out the sliced onion and bit into the flatbread. She hummed happily and went crazy with the condiments, but she had a proper dinner and lemonade.

Three pride meals in a day. Things were certainly different with an omega in the house.

Chapter Fifteen

Running out the time in Ambrose's lap while he checked on her bite every twenty minutes or so went quickly. Argus was getting progressively more tense as they watched the romantic comedy, and Olivia wasn't sure if it was the movie or the time.

She dozed in Ambrose's arms, and Dexter was sitting on the floor, absently giving her a foot massage that made her arch back into Ambrose.

This was the second movie, and it was just wrapping up with the dorky beta hero pledging his allegiance to the deceptively sexy beta heroine as she turned down the fascinating alpha.

"Aw . . . that's sweet." She spoke in the silence.

Three pairs of eyes looked at her accusingly.

"What?"

Argus murmured, "They made the alpha look like a bully."

"With anger management issues," Ambrose murmured.

"And bad fashion sense," Dexter muttered. "Who wears a leather jacket to an office?"

She chuckled. "So, the alpha was unfairly depicted?"

They all agreed. Dexter grabbed the remote and queued up the next movie. Another romance based on an omega singer and her three alpha bodyguards.

Argus went to get some hot chocolate when there was a beep, and it was coming from the kitchen. There was a blur with black hair and golden skin. Ambrose pulled his arms back. "Your turn. Fair and square."

There was a dark chuckle from Argus, and he sprinted up the stairs with her. Olivia clung to his neck, and she was surprised when he brought her to the nest again.

"My nest?"

He nuzzled her neck. "You relax more easily here, so it is the best place for the bonding."

"Will you let Dexter know when to start his clock?"

Argus laughed. "He doesn't need to wait; we just needed the first bond to lock in. You and Ambrose can each pull on and shore up the other. So, you can now accept other pride members."

"You make me sound like a private club."

"Oh, you are. Very exclusive." He peeled his shirt off and unbuckled his belt, unsnapping his jeans. She watched in rapt fascination as panels of muscle were exposed, and she dug her fingertips into her palms. She groaned when he stood there in tight boxers and socks, then giggled when he flicked the socks at her. She batted them away, and he tackled her into the nest, holding her carefully and landing on his back.

She giggled and covered his chest with tiny kisses. His hands gathered the folds of her dress and hauled upward, pulling it off over her head. She was left in the miniscule lacey bits that Ambrose had picked out.

Her hair was everywhere, but she clawed it into order and grinned down at Argus. She looked at him and took in the sparkle in his eyes, the dark, thick waves in his hair, and the pulse in his throat. "Hiya, Argus."

He smiled at her. "Hello, Olivia."

She nuzzled his neck and murmured, "Have I thanked you properly for coming for me?"

"Oh, nothing I want to do to you is considered proper, kitten."

She chuckled and licked his neck happily. He tasted like the best kind of calm, safe afternoon in the woods. The only place she had been safe.

She nibbled at him and felt her bra release and then slide free. She rubbed her breasts against his chest and rocked on his erection through the ridiculous barrier of her panties and the snug confinement of his briefs.

He groaned. "You learn quick, Olivia."

She was panting. "I find you . . . inspiring."

He chuckled. "Oh, honey, you make me dream of things I have never even imagined before. I certainly would never have cuddled with Ambrose before tonight."

She smiled and closed her teeth over one of his nipples, tugging softly. "That was nice. I like having all of you close and breathing you in."

He tugged at a lock of her hair. "Do you, Olivia?"

She nodded. "The scent is waking up and having breakfast in the woods. I was always safe in the woods."

His arms closed around her, and he pulled her head to his, kissing her softly before rolling over and pressing her into the soft blankets and cushions. "You have a way of breaking my heart and filling it at the same time."

She frowned. "I don't understand."

He brushed his lips over hers and smiled. "It will become evident soon enough."

It was the last bit of conversation as he took the lead on their encounter, and it felt like her blood caught fire.

She wanted to keep tasting him, loved the feel of his skin against her tongue. His scent got heavy around them, and hers was running riot. She rolled her hips against his, and he groaned, but then, he moved down her body until his lips were against the thin layer of lace, and he lapped at her with his tongue. He slid two fingers into her as his tongue dragged over her clit under the fabric.

She threaded her fingers through his hair, and she whined as her hips moved against his fingers and lips. Her body became one huge pulse, and she screamed as he slipped a third finger into her and thrust deep. She clenched on his fingers, and he chuckled.

He slowly stroked her through her climax and murmured soft words to her as she came down from the sudden spike.

When he withdrew his fingers, he licked them and sighed happily.

She blushed and reached for him, "More, please."

He laughed. "So polite."

He held the fingers that he had just had inside her to her lips. She licked, sucked, and slurped greedily. She heard him curse, and he grabbed her left wrist, returning the favour by mouthing and licking down her skin until he returned to a spot beneath her wrist and he bit. She moaned, and the link between them started forming. She felt more. There was just suddenly . . . more.

She purred softly, and he released her arm, licking at the mark that had pulled their consciousness together and made part of her echo at his frequency, or he changed to hers.

He purred heavily as he licked her wrist, and lust flickered through with something brighter and stronger. His mark would activate anytime someone grabbed her wrist. It was an alert system, and when he or her pride touched it, it would start her engine faster than cheap cocktails, or so she guessed. She didn't actually drink.

She shivered and whimpered. "Can you come inside me now? I feel hollow. I ache."

He paused and closed his eyes before opening them and leaning back to peel off his boxer briefs. Her underwear was dealt with by his claws, and then, he was leaning into her, and she was more than ready.

He pressed in, and she pressed back until his knot was nudging at her. He pulled out and slid back in on a slow stroke. Olivia sighed and fed him her satisfaction through the link. This is what she had missed. Argus. She wanted him to fuck her forever.

He pressed a kiss to her neck, her temple, and he licked at the inside of her wrist when she laid her hand on his shoulder. They rocked together easily, and she enjoyed the slow climb of pleasure until urgency crept in just before the peak. She tried to move faster, but he held her pinned and kept moving at his unhurried pace.

"Argus, faster." She plucked at his shoulders and fed him her urgency.

He shook his head. "No."

He continued his steady strokes, and she started to shake with every thrust and slide. She whined in frustration and heard and felt Ambrose come into the room. He moved in the nest and sat above her head, taking her arms and pulling them taut. Her balance was screwed, and she had no way to speed up the thrusts. Ambrose held her wrists in one hand, careful of the new bond mark. He reached down and stroked her breasts with the other, teasing and chafing her nipples. She moaned, and her body began vibrating faster until she shattered, and her body clenched down on Argus's cock, but his knot was out of her grip.

"Oh, there we are, love. Just squeeze me a little more."

She blinked and gasped, but when she reached some kind of benchmark that he had in mind, he thrust in and locked the knot into her. Her eyes went wide, and the breath rushed from her lungs. The long, low wail wasn't a sound she had ever made before.

He chuckled. "Easy, kitten. Just a little experiment to set the bond."

He took her left hand from Ambrose, and he turned it so that her bond mark was exposed. He began to tease them with the same dexterity and enthusiasm he had offered to her sex earlier. The first surge of slick coated his cock, and her eyes widened again as she realized what he was doing. He was using the bond mark as another erogenous zone.

He continued to simply mouth at the mark, and her breathing took up a whining hitch. His hips began to rock, and when she purred, he rutted in earnest, the short jerks of his knot against the band of muscle meant to hold him. He pounded against her, and the spiral of pleasure vectored sharply upward until she screamed and he roared.

The bond sent hot satisfaction between them, and she

smiled weakly. "Well, that worked."

He looked at her with a smirk. "It did indeed."

She sent her attraction and admiration and the feeling she had in her chest when she saw him. His eyes went wide this time, and he smiled softly before kissing her with an aching gentleness. She felt an overwhelming warmth through her body, and more fluttering clasps squeezed his knot. It felt like an emotional hot bath. It was designed to comfort and relax.

Their lips and tongues continued to meet and part while they waited, and when he separated from her, they started over again with her on her side and Argus at her back.

Ambrose licked and sucked at her breasts while Argus lazily thrust.

When he locked inside her, she moaned low and shook around him, her teeth clenched on a groan as the sensation of having him locked to her taking up space in her perfect memories. He stroked her throat, licked Ambrose's mark to send lightning through her, and traced his own mark with delicate fingers. His mark made her clench.

"Gods, Olivia, you are so fucking tight."

His words made her clench again, and he groaned, spilling inside her. She whined because now the countdown to him leaving her started.

"Aw, are you sad because I came? You wanted to feel me inside you longer?"

She nodded.

Ambrose chuckled. "I think you will remain her favourite. I am good with that. As long as I can join you occasionally. I think her face would be sweet if you were in her pussy and I was in her ass."

Olivia's eyes widened, and Argus chuckled and groaned. "She enjoyed that idea."

Ambrose smiled. "I know. It was like an electric lick through the bond."

He and Argus chuckled. Olivia groaned and said,

"Arrangements will have to be made in advance for that. The prep work would have to be set up."

Ambrose kissed her softly. "Helping you get ready for that would be my honour."

She shivered, and Argus grunted. "That is a weird honour."

He grinned. "Anything to make it easier for her to give yourself to us with no reservations."

She gasped. "Sounds like a title for my book."

They both froze. "Book?"

She paused and blushed. "The centre had me work on writing as part of my therapy. So, I already have enough for a book. Margot suggested that I continue with my first few weeks with you guys, just to wrap things up and give the readers a conclusion."

Ambrose asked, "Can we read it?"

Argus kissed her shoulder. "Me too."

She shrugged. "You know all of it. Well, the broad strokes."

Argus placed his hands low on her belly. "I like broad strokes, but I wouldn't mind knowing details."

She sighed. "You are going to get mad."

"Probably, but your past is part of you, and while it doesn't have any bearing on how I feel, I would like to be warned in case it rises again."

Dexter spoke from the corner of the nest. "I agree. Are you going to publish it?"

"Uh, doesn't that involve a long process of submissions and stuff?"

Ambrose grinned. "Not if you cheat. I designed a lake house this summer for the owner of a publishing house. I am pretty sure that she would take a look at it."

"I don't want to cheat." She frowned. "Is that cheating?"

Dexter chuckled. "It is being escorted to the front of the line. If the book isn't good or doesn't have a marketable hook, it won't sell."

Argus licked her ear. "Dexter's older sisters are in publishing. One is an editor, and one designs cover art in-house. He's the baby."

"Oh. Ohhh." She shuddered as their bodies slowly unlocked. Argus massaged her belly, and a rush of slick and cum followed his cock out of her.

A deep whimper left her chest. Argus kissed and licked her wrist, and her body relaxed against him again.

He murmured softly, "Dexter."

Their fourth moved in, naked and aroused but careful. Ambrose moved aside, and Dexter slid in front of her, smiling. "You consent to the mark?"

She grinned, and Ambrose winced, and she felt Argus tense. They hadn't gotten formal consent. It was implied consent and begging all the way.

"I consent to the mark, *Dexter*."

He lunged at her, licking and sucking at her mouth, and the kiss got progressively more dangerous as time went on. His hands gripped her waist and pressed her against him, rolling his hips to hers.

His affinity with Hector was marked in a few ways. He was also larger than standard, and he desperately wanted a mate.

It was excellent because she desperately wanted a Dexter.

Chapter Sixteen

She slid her thigh up to his hip, and the desperate eating kisses continued. Olivia was sure that having an orgasm from kissing was just something that women started dreaming about when sex hit their radar, but she was fucking close.

She rocked against him, seeking friction, but he kept his hands on her waist and didn't move into her as he drove her insane with the slip and slide of his tongue against hers. His purr was heavy, and he slid his thigh against her sex. She opened her eyes wide and clutched at his shoulders as her clit enjoyed the deep vibration he was providing her with.

She shrieked into his mouth and dug her nails into his shoulders as her control snapped and her orgasm hit. It felt like a punch to the abdomen followed by a hard squeeze, and she whimpered.

He lifted his head and looked to Argus and Ambrose. "That is . . . she's . . ."

She looked at Dexter and held her control. "If you want to mark me, I hate to rush you, but time is definitely a factor. I haven't ever . . . been free during a heat. It's coming on pretty quick."

He moved down her body, licking and sucking at her breasts before nuzzling the curve of her hip where he liked to rest his hand. He nuzzled, licked, sucked, and then bit. She moaned and twisted, but he caught her hands and stroked her thigh. When he raised his head, he murmured, "Easy, babe. Can you feel it?"

She closed her eyes, and the shimmering line of emotion and curiosity was stretched between them. She moaned, and he kept licking at her while he slid his fingers inside and curved them; this was a test; she could feel it. He moved carefully, and when she jerked, he slid his fingers rapidly over the raised area inside.

She went from a moan to a yelp to a silent scream while looking into Dexter's eyes. He kept a hand over their mark, and the heat that pulsed rhythmically through it was an added sensation. Her eyes went blind as she looked at him, and pleasure pulled through their link and lashed through him.

He shuddered, and she felt the sticky spurt on her belly, so she reached down and squeezed his knot, causing a deep grunt, and his hips jerked against her hand, his cock fought her grip, and his knot resisted, but the clasp was what he needed to drain the pressure.

She stroked a few fingers across her belly and licked them slowly. The scent was pumpkin spice, and the taste was Dexter.

Dexter shuddered and pressed his forehead to hers. "I didn't know you could do that through the bond."

Ambrose blinked. "What did she do?"

Dexter's features lit up. "Just for me? Aw, babe."

Olivia grinned. "It was a test for me, too, and since you weren't going to be inside me, I thought that sharing the pleasure was the best bet. It worked."

He grinned and bent to tend to the bite. His tongue was extra raspy, which made her skin super sensitive.

Argus bent her back and kissed her softly. "What did you do?"

"I fed him my pleasure through the bond while keeping the light connection between you and Ambrose. I look forward to sharing with you during my heat, but then, I won't have a choice. I wanted to test the choice because it was my last chance to make that experiment of my own free will. When I share with all three, I might lose that individual touch if I didn't practice it."

Argus grinned. "You are very clever. You are close?"

"Unfortunately. I think mating with all three of you has kind of set it off."

Ambrose was moving around, and he went to check on her. "Uh, Olivia, did you have an abdominal spasm and then a surge of slick?"

"Yeah. Why?"

He reached down and held a small piece of plastic on thin cables. She blinked in horror. "Oh, nonononono. Not now."

Ambrose stroked her thigh. "Don't worry. It can be replaced."

Dexter blinked. "What is it?"

Olivia was pale. "My birth control. The Omega Centre wanted me to have a controlled heat before I tried to get pregnant."

Dexter frowned. "We can get condoms."

She swallowed. "That won't do much with the cum that's still inside me looking for an egg. There is no way to undo that."

Argus held her tight. "We all want kids, Olivia."

She looked at him. "But, I just became me? I don't know if I want to be a mom yet."

Ambrose stroked her thigh, her IUD in his fist. "You have a lifetime to change who and what you are, but you will always be ours."

The calm that was washing through her was thick and warm. It was also heavy and taking her under. "Guys. Guys. Knock it off."

The calm eased up, but it was replaced by concern and at least one trill of excitement. Olivia glared at Ambrose, who was trying to play it calm. "So, DNA testing determines who the father is? Do you even have room here to start a family? Space seems pretty allocated."

Ambrose grinned. "I can totally put on an addition. I have one drawn up already and have tentative planning permission."

Argus murmured, "We could buy Ford's place. It is really huge and adjoins the rescue."

Olivia sighed. "Can't we just call the Omega Centre and see if there is a doc around that can implant a new one? They aren't exactly uncommon."

Dexter sat up. "They can do that?"

She leaned back against Argus. "Yeah. The one that came out should have made me inhospitable for a while yet. Sorry for the initial panic, but I have myself under control now."

Ambrose frowned. "I'll make the call. I'll be right back." Naked and unconcerned, he left her nest.

Argus stroked her belly. "Did it hurt?"

"No more than normal heat cramps and far less than what I used to go through, so . . . yes?"

Dexter scowled. "It hurts when you go into heat?"

Olivia took his hand and wove her fingers with his. "Everything stretches, fills with slick, prepares for a marathon. It is a deep ache, but my body starts it suddenly. It is like two hundred sit-ups in under a minute on a full stomach."

Dexter winced. "I am sorry."

"Don't be. With all of that going on, the ovaries launch and the uterus preps for visitors."

Argus chuckled. "You would have been fun to share a desk with in health class."

Dexter leaned down and licked at her mark. She twisted, and her breath shuddered out of her in a rush.

She squirmed against him, and she wanted nothing more than to wrap her thighs around him and ride him until he roared.

Olivia looked at him and Argus and blinked. "Uh-oh."

She fed them some of her heat, and they both stared at her. She passed it along to Ambrose, and she heard a thud and then, "Damnit!"

She chuckled. "So, that works."

Argus murmured, "Are you playing with us?"

"No, just trying to find the remote control to the bonds before things get weird. Hot. But weird."

Dexter opened and closed his mouth. "What . . . what was that?"

Olivia smiled. "That was a teeny, tiny portion of what you are going to be feeling in the next six to twelve hours, and you will be feeling it for three to six days. Your nerves will be on fire, your skin will take every touch as pleasure, and if you rub up against one of the other guys, it is going to be nearly as hot as touching me. You are going to want to get inside me every moment that my body is calling yours, and it is going to call constantly."

She looked at him with narrowed eyes. "You guys are going to fuck me until I pass out, and as soon as I wake up, you are going to start again. I won't eat, I will barely drink, and when it's over, I am going to need some alone time, or I might want to just crawl into a pile of my mates and sleep there. I have no idea. I just have gone over forty-three recorded descriptions of heats by different omegas, and this is the average I have figured out."

Dexter grinned. "I know; I just like hearing you say it. Best. Weekend. Ever."

Argus murmured, "And part of the week. You might want to warn your parents. They tend to fuss."

Dexter groaned. "This is not a call I thought I would have to make. *Hey, Mom and Dad, you know that nice lady you just met? I have to fuck her until her heat's over. Don't worry, I will be screwing around with our other bond mates at the same time. What? Oh yeah, I will see if they can all make a family dinner next week.*"

Argus leaned in as Dexter got to his feet. "He likes to rehearse."

Dexter flipped him off and left the room.

Olivia sighed. "Sorry."

"Don't be. They warned us two days ago that it was imminent. The only unexpected part was the birth control failure, and considering the circumstances under which it was inserted, I am not surprised it crawled loose."

She wrinkled her nose. "Neither am I. I hope Ambrose has some luck."

Ambrose walked in and headed to her closet. He walked out with some fabric over one arm. He was wearing a long, heavy silk robe.

"You know, for an omega in heat, they have someone who makes house calls. She's on her way." Ambrose smiled. "Get up, precious. We have twenty minutes, and we may want to take care of that other matter since it is going to be a long weekend. Dexter is ordering groceries. Argus has to let his family know as well, though their pack will be highly amused that he ended up with an omega, a bond, and a heat in the same twenty-four hours."

She extended her hand to Ambrose, and he took her wrist. She collapsed as her body reacted to the grip on her mark. Argus hissed. "Easy, Ambrose."

"Oh, sorry, man." He picked Olivia up and set her on her feet. He tucked her into her robe and escorted her dazed self to the restroom. "Come on, Olivia, before you want to slap the hell out of me."

Argus was still laughing twenty-five minutes later when Ambrose's cheek was still glowing slightly. It seemed that the lust-haze had worn off mid-prep, and Ambrose had said the wrong thing.

Olivia was sitting on the edge of the kitchen island—grumpy—and the doctor was going through all of the pros and cons of the IUD placement.

"Given the failure, I would recommend a pregnancy test in a few weeks, just to be sure. Are you sure that you want to use this? Your mates could use condoms."

Argus nodded. "We will, but we would like a backup."

Dr. Ursel smiled. "Good. Sensible. I wish more alphas

would think like that. Most are in a breeding frenzy. How long have you been together?"

Argus smiled. "Less than a day, but we have been pledged for five weeks. She also had medical complications during her last heat, so they asked us to make sure that she could have an uncomplicated one."

Dr. Ursel frowned. "Let me make a call."

The doctor left for a moment, and Olivia made a face, glaring at Ambrose. "The kitchen island?"

He grinned. "If you want me to set up an exam table with stirrups, I can have one here in an hour."

She paled. "No, that's fine."

He leaned in. "That's fine . . ."

She glared at him. "That's fine, sir."

He chuckled and kissed her slowly, she caressed his jaw, and when he leaned back, she tapped his cheek. His grin was unrepentant.

Argus asked, "So, what do you think Dr. Ursel is doing?"

Olivia sighed. "Getting my medical history or the salient points." She looked at him. "If the doc comes back grey, she got the details."

They were all in their robes, and Olivia was wearing light silk that Ambrose had picked out for her. Argus had thought that having pride robes with their favourite beasts painted on them was ridiculous, but he was happy for the option to get down to skin the moment the doctor was gone. He looked at the robe Olivia was wearing, the fabric outlining her tight nipples. She needed a matching robe, but he couldn't figure out what her cat would be if she even had one.

Dexter returned with the groceries, and he put them away, keeping a stack of sports drinks aside. Argus asked, "Dexter, if you looked at Olivia and had to figure out her big cat, what would it be?"

Dexter grinned. "Easy."

He walked over and whispered it in Argus's ear, and he shouted with laughter. It was pretty dead on. Argus said softly, "Let Ambrose know."

Dexter walked over to Ambrose, and after a short glance at Olivia, he went and grabbed his phone. The artist was about to get an email.

Olivia took the opportunity to ease to the edge of the counter in preparation to jump down, but Argus stopped her and said, "Just a few more minutes, kitten."

She wrinkled her nose. "I want you inside me now." She stroked his chest in the vee of his robe and pulled at the fabric, yanking him to her.

Argus was surprised by the aggression, but his omega had a need, and he was duty-bound to fulfill it. He tried to soften her heat with gentle kisses, but if he didn't mistake himself, she was spelling his name against his lips with her tongue. "Oh, fuck, kitten."

A feminine throat cleared. "Olivia, I understand the need for this device, even as a temporary measure. Argus, was it? Please stand aside. Oh, you might want to hold her hand. This is not comfortable."

Olivia sighed and lay on her back, pulling her feet up and tucking her heels next to her hips. He had never seen her from that particular angle, and it was perilously close to presenting to her alphas. The doctor took a look and sighed in relief. "Well, at least you haven't been at her yet."

Argus and the others looked at each other, "Uh, doctor, we have been at her for the last twenty hours. What are you seeing that we aren't?"

The doctor set to work, and Dexter went to hold her hand. The doctor spoke conversationally. "You are feline alphas, and your knot has a ridge of small abrasive spurs, right?"

They all agreed.

"Well, Olivia hasn't any of the signs of abrasion or inflammation that I normally see after a woman has entertained one of your sub-designation. Felines don't easily breed for that reason. It is hard to get repeat matings." She finished what she was doing and withdrew her tools, putting them in a bag.

Olivia was breathing heavily, and Dexter was stroking her forehead.

"The pain and cramping will subside in a few minutes, possibly an hour. If there is excessive bleeding, call me. If you dislodge it again, call me, but you might want to consider just taking your chances if chemical contraception won't hold, risking the ten percent chance of conception during your heat might be a suitable alternative."

Argus was shocked. "You are telling her to just roll the dice?"

"More or less. She's an omega; they were born to breed with alphas. You are alphas, and you have found an omega who can tolerate your particular mutation. Enjoy it. My granddaughter has been fighting her designation and has found nothing but misery. Olivia has a terrifying back story, but she has the men she wants."

Argus grunted. "Are you sure about that?"

Dr. Ursel took out a set of scissors, and she was about to cut the strings when Olivia muttered, "Cut them as short as possible and roll them up, Doc. I am pretty sure that the last one got . . . uh . . . snagged on someone."

The doctor paused. "Right. The barbs. Excellent logic, Olivia." The strings were clipped and rolled up before she tucked them inside.

Dexter helped their mate sit up, and she winced and got her robe back into concealing lines.

She gave Argus a smile. "Well, that dumped some ice water on my hormones."

He rubbed his cheek against hers and purred. He looked to Dexter and Ambrose. "Group hug."

Argus held Olivia in his arms, and Dexter and Ambrose came in. They started to purr, and Olivia looked up at him. "Oh. You bastards."

He grinned, and their purrs got deeper and rougher. Dexter slid a hand to cup her groin, and she shrieked, and her knees gave way.

The doctor was looking at them as they chuckled and parted, leaving Argus holding their throbbing mate.

Dr. Ursel looked at them and nodded. "Wow. That is the first time I have seen that move. I can feel your purr at the back of my throat from several feet away."

Olivia mumbled, "My throat is not where I am feeling it."

Argus chuckled. "Give us time, kitten."

She bit his chest lightly and looked at him, a slight grey ring around wide, dilated pupils. "Time is something that just ran out."

Chapter Seventeen

The standard ibuprofen was taken, and she had a snack while the guys looked at the instructions on the pamphlet from the IUD.

"You guys are sure hooked on pamphlets." She finished her veggies and dip after they had expressed their dismay at how things had been done in the wrong order.

Argus smiled. Ambrose answered. "Most men say that women don't come with instructions, and if they did, they wouldn't read them. We are determined to gain any insight into you, and if it only comes in pamphlet form, we will read it."

There was something that had happened during the doctor's visit that was sending little curls of pleased lust through the links, and she could feel it in all three. "You guys are happy about something. What?"

Ambrose grinned. "We didn't hurt you."

She snorted. "With the amount of slick you have been inspiring, I would doubt that you could."

Argus chuckled. "She couldn't tell that we had been frolicking for nearly a day."

"There were intervals."

Dexter rumbled, "But you weren't stretched out or swollen or anything."

Olivia covered her face with her hands. "Right. Got the idea. Thank you. Armour-plated, latex vag. Got it."

Dexter snorted. "Not hardly. You are all slick, soft satin, and tight, eager muscle."

She thudded her forehead against the table.

Dexter murmured, "Shouldn't I have been honest?"

Ambrose chuckled. "You described her very well. I would have gone with oiled velvet, but yeah, she clenches hard enough to grip a single finger, so no wonder she can milk a knot. The miracle is that she has space for a knot at all."

Olivia got up abruptly and said, "Uh, I don't need to be here for this discussion, do I?"

She headed out back to the brick patio, and the boys ran up to her. They had an enclosure at the house, but they knew how to open it.

She went to a lounge chair and had a seat, the boys on either side, their heads on her lap. She must have fallen asleep because a voice she didn't know called her out of her nap.

"Well, well, where did they find you?"

She jolted awake and saw the man standing six feet away. He was living midnight, and his expression was admiring. He had a nice scent. Baked apples wafted toward her.

She looked at his black hair, blue-black skin, and dark amber eyes. "Hello."

He smiled and walked toward her. "Ford Rathsmussen at your service, dear creature. Did I catch you before or after one of the cats mauled you?"

She frowned. "I don't understand."

He crouched next to her, and he chuckled. "Which of the pride do I have to negotiate with for your body. I will only deter you for a few hours, days, weeks. Probably weeks. I am very generous with my lovers. You will be compensated for your time."

She pulled on her links and swallowed. "Um, I am not interested."

He leaned forward and was speaking when he realized, "Your scent tells . . . wait. Where is your scent?"

She sighed in relief when she heard the rustle of her guys behind her.

She got up and walked around the chair, straight to Argus's arms.

Ford came toward Argus. "If she's frigid, I can thaw her out for you."

Ambrose snorted. "Not necessary. Our omega can withhold her scent."

"If that is an omega, I am going to hang up my dancing shoes."

Argus chuckled, and Olivia saw the question in his eyes. He kissed her and purred. She was ready in less than a minute, panting and rubbing against him.

Ford spoke while she was making out with her favourite mate. "Peaches? You find an omega, and she smells like peaches?"

She said, "When Dexter, Ambrose, and I get together, it is like a fucking bake sale."

Ford paused. "Is she making a joke? She has a sense of humour? I had pinned her more for an inflatable doll."

Olivia growled and started to turn to smack Ford when Argus pulled her back.

Argus held her with an arm under her breasts, and he licked at Ambrose's mark before he tended his own.

"Bonded? I just meet the love of my life, and she is already bonded?" Ford chuckled. "How are you two dealing with that?"

Dexter joined them and kissed her softly, sliding a hand inside her robe to caress her hip, which nearly exposed her to the other omega. Ambrose wrapped himself around the other side. "She's our bonded mate, and she is in heat, so do excuse us, neighbour."

His eyes gleamed with excitement. "Wait. So, she's a pride mate? Are you accepting pride applications? I have been looking for some boring men with a fun female to attach to. I come with four alphas of my own, none bonded."

She frowned and didn't know what kind of a joke he was making.

Ambrose had frozen in place. Dexter's hand squeezed, and her body throbbed, and she whined, slowly moving her hips against Argus.

"We are heading inside. We'll be in the nest." He lifted her carefully and nuzzled her neck before nodding to Ford and carrying her inside.

Olivia held tight to him as he carried her up the steps and down to her nest at the end of the hall.

"Why was Ford here?"

"He was probably here to borrow some lube or liquor or both."

She laughed. "Was that flirting? I am not really good at spotting it."

"Yes, kitten. That was flirting; I thought there were elements of seriousness in it. He's been looking for a female omega to partner up with, and I am delighted that you were bonded to us first. He has a powerful draw."

She smiled as he set her down in her nest. "Does he? I didn't notice, and what? Two omegas together? That would be non-stop screwing."

He grunted as he untied her robe. "Yes, please."

She chuckled. "You wouldn't get anything done."

He groaned. "But . . . it would be so nice to have you two to watch."

She pinched him; it took a bit to find a piece of skin that wasn't taut over muscle. "You haven't even seen me through a heat yet."

Argus leaned in and nuzzled her cheek. "How hard could it be?"

She sighed and let the rising heat bleed into their bond. "Let's find out."

His eyes went wide as she shared the full force of the burning in her blood, and he slipped her robe from her shoulders and pressed her back into the softness of her nest. When he slid into her, she started the countdown. She normally burned for three days, so she was curious to see what an actual free heat was like.

As he thrust into her, she wrapped herself around him,

and her scent was freed. It was the beginning of a long three days.

Olivia was sitting in a large tub with her three exhausted alphas when she came back to herself. She murmured, "What did I miss?"

As she moved, flickers of memory started to rush back, as if her brain had ignored making memories to concentrate on drawing more out of them.

Argus kissed her neck. "You didn't miss anything. We have a surveillance camera in your nest if you want to watch a replay."

She blinked. "Why?"

"We didn't think things would go this quickly, and we wanted to make sure you didn't say you were happy here when you weren't," Ambrose murmured and reached for her.

She settled easily against him, and an ache in her backside reminded her of where he had spent a good portion of his time. "Where are we?"

Ambrose smiled. "My room. A large bed and bath were set up for the hope that we would grow into them one day."

Dexter had his arm around Ambrose, and Olivia knew exactly when that had happened. Argus had been under her, Ambrose in her ass, and then, he grunted as Dexter worked inside him. The waves of pleasure that ran through all four of them had swirled in her, and she gave them back, so everyone was on the same level as the thrusting and rocking brought her to another fast orgasm.

Dexter was humming with happiness. He had lovers for the first time in his life, and his purr was tremendous when he eventually took her on his lap and rubbed his hands over her. "Are you all right? We are fucking flattened."

She smiled and opened her thighs as he stroked his fingers against her bare sex. At some point, Ambrose had shaved her pussy, and then, things had moved along faster. Everything got a lot more slippery.

She glared at the oldest alpha of their group. "We are going to have a discussion of appropriate grooming suggestions and why doing that during a heat is not something I will be a fan of again. It will be a waxing appointment a few days before. I ended up with a bit of razor burn the first day."

Ambrose frowned. "You didn't say anything."

"I was trying to lick my way down your happy trails; my mouth was busy."

He grinned.

She was being assailed by memories of slick and filthy groping, laughter, groans, and more sex than she considered physically feasible. She was a little tender, but that was it. She really was made for it.

She pulled away from Dexter and ignored his sad sound. She moved back to Argus and wrapped herself around him, straddling his lap. He had always been careful with her, had made sure she was comfortable when the others pushed the limits, and his scent still made her feel at home.

"Aw, kitten. You're sleepy?"

She nodded. "Yeah. Just a little rest, and I will be fine."

She burrowed against him, and his arms wrapped tight around her, and she slept.

Olivia woke up sandwiched between Argus and Ambrose with Dexter's hand on the curve of her hip, over his mark. She looked around the room, and they were in Ambrose's room. He was the oldest, so it was the only thing that elevated him from the rest. She slid a leg out of the pile, and the arms holding her tightened. The deep purring started, and she dozed off again.

She stretched and rubbed her nose against Dexter's chest. They were alone together, and she blinked sleepily. "Where did they go?"

"Argus had to put out some kind of emergency on a

jobsite, and Ambrose is talking to a client while making lunch."

She squirmed. "What day is it?"

He smiled. "Wednesday morning. You had three intense days and then one recovery day. You did good, Olivia. I'm exhausted."

She felt the bone-deep satisfaction in her body. "So, do you want to get up and get dressed or slow sex?"

His hand was moving smoothly between her thighs, and he was purring like a maniac. She rolled him to his back, and his purr went up a notch. He grabbed a condom from a bowl next to the table, and she grinned. "Thanks. Do you want to help? I flunked that course at the centre."

He laughed and opened the condom and rolled it down and over the expanding knot. She crawled over him and pressed him into her, sighing happily at the heat ever-so-slowly making room for itself inside her.

He clenched her thighs and shuddered. "Oh, babe, you are killing me."

She continued her slow progress to take him in until her thighs rested on him. She looked down and grinned. "Huh. It went in."

The veins in his neck were standing out, and he gripped her hips. "Oh, god. You feel . . ."

She braced a hand on his belly, and she squeezed around him, clenching hard.

His groan as his cock flexed inside her was adorable. She started a slow undulation to rock herself in place, stirring him inside her and driving herself higher, using the small range of motion that his locked knot allowed. She took Dexter's fingers and pulled his fingertips to her clit. He caught on, and then, he started that deep motorcycle purr of his.

She continued the slow ride, and when she was panting over him, he reached up and cupped her right breast in his hand, squeezing her nipple with just enough pressure to send her over the edge. She screamed softly and kept moving her hips through the spasms until she slowed and collapsed over him, lying on his chest. His purr still rattled him inside her, and she clenched again. He groaned, and she felt him flex again.

A low whistle from the doorway got her to turn and look. Ford was standing there with a tray. "That was lovely . . . and now, I want pie."

Olivia looked at him, and he settled on the bed as casually as if he owned the place. Dexter was still relaxed, so Ford's visit must not be unexpected. She snorted mentally; he had a view of the doorway that she didn't have access to. Dexter had seen him watching.

She leaned up on Dexter and looked at Ford. He checked out her breasts and belly and the position she was in that resembled doing the splits.

"Aww, pretty. You still stuck?" He raised his brows.

She nodded. "I am straddling a guy I have known less than a week when a new strange guy wanders in, and I am not diving for a robe, blanket, towel, or closet. What do you think?"

He grinned. "I will admit to timing my entrance. So, where did they find you?"

Olivia looked at Dexter, and he shrugged. "On my knees trying to claw my way into a soundproofed shed so I could scream my way through a heat. I am assuming they moved in after you?"

Ford picked up a piece of fruit and held it out to her. She took it obediently, and his eyes lit up. She noted that it was a peach, but she just shook her head and smiled. "So, you have been friends with the pride for a while?"

"I used Ambrose as an architect when I bought the lot next door. He designed my house. Then, he and Argus linked up on the job and moved in here. It has been torture having such gorgeous alphas next door, and when Dexter moved in, my heart broke. So much pretty, and they had no interest in me."

He fed her some more fruit, and she leaned forward and gave Dexter half. His eyes gleamed. "Thanks, babe."

She snorted.

"You are an interesting creature. You look soft all over, but when I look in your eyes, I see the keen intellect of an educated alpha." He held out a strawberry, and she took it, then licked the juice from his fingertips. He shuddered. "That was mean."

She grinned, and the strawberry appeared between her teeth, and she shared with Dexter again. He was fondling their bond mark. It had healed during her heat, and now, the contact created a warm hum in her body with his fingers over it.

Olivia cocked her head. "Why are you here?"

"Ah, two omegas in the same neighbourhood is unheard of. I thought it would be fun if we became friends. I have all kinds of events that I can bring you to. You would gain quite a following."

She looked at Dexter. "Why would I want a following?"

He grinned. "Omegas crave attention."

She shuddered. "Not really. I really just want to figure out an occupation and keep myself busy, then have cuddles and messy sex with the guys."

Ford's eyes lit up. "What kind of occupation? Porn?"

She blinked and leaned back. "No. I give it away; I don't charge for it."

Ford laughed.

Dexter sat up and wrapped his arms around her. "She's written a memoir."

Ford leaned in. "I know dozens of folks in publishing. They are deadly dull but are always looking for someone to have dinner with. Apparently, they like eating."

She clapped a hand over Dexter's mouth. "It was a memoir as an assist to therapy. It isn't finished."

Ford reached out and stroked her thigh. "Let me read it. I

like reading stories about cute omegas and their coming of age."

"Uh . . . that isn't exactly the story."

Dexter traced his tongue on her palm. She let his mouth go. "Yes, pet?"

He raised his brows. "Pet?"

"Scooter? Junior? You can pick a name if I can replace . . . babe."

He chuckled. "My dearest, honey-dripping omega. Let him read it. I have his email. We can send it to him after we uncouple and Ambrose stops leaning in the doorway."

She was appalled. "You are not calling me *that*."

A silky touch caressed her cheek, and Ford was extremely close. He whined. "You smell good. Sooooo . . . good."

Dexter snickered. "Your scent comes out when you are aroused or irritated."

"Good god."

Dexter's knot let her go, and the rush of scent caused Ford's eyes to roll back in his head, whimpering. "Oh, my god."

His head was suddenly at the point of connection, and Olivia squawked as he started licking. Thinking that he wanted to get at Dexter, she separated them and moved back. Ford tackled her and buried his head between her thighs as he licked and sucked ferociously.

Confused, she looked at Ambrose and saw that he was surprised and amused. "Ford is impulsive, and he won't go further, but despite him surrounding himself with male alphas, he prefers females. Are you uncomfortable?"

She blinked as his tongue swirled around her clit and his fingers entered her. "No, but this is kinda strange. The betas back home don't do this a few minutes after meeting someone."

She arched as the fingers hit that spot inside her, and she mewled, twisting her hips against his hand. His mouth sucked and nibbled; she felt the building in tension, the air filled with peaches and syrup. She panted, writhed, and locked her fingers in his dark hair as she started to shake. Ambrose kissed her softly. "It's okay, precious. Let go."

She wailed, and her control shattered. Ford continued to move his fingers inside her, but he licked around his fingers, gathering the slick against his tongue. She moaned and shuddered as he swirled his tongue around and around.

She had just calmed when she started climbing again. Green apples filled the air, and she squirmed. "Whoa. Wait. What's going on?"

Ford looked up, his mouth shining. "Can I have more?"

She blinked. "Why?"

He whispered, "You taste so good. Please?"

She glanced at Ambrose and Dexter. They shrugged. She sighed. "Fine. But this is the last time. I want to take a shower."

He chuckled. "That is possibly the least sexy invitation I have ever gotten, and yet, it's the most irresistible."

He dove back into her—or rather his—happy place. She sighed and panted lightly as he went on, but when Dexter and Ambrose decided to help, she was lost. They painted her nipples with fruit and sucked both breasts at the same time. Her marks were all stroked with slippery fingers and focused tongues. She moaned, whined, her hips moved violently, and her body took on that peach nectar scent. Ford was moaning, and she finally came with a silent arching of her back as every nerve was locked and on fire.

She clamped on Ford's fingers, and he let out a low moan, and his scent splashed over her in a wave, which set her off again. She screamed and clenched so hard, he hissed, the waves of enjoyment sent her off, and she slowly came back to herself with a stunned Ford looking at her and Ambrose and Dexter stroking her hair and torso slowly, purring to calm her down.

She was panting, and Ford has his hand wrapped around her ankle. "I swear to god, if you try and put your dick in me right now, I am going to cut it off. As much as it seems like the best idea in the universe."

Ambrose raised his brows. "Really?"

"Yeah, his scent hit me, and I went off again. I wanted nothing more than to just crawl over him and get him inside me."

Ford whined. "Why didn't you?"

She winced. "Wow. Not a good look for you. It is bad enough when I do it, but I am usually blacked out with lust."

He gave her a wry look. "I came from just watching you the second time. That hasn't happened in . . . well . . . ever."

"Oh. Good. I am going to take that shower now. Which way was my room?" She was disoriented but needed to get away from Ford.

Dexter helped her off the bed and led her to her room, where the nest had been stripped, and the clean pillows were stacked and waiting. She wanted to fix her nest, but a shower was more important.

She told Dexter that she wanted to shower alone. She gave him a slow kiss and pushed him out. She climbed into the shower and fought the wave of shame that came over her. Tears fell hot and fast, and her throat swelled. What she had had with her alphas had been special for her, even if the memories were swelling and fading into her thoughts. Reacting like that to Ford filled her with humiliation.

Ambrose picked up his phone. "Hey, Argus. What's up?"

"What the hell just happened?"

He and the others were in the kitchen, and he paused, seeking the bond. It was placid.

"What's going on, Argus?"

"She . . . fuck . . . I don't even know what she's feeling right now. Shame? Anger at herself. Disgust?"

Ambrose frowned. "Ford asked to play, and we said she could."

Argus growled. *"Did she bring it up, or did he?"*

"He did. Why?"

"She's a people pleaser. She won't say no to us. Ever. What you just told her was that you would let other people have her, and her opinion wasn't required."

"But, everyone wants Ford."

"Yeah, and we all know that Olivia is everyone. That she has no self-control." Argus growled. *"I will be home in an hour. I want her dressed and being cuddled in the living room, but she needs to know that you aren't going to start offering her to neighbours."*

Ambrose heard Dexter forcing the bathroom door. "Dexter went to get her."

"Good. Take care of our mate. She doesn't know anything about social or sexual relationships. She is learning from us and . . ."

"Got it. Get home when you can." He hung up and touched the link again, and his knees shook. Her actions during her heat had been explained to her as normal and natural. Having a strange male omega go down on her while her mates watched wasn't.

Ford raised his brows. "Something up?"

"Yeah, you need to leave. Olivia is having a crisis of conscience because she doesn't know what happens after her heat."

"Oh, come on. Everyone knows omegas have a nearly limitless capacity for sex." He chuckled. "This also isn't her first heat."

Ambrose pinched the bridge of his nose. "Olivia isn't most omegas." He gave Ford a shortened version of Olivia's history.

"She was told that her pride would be her mates, and no mention of outside partners was ever mentioned. Reacting to you feels like a betrayal to the pride."

Ford nodded, chewing on a carrot. "I am not going to go."

"What?"

"Having me scuttle away will add to the shame. When she comes downstairs, let me hold her. If her attachment is linked to mating, I can help her with that. I can also explain a bit about being an omega that those stuck-up betas at the centre won't have shared with her."

"Argus will be pissed."

"Argus has absolutely no interest in me if I am not in heat. You and Dexter are a little more flexible."

Ambrose sighed. "Just because he doesn't want to have sex with you doesn't mean that Argus doesn't like you. You just don't stop flirting long enough to have a conversation. He's really a chatty guy and has a lot of other interests. He would be a good friend if you put in the effort."

Ford glanced upward. "You think he will let me after today?"

"Yeah, but I think I am going to have my ass handed to me." He didn't think it, he knew it, but he liked to pretend that there was a chance it wouldn't happen.

Chapter Eighteen

Olivia sat on Dexter's lap while he soothed her. She wore the dress with the buttons from the first day, and she inhaled Dexter's scent. She had been surprised when he broke the door to her bathroom and shocked when he started cuddling her. She was still confused about what was going on, but looking over at Ford made her wonder what was going on.

Ford smiled. "Are you calm now, Olivia?"

She nodded. "Better. Why?"

"Come sit with me."

"Why?"

"Because it would make me feel good, but it will also make you feel good. You like the way I smell, right?"

She nodded. "Yeah, but . . ."

"And I like the way you smell. That is basic attraction. I am not going to do anything sexual, and you are safe here with your pride mates. Right?"

Ambrose and Dexter nodded. Ambrose said, "We only thought that he would make you feel good earlier. If I had thought about it for a minute, we would have taken you out of there. We keep forgetting that this is your first relationship. You just settled in with us so naturally."

Dexter smiled at her. "If he tries anything, I will claw up his pretty face."

That seemed to be what she needed. Her body told her that being with Ford could be so much fun, but her consciousness said she was a whore for thinking about it.

"Born to be a whore. Stop that stink!" Her father's fist hit her in the jaw and knocked her to the ground.

She blinked and pulled herself out of the memory. Dexter

looked at her warily. "What happened there, babe?"

"Uh, memory. Bad one. Therapy starts this week. Again."

Ford asked Olivia. "Will you sit with me?"

She looked at him in his position on a comfortable chair. He looked so tempting, but she wasn't sure she wanted to risk irritating her bond mates.

Ambrose blinked, and he said, "If you are attracted to him, it doesn't damage our relationship with you. We get echoes of your pleasure through the link, but it doesn't hurt us. We *know* you chose us."

Dexter sighed. "Besides, he's an omega. He isn't a challenge to us when it comes to you."

She blinked and smiled.

Ford chuckled. "What Dexter is trying to say is that it is unlikely that you will get pregnant if we have sex, even during your heat or mine." Ford held out his hand. "Come on, baby omega. I can answer most of your questions."

She blinked and left Dexter's grip.

She walked toward Ford, and he smiled, his white teeth blazing against his dark skin. He held his hand out to her, and when she slid her palm along his, they both narrowed their eyes. He chuckled. "Feels nice, huh?"

She nodded. "Um, where do you want me to sit?"

"Honestly or for the sake of your comfort?"

"We are going to say for the sake of my comfort."

"However you want to sit."

She walked in close and sat with her back against his chest as if he was a throne. He chuckled in her ear. "Interesting placement choice. I would have you pegged for cuddling like a kitten."

"Not with you. Not now." She grabbed his arms and wrapped them around her waist.

"Slightly better."

She placed her hands over his, her fingers lacing with his.

"I am not letting you weasel your way through the buttons." She murmured, leaning her head back on his shoulder. "I thought omegas were all small."

He grinned. "I am small for an alpha. I am slightly above average for a beta. Omega males are all over the board."

She nodded. "How do you make money?"

"I am a video producer. I make micro-movies with a musical background."

Ambrose added. "He wins tons of awards every year."

Dexter grinned. "We get invited to the parties, but we don't often go."

She nodded and asked Ford, "You don't have bonded alphas?"

"No, but I have always had my eye on your guys."

She tensed.

"They have chosen you, bonded to you after only knowing you for a few days, and you weren't even in heat yet. There is something there, Olivia. Your links are strong and bright?"

"Yeah."

Dexter tickled her through their connection, and she smiled.

"Then, don't worry about it. If you do anything to tick them off, hurting you would mean hurting them. You have a bond. If they don't want you to be near someone, they will say so, and you will feel it."

She blinked. "I am just getting used to them."

"I know, but with the link, they feel like you have always been there. They forget." He kissed her neck softly and nibbled her ear.

"What are you doing?" She needed it stated.

"Trying to get you comfortable with me in the way that always works for me."

She stiffened in his grip.

"Olivia, do you like my scent?"

"Yes."

"I like yours a lot." He rolled his hips against hers.

"That has become apparent."

"So, I want to get closer to you, and as we are neighbours,

it stands to reason that we will spend time together. I like your guys and get along with them. When we get together for social stuff, I would like it if you would come along. What would you like?"

"You work with music?"

"Yes." She felt his wry acceptance of whatever she was going to ask.

"Do you dance?"

"Of course."

She leaned to the side and looked at him. "Can you teach me?"

Ford blinked. "What?"

"Can you teach me to dance? I don't know how. Never learned. The guys have already had to put up with me learning how sex works, so I don't think I should punish them by making them live through my stomping on their feet."

He smiled slowly. "You are willing to stomp on me?"

"Yup. You want to get close enough to me that I will consider having sex with you? The price is teaching me how to dance."

Argus came in, and he looked at Ford and Olivia, scowled, and then took in Ford's expression. "She just said something that stunned you, huh?"

Ford nodded. "She is saying that she might sleep with me if I can teach her to dance. Who will be the judge of whether I have done a good job or not?"

She smiled and looked at her guys. "They got me into this; they can judge."

He grinned. "But, my treasure, that will be fun for me. Call it extended foreplay. What can I do for you to speed the seduction?"

Argus sighed and whispered in Ford's ear. Ford looked at him and said, "Seriously?"

Argus looked at her and leaned in to kiss her cheek. "Seriously."

She looked at him curiously. She twisted on Ford's lap. "What did he say?"

Ford looked confused. "He suggested that I invite you to my place."

She looked back at Argus in confusion.

Ford finished, "And tell you that you can swim in my Olympic-sized pool anytime."

She started to hum with excitement, and a heavy purr emerged from her chest.

Ford muttered, "What the hell?" He craned his head around and took in her flushed cheeks and obvious excitement.

He looked at the guys. "Can we go now? I would be disappointed if this wore off."

Argus smiled and crouched near her, extending his hand to her. "It won't. She loves swimming, and it has been on the forbidden list for the last decade and a half. If you let her, she will be sprinting over to your place every freaking day."

Argus kissed her palm. "You will have to put down rules about how long she can swim per day, or she will be perpetually pruney. Any relationship you two pursue is your own business. I will just be happy if she comes home to us every night." He glanced at Ford, "Or if she comes to us for her heats."

She blinked, and fat tears started their way down her face. The guys jolted, and she opened the links and dumped her howling loneliness into the link. They clutched their heads, and she broke from the confused Ford's grip and started up the stairs. She didn't have a plan, but if they didn't have any problem with her being gone, she would go. It would hurt less than having them shove her at other people.

Ford tackled her when she was on the steps, holding her carefully to stop her from bruising herself. "What the hell is going on?"

She blinked. "They don't want me. You heard them. I can go, and as long as I come back for my heats, they are fine with it. I am in the way." She gulped air.

He nodded. "Right. In that case, I will do the neighbourly thing." He got to his feet and picked her up, carrying her out of the house through a side door.

She blinked. "What are you doing? Where are you taking me?"

He chuckled. "My house. Things happened suddenly, and they got physically ready to have you there, but they didn't realize that your situation requires a bit more maintenance than they were prepared to offer. You can stay with me, you can fuck them in your guestroom, but I have a schedule that I can manage, and I can take care of you." He chuckled. "Who knows what an omega needs better than another omega?"

She looked at him. "The centre is going to be pissed."

"You aren't their concern. They signed you over to Ambrose and his lot. They may have meant well, but their natures mean that they aren't going to deal with a little bundle of emotion like you. Alphas with canine or ursine characteristics are far easier to deal with. They would worship the ground you walk on."

She looked at him. "I chose Argus."

"Yeah, he gets it, but he knows that the others don't quite see you as anything other than a fuckbuddy yet. Did you really write a book?"

"Yeah, but my laptop is in my suitcase." It had been one of her presents from the guys. "I don't know if I should get it. It was a present."

"I will have some of the guys go and get your stuff. Call it a sleepover."

She blinked. "I don't really want to move in with you."

"I know, but I don't want you there when they all go back to work and realize that they would have left you alone in a new house in a strange city where you didn't know anyone. I am going to make sure that you know *everyone*."

She blinked. "Oh."

"A lady as sweet as you deserves the best, and if I can't be it, I can certainly pretend to be your fairy godfather."

She looked at him and cocked her head. "You want me around for your heat."

He grinned sheepishly. "That may be part of it. I am a little tired of being surrounded by men, and most betas can't keep up. Don't worry, it isn't happening for a few months, but the groundwork has to happen sometime."

She rolled her eyes. "I can barely remember mine. I just remember they had to keep switching out, and there was a lot of them falling down exhausted. Three was barely enough."

He let out a happy sound. "Aww, honey, that is just what I wanted to hear. I have never done it with another omega. The ones I have run into have packs, and they want me to join. I like my specific niche in the universe."

He rounded a tree, and a buff stone building loomed complete with the Olympic-sized pool. She whistled softly. "Wow."

"Yeah, Ambrose does good work. Have they started talking about kids?"

"We have started discussing it, but we were doubly safe during this heat. They used condoms, and I have an IUD."

He exhaled. "Well, that shows that they care for you. You are more than just a womb with legs to them."

"I think getting someone as fucked up as I am is more than they could handle. The sex is fine, but I need a lot of work, and there doesn't seem to be a place to start. It is very much a deep-end situation. They have to get back to their lives, but I need to start mine. Different places at the same time."

He nodded. "I think a little space is what is needed. They need to think of ways to reach out, and you need to meet new people. I know tons of new people who will be delighted to meet you."

"Um, isn't it dangerous for me to be out on my own?"

"It would be if you weren't with me. I hire bodyguards,

and they come with me everywhere I go. They fend off other alphas and betas who want to try me out. I like my life the way it is."

She nodded. "Why are you carrying me?"

"You didn't have shoes on."

She looked at him and laughed. "I lived in the country. Shoes are an afterthought."

He paused. "Country? Like chickens and stuff?"

"Chickens, goats, and some pigs destined for ham, but Argus had them all taken in by rescues so that it would be one thing off my mind."

"But, you did all that stuff?"

"Sure. Mowed lawns, fixed plumbing, put in windows. Catered weddings and parties. Ran a bed and breakfast."

He whistled. "So, which of those do you really like doing?"

She smiled. "I like cooking. I loved swimming when I could do it. I would like to start training again. They didn't let me use the gym at the Omega Centre. They were afraid I would hurt healing tissue."

"Yeah, what happened there? Ambrose was a little vague."

He nodded for her to open the door, so she reached for the handle. "My dad had me stitched shut during my first heat."

He froze, shaking. "He what?"

"You heard me the first time. And beat me when my scent was detectable. So . . ."

"So, you keep your scent back. I didn't know we could do that."

"Oh, I was motivated."

He hugged her to him.

"Hey, hey. No blubbering."

He looked offended when he straightened. "I thought you needed a hug."

"No, I had to live with it for over seven years. It's over." She wrinkled her nose. "I have a list of things I want to do, but I feel weird about the guys paying for stuff."

"They have bought into the idea that female omegas are

helpless and need to be tended. Me? I can see what you are capable of, and I am going to pay you for stuff around the house."

"Like what?"

He was moving through a kitchen even larger than the one that the guys had. "Make me breakfast to order. My bodyguards usually make something, but I would prefer for it to be what I want on a particular day."

"I will, provided that I don't have to go shopping. I don't have a car and don't even know where to start."

"That's fine. Do you have a license?"

"Yeah, the guys have it."

"Cool. Can you drive stick?"

She looked at him, but he was serious. "Yeah."

"Nice. You can be my driver to some of the evening events. Wait. Strike that. I want you on my arm during some events. We will present you as my escort for the evening, and I am going to have to find dresses that show off all your bond marks so no one will get a funny idea."

He set her down on a couch in front of a huge television. He dropped next to her and smiled. "Let's get a pizza and discuss your future. No one knows who you are; no one knows who your guys are. They will assume it is a pack and try to figure out who they are. You are a woman of mystery."

She snorted. "I am a rural girl in an urban setting, and I am sitting and talking about flashing my bond marks to a bunch of strangers."

He grinned. "And the international press. This is going to be so much fun. First, we need to teach you to dance. So, did you ever box-step?"

"Uh, when I was twelve."

"Cool. We will start with a waltz then and work our way to hip-hop and club dancing."

"Uh, is this going to be complicated?"

"As much as you make it. The more you trust your partner, the easier things will be." His eyes twinkled, and he got to his feet, holding his hand out to her. "So, we will start building trust. The waltz while we wait for pizza."

She got to her feet. "I still don't have shoes on."

He kicked his sneakers off. "There. Now we are on equal footing, so to speak." He touched a remote and walked her to the open area when the music filled the air around them. He smiled. "I go forward, you go back. The opposite of fucking. We don't want to meet in the middle. This is chase and retreat."

Ford started dancing. She moved with him, and after a few false starts, she had managed to make one circuit of the room with him. She saw dark figures watching them, and he murmured, "The bodyguards. That dark one is Rick; the blonde is Andrew."

"Why are they watching us?"

"Because you weren't introduced. They think you are a groupie out to have your wicked way with the poor, helpless omega in your clutches."

She sighed and raised her voice. "Guys, I am the omega from next door. Ambrose's pride's bond mate. Ford is giving me a dance lesson because I am hopeless, and I am probably staying in a guestroom."

The two guards grinned. Rick called out, "Like fuck you are an omega. None of the girls would pass up a chance with Ford."

She grinned as Ford twirled her. "I just came off my heat. I am fucked out."

The guards blinked.

Ford grinned. "And her cum tastes like peaches."

She blushed and elbowed him, but they kept dancing. The music faded, and she stopped.

She bit her lip. "So, how bad was it?"

"It was agony; it was torture. We are going to have to bring a professional in. Rick! Get over here."

Rick groaned. "This isn't in my contract."

"Yeah, but you are a choreographer at my heels. Dance is

160

in your blood. I am much better at seeing how things are going through a viewfinder."

Olivia looked at the alpha in black. "You looked less scary at a distance."

He paused and smiled. "It is not the first time I have heard that, but it is the first time someone has stepped into my arms a moment later."

The music started, and he danced with her. "Relax a little; you are a bit stiff."

"Nervous about your shoes and my feet, but I get that this isn't the job you are here for, so thanks."

He nodded, and they began to move around the space. He spun her, pulled her back, and kept the decorous space between them at all times.

Ford smiled. "That looked beautiful. Rick, isn't it amazing that she can keep her scent locked down like that?"

Rick nodded. "I haven't ever heard of an omega doing that. How do you do that, Miss?"

"Practice."

Ford chuckled. "You are going to have to read the book."

"There's a book?"

Olivia huffed. "Not yet. It's a memoir."

They danced, and the music changed. He put his hand on the centre of her back, and their movements changed into something more sweeping, less rigid.

Rick smiled. "Have you ever slow danced? Like at prom?"

"No prom for me." She smiled tightly.

He slowed and put his hands on her hips. She blinked and hissed, "Where do I put my hands?"

"Chest, shoulders, arms. Waist, back of the neck. Wherever you are comfortable."

She flexed her hands and put her hands on his biceps.

"I have never seen an omega this afraid of contact."

Olivia bit her lip. "Yeah, well, I am one of a kind. You aren't one of my alphas, and I don't like contact with strangers."

"How did Ford end up tasting you?"

"I was coming down, and my alphas had just been sexed up, so they were amenable to have someone else taking the bullet, so to speak."

Ford sighed and put his hands behind his head. "You should have seen her riding Dexter. She was breathtaking."

She blushed. "Shut up, Ford."

He chuckled. A bell rang, and Andrew went to get it.

He came back a few minutes later with a stack of pizza and Dexter. Olivia looked at him, and he looked weirdly helpless for a guy that big. She left Rick, and she went to him, holding him tight.

Chapter Nineteen

"I didn't think they would let you go," Dexter whispered.

"I am not gone, but I don't fit, and you three don't have room to let me fit." She held him and ran her hands over his neck, arms, chest, and held him with a solid grip around his waist. "With the heat over, everyone is a little disoriented, and we didn't have a chance to learn each other before it hit. Frankly, all Ambrose knows is that I don't like humiliation play."

Dexter held her tight. "They both came from larger packs. There were so many people to attend to their omegas that I doubt they saw what was necessary."

She rubbed her cheek against his chest. "I will work on being more self-sufficient and figure out how to make my own way in the world. Don't worry about it. I will come back to you for my heats."

She looked up at him and tried to give him an encouraging smile.

"You think I am here because of that? He was touching your mark, and I want to rip his fucking throat out, but you were talking to him and smiling, and I realized that you wanted to learn how to dance and not one of us offered to help."

Olivia blinked back tears. "You know how to dance?"

"Yeah. My dad made me learn."

Ford laughed. "Show me. This I have to see."

Dexter snorted. "I know a challenge when I hear one."

He took Olivia's hand and said, "Will you dance with me?"

She smiled. "Yeah, alpha, I will."

He took her in his arms, and they moved smoothly. The

music picked up speed, and Dexter murmured what he wanted her to do, and she did it. She spun with him, he lifted and turned her, and she noticed that he touched his mark every chance he got. Peaches and spice filled the room as they moved together. When the music got heavier and more intense, she laughed as she ground her hips against him. The music stopped, and she looked at Ford with a sheen of sweat.

He chuckled. "The pizza is getting cold . . . again."

She grinned at Dexter and headed for the pizza.

"Ambrose doesn't want her eating junk food." Dexter hesitated.

Olivia looked at him as she ate her slice. "Ambrose doesn't want *me*. Any warm fuckable omega would do. He wants to say that his pride has one, not that he actually knows her name or what she wants to do with her life."

Dexter took her hand. "That is only partially true. What do you want to do, Olly?"

"I don't know, but I need to find out, and you guys all have jobs and family to attend to. I have a whole bunch of free time and no one to help me find out what I can do here. At home, I had a tiny domain that I was trapped in, but my days were laid out. There were animals, building, repair, and guests. That was my life for a lot of years, and now that is over, and I have to change things. I am starting at the bottom in an unfamiliar place. You guys are my foundation, but I need to know where I can go from here and how strong the foundation is."

Dexter nodded. "That's fair."

Ford leaned forward. "I will take care of her, but I understand the split between what you were born to be and what you want to be; she also has to deal with what she has been crafted into. We are just next door, and her bonds are strong. You are with her, Dexter."

She leaned against her youngest alpha. "It's fine, Dexter."

He whispered, "You say that a lot, and it is always something that hurts you."

She shrugged. "It's a survivor thing. Don't irritate the predators. Alphas or betas, they still have a physical advantage."

Dexter looked at her with horror in his eyes. "You don't think we would ever . . ."

"Ask Ambrose that when he threatens me with his favourite pastimes. He can go play with someone else. I am not interested in being hit, no matter the playtime implications. No physical abuse victim signs up for that."

Ford blinked, and his eyes widened. "He said he was going to . . ."

"Yeah. He can hardly wait. Yay for him. I can fucking wait."

She finished her pizza and asked Ford, "You said you had a guestroom I could use?"

Ford nodded. "Uh, yeah. Come with me."

She swallowed around the lump in her throat, kissed Dexter softly, and followed her host up the stairs. She paused and asked Dexter, "Can someone bring over my bag from the centre and the phone, and maybe my license?"

Dexter nodded. "Sure. No problem. Do you want your wallet?"

She shook her head. "No, that's yours."

He blinked, and his shoulders slumped. "Right. It's ours."

She blinked and pressed her hip, where the bond between them ached.

Olivia followed Ford and hoped that there were enough pillows to make herself comfortable.

"The nearest guestroom is down that way, but I think that tonight, you should spend it in my nest. Nothing funny, but you need to be held tonight. Is that okay?"

She nodded. Her throat was thick with tears. "We never got to that point."

"What?"

"Them holding me while I slept. It was too much too fast, and nothing had a chance to start before it was over."

Ford paused. "Fuck. Okay, this way."

He opened the door and opened another after it. The inside was dim and comfortable and smelled like apples. She chuckled. The nest was dark and soft and covered with fuzzy throws and pillows. There was satin and silk, but mostly, it just looked comfy.

"I will be right back. You get comfortable, and I will be right back."

She nodded, sniffling, and walked to the edge of the enclosed half circle filled with the most comfortable things she could imagine. She lifted her dress and slip, removed them and folded them, then she removed her bra and panties, folding them as well. She slipped into the nest and grabbed a dark pillow, pressing her face against it until all she could smell was apples, and her mind hummed pleasantly with arousal.

Ford came back, and he spoke softly, "Olivia, are you awake, honey?"

She peeked at him over the edge of the furry throw she had commandeered. "Hey, Ford. Nice nest. Mine got messed up in the heat."

"I am sure they put it back the way it was before you rested."

She cocked her head. "No, they moved me to Ambrose's room."

"They really fucked up."

"The only thing that felt right was when we were together. Everything else felt like something bad was going to happen."

Ford peeled off his t-shirt and removed his socks. When he unbuckled his belt, he paused. "Honey, what are you wearing under the throw?"

"Nothing. I don't like to sleep in anything."

He groaned. "Me neither. If I try to have sex with you in my sleep, just pinch me awake."

She chuckled, and it was a throaty sound that surprised

her. "You will stop?"

"Probably not, but I will enjoy it more if I can remember it."

She snorted and looked at him. He was stunning. He was all rippling muscle and an erection that was impressive even by alpha standards. He crawled into his nest next to her and pulled her against him, the throw between them.

"Seeing your eyes over the edge of this fur gave me an idea for a video. Do you want to come to work with me tomorrow?"

"Are shoes an option?"

"Of course. I asked Dexter to send over clothing that you would be comfortable in, not what Ambrose picked out for you."

She sighed. "Jeans it is, then."

He chuckled. "And you have the ass for them."

She smiled. "I think in their heads I became a damsel in distress, but they didn't realize how far from a damsel I was. Ah well, I shouldn't bug you with this. I think I have a shrink appointment on Thursday."

"How will you get there?"

"Um, don't know? Walk. Public transport. I have no idea. I will figure it out. I always do."

"If I am working, I will send you with a car and one of my guards. They will bring you home or to where I am afterward."

She smiled. "Thanks. There is a lot of new here."

Ford sounded plaintive, "Honey?"

She knew what was coming next. "Yes, Ford?"

"Can I feel your skin?"

She nodded. "Yeah. Come on under."

He lifted the throw and scooted against her. She was finally being held by someone while she slept, and it wasn't Argus. She touched her bond mark, and Ford kissed her cheek while she cried silent tears. He cuddled her close and held her until she hiccuped to sleep.

Argus hit the heavy bag as the waves of sadness washed through him. He paused and breathed as it slowed and then stopped. She was asleep.

"Goddamnit!" He plowed his glove into the bag.

Ambrose looked at him. "What's the problem?"

Argus was about to talk to him when Dexter came through the door to the gym. He went for Ambrose and tackled him to the mat with a roar.

Argus got his gloves off and went to pull their younger member loose. Dexter was snarling and glaring at Ambrose as the older man sat on the mat.

"How could you say that to her?"

"Be specific? I am chatty during sex." Ambrose was wary.

Dexter growled again. "How could you threaten to hit her?"

"Hit? No. I just said I looked forward to when I could spank her." He shrugged. "That isn't hitting."

Argus paused. "What?"

"You know what I like. I just told her I could hardly wait until she was up for a little of that kind of discipline."

Argus sat back, his forehead against his fists. "Shit. I am beginning to see how badly we have fucked this up."

Ambrose scowled. "What?"

"She's a physical abuse survivor. How would you like someone to take your worst terror and make a game of it for their own enjoyment?"

Ambrose opened and closed his mouth. "I . . . didn't think of it like that. When she got here, I was only thinking of what I could do to her."

Dexter growled. "Do to her. Do with her. Not do for her. The canines have it right. They serve their omegas. It doesn't make them weak; it makes them stronger. Gives them a focus. We had her, and we tore her in so many directions it is no wonder she started coming apart." He blinked. "I went over to the most notorious horn-dog's home, and do you know what I found? He was getting one of his staff to teach her how to dance, and he was making notes on how she could improve her stance. That was what he was doing *for* her. We offered to help her with her goals, but she would have to find them on her own. From here. With no way to navigate the city, and none of us even volunteered to take her to the park."

Argus lifted his head. "There wasn't time."

Ambrose was silent, and he ran his hands through his hair.

Dexter looked at him. "She said you can take those impulses out on someone else."

Ambrose looked like he had been slapped. "I don't want . . . I need . . . Oh, damnit. I don't want anyone else."

Argus muttered, "Well, you aren't going to strike her. No spankings, no whips, paddles, any of that."

"It's fine. I don't want to. I said that before the heat. I was flirting."

Dexter snorted. "Asshole. Idiot."

"What else did I do wrong?"

"She hadn't left her property in years. She doesn't know about flirting and witty banter. She hasn't even had a date, and we spent days inside her."

Argus looked to Dexter. "What do you suggest?"

Dexter sighed. "First, I think we can use some group therapy, and second, I think we need to court our mate."

Argus paused, and a flicker of hope started in his brain. "What did you have in mind?"

"If she was a woman we were interested in, in the normal span of things, what would we do?" Dexter smiled. "I would take her out for dinner and a movie."

Ambrose looked grim. "The theatre. I would take her out to the theatre."

Argus chuckled. "And I . . . will ask her to paint ball."

Dexter blinked. "Paint ball?"

"She's a physically active girl from the country. She can shoot."

Dexter paused. "My parents want to have her over for dinner on the weekend."

Argus nodded. "Stall them. We have months until her next heat, but I don't want to spend that time with Ford sheltering her the entire time. I want her home by her own free will."

Ambrose nodded. "So do I."

Dexter grinned. "Me, too. Oh, and Ambrose? Ford is feeding her junk food."

Ambrose's eyes burned. "Bastard."

Argus snorted. "If it's the calories you are worried about, she burns them off."

Dexter shook his head. "Not if we aren't with her."

Argus raised his brows. "You forget that we gave her free agency, and our neighbour is one of the most successful seduction experts in the country, and she's fresh off a heat."

Ambrose's face tightened. "Bastard!"

Olivia was warm like her body had been filled with hot honey warm. She stretched with her arms above her head, and she felt a warm chuckle against her belly. She exhaled slowly as Ford tongued her stomach. "I thought I was supposed to be up and getting you breakfast."

He chuckled. "I need to place my order."

She swallowed as he stroked her breasts carefully, learning their shape and their sensitivity. For a busty gal, they were a little on the touchy side.

His fingers trailed along her ribs and caressed her hip.

"Having fun taunting Dexter?"

"If anyone deserves to wake up with this running through his blood, it's that young man."

He skated his fingers over her belly. "You are so soft. Made for touching."

She caressed his shoulders, "I could say the same."

"Ah-ah. This is my breakfast order, and I am in the mood for peaches." He chuckled at her gasp and parted her thighs before settling against her sex with his feverish mouth and careful fingers.

She moaned and stroked her fingers through the waves of his hair, bending her knees and spreading her thighs wide while he laughed.

This was her favourite sex thing. It was all for her, and she could be greedy. Her peaches mixed with his green apples, and she was suddenly craving fruit salad. Ambrose would be so pleased.

She gasped as Ford's tongue swirled, lapped, and he sucked at the slick that started coming and didn't stop. Her hands flailed as she fought to find something to grip, and as she wailed and shuddered against his tongue, she was digging her nails into his shoulders. He kept working her until she had shuddered to a halt, the slow throb of her body continuing as he raised his head. She smelled blood, and her eyes widened. "I am so sorry."

He moved up and lay flat on her, bearing her weight into the mattress and cushions. "Don't be. It has been a long time since anyone dared to mark me just because I was rocking their world."

She looped her arms around his neck. "It was rocked. Thank you. Now, what do you want for breakfast?"

He nuzzled her, getting his scent all over her. "Second helping. You are addictive."

Olivia blinked, and she cocked her head. "You don't want to have sex?"

He paused and then shuddered. "Don't do that to me in the mornings, Olivia. I think that I will be happy with a taste of you. When you actually want me, let me know. I am standing by." He chuckled. "Sort of."

She frowned. "How am I going to know?"

"How do you feel about Argus?"

"Like I want him inside me all day, every day."

"When you feel that you want me inside you and you don't mind your guys knowing it, it will be time. Until then, I will content myself with my favourite thing." He sucked and licked her nipples on the way down, and then, he returned to his favourite snack spot between her thighs.

"Dexter brought your bag over. This was in it. I think the boys are courting you." Ford grinned as he held out the bikini.

She didn't understand what he meant until she took the garment and caught the heavy hit of Argus's rutting scent. It was different than the normal scent and far more wild. Her body responded immediately, but she ignored it. There was a note inside the cup of the bra. *Paint ball, Friday at 2 pm?*

She grinned. "I think he is asking me out on a date?"

"Smelling like a rutting moose?"

She twirled the swimsuit on her fingers. "It has a certain charm."

He inhaled it. "Yeah, it does. Quick, go swimming and wash that off."

She slid her slip off and put the swimsuit on. The bust nearly fit, which wasn't bad considering they had to purchase off the rack. "I have gotten turned around. Which way to the pool?"

He had his jeans on, and he walked her through the house and to the pool, showed her where the towels were and then headed inside. She walked to the edge of the pool and remembered the feeling of swimming. No time like the present. She bent, arched through the water, and promptly lost her top. She ignored it and started to do a crawl through the water with enthusiasm.

Time ceased to have meaning, but when her limbs felt heavy, she pulled herself out of the water and sat at the edge of the pool.

Ford handed her her top. "You lost this."

"It jumped ship on the first dive."

"You can swim naked for all I care. I just thought that you would be more comfortable in a suit."

"Getting a sport suit for me is tricky."

He wrapped an arm around her, across her chest. He kissed her neck. "These things pop up, and we will deal with them."

"Things? Like my breasts?"

He squeezed her. "Yeah. I will give them a stern talking to."

She snorted and went to grab a towel. "How long until you have to be at work?"

"About ninety minutes."

"How far away is it?"

"Twenty minutes."

"I am coming with you?" She looked at him seriously.

"Honey, I am counting on you to drive. I will be your GPS. The guards will be ahead and behind us. Ready for a shower that will hit the borders of molestation?"

"As long as it doesn't cross the border." She walked into the house with him, and he introduced her to the shower. She washed her hair, soaped up, and stood with her hands against the wall while all the sprays hit her from all the angles. She was gasping and tingling but clean as hell when she got out.

Ford grinned. "Need a cigarette?"

"No, but it was a very, very near thing." She glanced back. "I think I want its number."

"It never calls." Ford laughed.

She dried her hair and brushed it, then braided it into a loose braid, and Ford handed her a hair tie.

The clothes in the suitcase were a surprise. Actual underwear that wasn't entirely made of lace and moonbeams, jeans and boots, a babydoll shirt and a gauzy kimono wrap.

Ford chuckled. "I don't know who packed this, but it wasn't Ambrose."

She scented it. "Dexter and Argus. Well done, boys."

She got dressed, pulled on socks, and when all the fabric was on, she put on the boots and zipped them nearly to the knee. She looked at herself in the mirror and smiled. She actually looked like the Olivia she remembered from way back when. She looked like the Olivia she had wanted to be when she grew up. A thrill of happiness ran through her.

It was one of the first times that she had felt like herself in the last decade.

She looked at Ford. "Now, can I make you breakfast?"

He looked at her and smiled. "Yeah, I think that would be fun."

Chapter Twenty

Ford looked a little nervous, but he settled when she kept pace with his bodyguards on the way to the shoot. She wove in and out of traffic and shifted easily. The car purred, and she missed her guys.

Ford blinked. "You are really good at this."

She chuckled. "I helped neighbours all my life, herding their cattle. This is similar and less dangerous."

"I thought you didn't leave your home. That was the implication."

"No, I wasn't *allowed* to leave my home. My sister charged the neighbours for my services. So, I did the work at their farms and was taken home every night. I was only allowed to drive on private properties."

"Wait, so you use vehicles to herd cows?"

"Sure. This is the twenty-first century. Trucks, quads, you name it. The horses are just for moving them in a relaxed manner and in areas where the vehicles couldn't go." Riding the horses had also been impossible for her after her father's actions.

"Oh. Cool. Can you ride horses?"

She smiled slowly. "Definitely."

"Motorcycles?"

"Of course."

"Excellent." He had an idea.

They headed to a warehouse district, and their little motorcade came to a halt near a group of other vehicles. She parked, gave Ford the keys, and he put them back in her hand, folding her fingers over them. She chuckled. "Dude. I don't actually have pockets on this outfit. The jeans are so snug that I am amazed I can sit."

He sighed. "Yeah, they are. Dexter?"

"Argus."

"Nice."

They got out of the sleek dark vehicle, and some folks rushed toward Ford. "Oh, thank god, Ford. We are ready to start, but I think something is missing."

Ford nodded to the man with the pink shirt, pinker hair, and enough piercings in his face to give Olivia the impression that he had been too close to a nail gun while drunk.

Ford chuckled. "I will take a look. This is Olivia, and I want her to see what I do for a living."

The pink man looked at her and pursed his lips. "It isn't like you to bring a woman . . . anywhere."

Olivia chuckled. "Oh, I am special. I am also his neighbour. I just moved in."

Ford grinned. "Spoiling my fun, Olivia. Come on. Let's go."

She took his hand, and they headed toward an area lined with cameras. She saw motorcycles lined up, and folks everywhere were dressed in post-apocalyptic tribal. She grinned. "It's like a costume party where everyone has to go to work."

He looked at her and narrowed his eyes. "Yeah. Did you want to play dress-up?"

She gave him a dark look. "Dude. I just got jeans back. No one is parting me from them. Not without me actually trying some cocktails."

His eyes widened. "Oh. Right. It's on the list."

"List?"

"Things that you should try in private and then public."

She grinned.

He chuckled at her expression and walked her toward the cameras. He got her a chair, showed her the safe areas where she wouldn't affect the filming, and she sat and watched with a coffee in her hands.

A *lot* of people stared at her, and she sat quietly as folks got in position, and they fired up the playback so that the actors and dancers could pace themselves to the music. It was a surprisingly sweet story being told by the song, but the counterpoint of the makeup and costumes lent it a whole new subtext.

Rick was speaking with the choreographer, and they seemed to be talking shop during one of the resets for the scene.

A woman was speaking urgently with Ford and putting her hand on his arm. He calmly slid the woman's hand off his skin and spoke gently. She paused and blinked. He loved touching her. He had been holding her hand during most of the shooting.

He smiled slowly and turned toward Olivia. "Honey, come here for a minute. This is Leora, and she is the talented musician and songwriter behind today's project. She thinks that the female lead needs more edge. What do you think?"

"She isn't wrong. The lead looks too helpless. During the motorcycles circling her, she just wrings her hand. Who thought that up?"

Ford shrugged. "Last week I thought it was a great idea. This week I think edge is what she needs. Could you get into makeup and be the body double? We are signing you up for a guild membership so you can get paid for it."

She crossed her arms over her chest. "How much?"

His eyes sparkled. "I will tell you at home."

Leora looked at her and smiled, walking around her. "She has the right look for it. Body double? I think she could do the whole thing."

Olivia blinked. "Uh, I am really new to all this. I can't act."

Ford stroked her cheek and neck. "No, but you take direction so very well. We will put an earpiece in, and you just need to do what I say. Got it?"

She glared at him as he stroked her lower lip with his thumb. "No playing on company time."

He laughed, and Leora blinked. "That . . . I haven't seen that before."

Olivia smiled. "I am complicated." She bit at the tip of Ford's thumb. She sighed. "What do you need me to do?"

Things exploded into action. She signed into the actor's guild and signed onto the shoot insurance. Her clothing was carefully set aside; she was put into the gauzy gown and soft doeskin boots. Her makeup was fun, but they covered her bond marks. That gave her a pang. She looked at herself in the mirror with Dexter's and Argus's marks hidden to the frontal view, and Ambrose's had been dabbed over.

The makeup artist looked at her. "You really bonded to three alphas? Why?"

"It seemed like the thing to do at the time."

They had to settle for ear cuffs on the makeup front as Olivia's ears weren't pierced, and no one had a kit with them.

"I am just going to hold the place. I think. I dunno. Ford had a funny look on his face."

"That just means he had an idea. He gets them now and then, and when that gleam is in his eyes, we all get to charge more for our next gig. The awards come."

Olivia grinned, and when she was dismissed and dressed like an after-disaster princess, she headed to the set.

She knew the look in Ford's eyes. She had seen it that morning when he looked up at her from between her thighs. She pressed her hand to his chest. "Down, boy. Now, get me the earpiece and tell me what you want me to do."

"Me. I want you to do me." He grinned.

She chuckled. "It wasn't in the earpiece, so that doesn't count. Now, lets' get going. I want to find out if this princess can actually throw the bola to catch the bad guy."

His eyes gleamed. "I don't suppose you can . . ."

"I am a bit rusty, but I can probably snag someone's legs."

"Can you practice first?"

She shrugged and walked to where the stunt folks were waiting. She picked up the hollow bola, and the coordinator walked her through a toss. She waited until they were at a safe distance, wound up, and threw. Then she did it again. And again.

The alpha came over with a pleased expression. "Can you do it on camera?"

"I don't know how I would get up onto a camera, so probably."

He snorted and clapped her on the shoulder then frowned. Her skin was bare, and she knew from contact with Ford that omega skin felt different. She smiled. "Congratulations, Ben. You found the one spot where they didn't have to hide a bond mark."

He was startled. "You are a bonded beta?"

She patted him on the arm. "I am bonded. 'nuff said."

His nose was going crazy trying to catch her scent. "Ben, don't hurt your sinuses. I just don't perfume like normal. Now, which way to the set again?"

He walked with her. She realized that he was acting as a bodyguard of sorts, and she blinked in surprise. Ford looked at her, and he grinned then he looked past her. "Ben, you are here to watch the scene?"

Ben nodded.

Ford grinned at Olivia. "Ready?"

"Sure." She got the earpiece, checked to make sure it worked and was secure, and walked out to starting position. She needed to stand in a windstorm with the bikes circling, throw the bola, and then get on one of the bikes when the stuntwoman would take over.

Ford grinned and rubbed his hands together. Olivia was going to make a splash in his circles, and it was going to start today.

The playback started, Leora lip-synched on her podium, and Olivia acted like the terrified omega she was supposed to be, all cute and soft and irresistible to the big bad alphas. She fell to the ground and kicked back with her legs, catching the bola as the leader of the pack came toward her. She waited until he got to the strike zone, her gaze hardened, and she rose to her knees. The bola spun, released, and took the surprised stunt guy down. She scrambled to her feet, jumped over his grasping hands, and Ford murmured, "Get the drones ready."

"She's just going to get on it, isn't she?"

Ford chuckled and murmured into his mic.

Olivia got on the bike, started it expertly, planted one foot, spun the monster, and shot past the stunned villains, and then, they got the order to give chase.

The drones were careful not to be in the shadow, but they showed Olivia streaking across the barren landscape, and the pack was coming up behind her.

"Cut it! Olivia, return to the set."

He watched the drone feed, and to his shock, Olivia was having to actively dodge the alphas who were coming after her. Shit. Rule one of being an omega. Never run.

He called his team, and they got ready. When she roared back to the set, she got off the bike and climbed up one of the sets, getting high, and to Ford's astonishment, she used one of the support ropes to get to an inaccessible part of the set. She knelt, breathed, and calmed down.

He watched. "Holy shit."

She was crouching on the platform and watching the pacing alphas below.

Rick tossed a canister of scent nullifier, and it swirled and spiralled out until they were all looking sheepish. Olivia dropped twenty feet and landed daintily in the cloud. She walked through it and headed toward Ford.

He wanted to console her, but she asked, "Any more shots for me today?"

He shook his head.

She smiled. "Good. I really like driving motorcycles, so you are going to have to have that bike scrubbed with nullifier."

His eyes widened. "Got it."

Under the chemical scent clinging to her, peach was rising strong.

"I am going to put some jeans on. Back in a few minutes." She patted his arm, and he bemoaned the chance to console her. She didn't look upset. She looked like this was just something that happened daily.

He looked to Ben, and his friend was staring. "I have never seen an omega hunt before. That was . . . intense. Is she really an omega?"

"Yup."

"She has bond mates, a pack?"

"A pride. Yeah. They are my neighbours and are having difficulty in adapting the transition from independent to having an omega." Ford shrugged. "She deserves better, but she has to meet the world out of her bubble."

"She's . . . impressive." Ben cocked his head. "Do you think it would be possible to kill her mates to break the bond?"

Ford blinked. "No. She would gut you in your sleep, bond or not. Don't let the soft exterior fool you. She's made of more steel than you have seen in a lifetime."

Ben glanced back toward the makeup trailer. "I can see that. She is the calmest omega I have ever seen."

Ford smiled. "She goes wild, but she does it when she's safe. Currently, she is my favourite thing."

Ben blinked. "I haven't heard you talk like that before, boss."

"Yeah, well, she has created a new way of thinking. She makes folks around her want to be better. I plan on stepping up. Besides, have you ever fucked an omega? We are *amazing* in bed."

Ben flushed. "Um, no. I only knew what she was because I touched her arm. She was so *soft*."

"Yeah, like peach fuzz." Ford sighed happily.

They changed the topic and discussed the shoot, looking

at the footage and making notes with Leora.

Olivia bounced out of the trailer, her hair back in the braid and her casual clothes back in place. Her marks were also visible when she raised a hand to say hi. "I am back. I think she scraped five layers off."

Ford plucked a few strands of silver thread from her hair. "They missed a spot."

She smiled. "Kiss?"

He leaned down and kissed her, stroking her cheek and cupping her jaw. Their tongues duelled, and he slowly raised his head. "What was that for?"

"Your scent is stronger than mine. I am using you as bait." She waggled her brows at him. "They won't look at me if all they can smell is you."

He chuckled, and Ben hooted with laughter. She was definitely complicated.

After lunch with the crew, where people kept staring at her, she sat next to Ford and chatted with Leora, who wanted to know where she trained and how she learned to ride a motorcycle.

Olivia talked about growing up hours beyond the city where kids didn't have access to the internet, but motorized transport was plentiful. And four-legged transport as well.

"Horses scare the shit out of me." Leora chuckled. "I have had to be on horseback for videos before, but I am really freaked out."

Ford snorted. "Olivia has been riding alternative four-legged transport lately."

He showed her the video and Ambrose's voice saying, "And there my buddy goes . . . with my mate. Get back here, you asshole!"

She watched her hanging onto Caesar for dear life. Romulus and Remus were chasing them, low to the ground and flat out.

Leora blinked. "That is some kind of CG, right?"

"Uh. No. My mates run the big cat sanctuary next to Ford's house." She smiled fondly. "That's Caesar."

"Are they tame?"

Ford snorted. "No. But the big cats like who they like, and they like Olivia a lot."

Leora smiled slyly. "Could we work them into the video?"

Olivia frowned.

Ford closed his eyes, and he tapped his fingers. "We could put her into makeup with green dots and put your face in with the register marks. You don't mind being invisible, do you, Olivia?"

Leora shook her head. "No, I meant Olivia's face and body. Not mine. I don't think a big cat would like her to sing in its face."

Olivia chuckled. "I could try it, but Caesar is a bit of a bully."

"Stick with the jaguars. They are a better contrast against her skin. Now, we just need to get Argus to agree." Ford tapped his fingers together.

Leora blinked. "Wait. Did you say that these guys are your mates?"

Olivia blushed. "Yeah. They haven't really explained how things work, but I think the animal rescue is Argus and Ambrose. The jaguars are Argus's buddies."

Ford smiled. "They like her very much."

"Uh. Maybe. They like him more."

Ford said softly, "Can you ask him?"

She blinked. "Are you whoring me out for jaguars?"

Leora stared. "I thought you were their mate?"

"Things are working a little backward." She pried her phone out of her skin-tight back pocket and sent a text.

There was a pause and a message. *Where are you?*

Video shoot with Ford. I got to be a body double!

You want to shoot with the boys?

Yeah. May I?

How much is the rescue getting?

She looked at Ford. "How much is the rescue getting?"

He snorted and sent a text to Argus.

Done. Are you going to be dressed up, kitten?

"Uh, am I going to be dressed up?"

Ford grinned. "You are. I know just the thing."

Leora laughed. "That is an evil look, Ford."

Olivia snorted. "That isn't evil; that's horny." She paused and looked at Ford. "Aw, hell."

He laughed. "This is going to be a fun afternoon."

They moved location, and when she came out of the wardrobe and makeup area, she looked at Ford with narrowed eyes. "You are going to pay for this."

"You will be paid for it. The rescue will be paid for it. You look spectacular."

The jaguar body paint and the same hairstyle that she had been wearing during the other scene. The only saving grace was that only her eyes were recognizable. The rest of her had been highlighted and contoured into a very feline aspect.

Her body was clad in tight black trousers, an overskirt of sorts was made out of woven leather. Leather bands on her wrists and a bra made of crossed strands of soft leather an inch wide.

"How is your range of motion, honey?" He grinned.

She dropped and did some push-ups, lunges, and lowered herself into slow splits. She looked up at him with a challenge. "Pretty good."

He let out a strangled sound, and she grinned. "There." She got back to her feet. The boots were the best part of the outfit. She loved boots.

The guys from the rescue were bemused, and they saw her and waved. "Hey, Den, Jerry, Harry. So, this is odd."

They chuckled. "Argus said to cooperate, but you need to keep to the cats you have met."

She asked Jerry, "How is Hector?"

He beckoned for her to follow him. "This has to be seen to

be believed."

She followed him to the enclosure, and Hector had pinned Caesar and was grooming him. She giggled. "Is she pregnant?"

"No, but we are starting to think *he* might be. She has him completely whipped. It's hilarious."

She stood next to the fence, and Hector's jaw jerked upward, as did Caesar's. They both came to the gate and rubbed against it. "Hiya. So, you two knocked boots, huh?"

Hector looked pleased with herself. Jerry looked at her. "If you want to go in, you can."

She smiled and walked into the enclosure, where she was rubbed and hugged by huge cats.

She patted the cats, and they moved to block her in. "Jerry?"

"Yes, Olivia?"

"Can you call Argus? I am kinda stuck in here."

Jerry was laughing. "Yeah, I can see that." He took out his phone and made a call. "Yeah, Ambrose, are you working from home today? Great. Uh, Caesar and Hector have pinned that mate of yours and aren't letting her out of the enclosure. Can you come down here? Great. Oh. Sure." He chuckled. "Yeah, she's all decked out for the video. She looks hot."

She flipped him off. Jerry hung up and snapped the picture. He was quick.

She huffed, and when Ford came to find her, he started laughing. "Sorry, honey. I wish I could help."

She was lying on Hector, and Caesar was still watching the door. It was a fairly comfortable place to rest if she ignored the drones.

Chapter Twenty-One

"Hey, Ford, what's she up to now? It's only been a day." Ambrose's deep voice rang through the air. He directed his question to Ford and then turned to look at her. "Holy shit. Precious, you look amazing in leather."

She grumbled. "It has always been a personal preference. Can you get Caesar to let me out?"

"I don't know. I think he needs you there to keep Hector under control. How many people are taking photos right now?"

She looked around and leaned up on Hector. "Six phones and two drones."

The tiger chuffed to Ambrose. He responded.

"Well, if I rescue you, you owe me, precious."

She tensed, and Hector growled. "What?"

"After you finish your shoot for the day, come to my studio dressed like that." His eyes were heated.

"This isn't my outfit. I think it's Ford's, though I don't know how it would fit him." She was wary. Ford was grinning and watching.

"Hmm. Perhaps a compromise." He opened the gate, and Caesar rubbed up against him, chuffing happily. "Yes, you caught her, just like you said you would. Thank you."

Outrage ripped through Olivia. "You jackass!"

She got up and scratched Hector's head when Dexter arrived, and Hector went apeshit, doing figure eights and other patterns because she was happy. Dexter walked over to Olivia and smiled. "That's a fun look."

"Thanks. It took a few hours, and we are losing daylight. I need to get out of here."

Dexter nodded. "Fine. Kiss."

She walked toward him."

"Ambrose."

She paused and looked at the smug blond leaning against his lion. "This is a lot of negotiation for being held hostage by big cats."

Ford laughed. "We are losing light, honey."

She looked at Ambrose. "Will you accept a kiss to let me out?"

He thought about it for a moment, and then, he nodded. "I will, but further negotiations won't be this easy on you, precious."

She blinked and narrowed her eyes. "Fine."

"Come here, precious. Let's get that door open."

She knew he wasn't referring to the enclosure, but she walked to him. He wouldn't bend, so she grabbed his shoulders, jumped, and wrapped her legs around his waist. He blinked in surprise and caught her. She pressed her lips to his and coaxed him into joining in. When her tongue slid into his mouth, he started purring, deep and heavy. His erection was growing against the seam of the leather pants, and she rocked against him as their kiss continued. He reached behind her and stroked the mark, and she moaned. Dexter's hands cupped her hips, and his purr was intense. She gasped and rocked between them until her orgasm ripped through her. Keeping it silent meant that she was staring into Ambrose's eyes as the pulses rang through her.

He sighed slowly. "I accept your payment. Caesar, stop being an ass."

She dropped to the ground, and when she was out of the enclosure, she muttered, "You are going to either wipe off the lipstick or get a touch-up. It's a good colour on you."

The makeup lady was doing the touch-ups as they walked, and the boys were happy to rub against her, and Ford was in her ear, telling her what he wanted her to do, how to sit, lie, stand with the drones and the artificial wind whipping her hair.

She heard him tell her that she could do whatever she wanted, she glanced at the drones, nodded, and she and the boys burst into a run. They bolted past her and turned around to see why she wasn't keeping up, but she kept running, and they returned to her and loped at her side. She heard shouting behind her and grinned as Caesar ran up next to her. She jumped onto his back, and he took off with Hector and the boys until they reached the end of the open spaces, and then, he turned and trotted smugly back toward the cameras and the shocked spectators who kept silent until the cats were back in their enclosures. Ford kissed her and bent her back into a deep dip.

"That was spectacular, honey. We got so much footage. We want one of you kissing Dexter, though."

"What? Why?"

"Because we got him all dressed up, and we need a couple shot for the end of the video."

She turned, and Dexter was wearing the apocalyptic gear in brown and black leather, and he talked to Ben. Her heart tripped in her chest, and her sex tried to purr on its own.

Ford grinned. "Isn't he pretty? I can see why Ambrose wants to top him."

She opened and closed her mouth. That wasn't the way it worked with those two, but if everyone was content to think so, it wasn't her place to correct them.

They stood on a rocky platform, the cameras surrounded them, and she followed direction, slowly looking up at Dexter. The kiss happened without any prompting. The playback in her head started, and she and Dexter started to dance. It was far more intense than she had anticipated, but it might have had something to do with Ford whispering filthy nothings into her ear.

They finished twisting, spinning, standing in a variety of embraces until the red light of sunset cast across them and Ford let them rest.

She was breathing heavily, and she looked up at Dexter. "Um, thank you for this. It's my first day out in the world. I feel like I just came out of an egg, and there is so much to try and do."

He chuckled. "This is going to do it. You look super cute as a jaguar. You are definitely more cougar, though."

She coughed. "Right. How old are you again?"

He grinned. "Wouldn't you like to know?"

"Yeah, I would."

He laughed and then sobered. "Are you having fun?"

"Yeah. I am meeting people, talking to strangers, getting stared at, and riding a motorcycle across the open fields. So much fun." She grimaced. "I am also learning that I am going to have to hire bodyguards if I want to move around on my own. It is weird, but an idea that is becoming acceptable as necessary to me."

She shivered as she remembered the motorcycle chase.

"What happened, Olivia?"

"Nothing. Thankfully. But I now know what a nullifier canister looks like." She smiled weakly.

His expression went dark. "You are coming home."

"To do what? Wait until one of you can find time in their schedules? I have been waiting for others all my life, and I am done waiting. I want to live for a while, and then, I can crawl back into my nest and stay there until you guys come to visit."

He sighed. "That isn't what I meant. I am worried about you."

"If I had a life before I met you, it wouldn't be an issue, but I didn't have anything. I was in a holding pattern. I need to live a little, and life can be dangerous." She stroked his cheek. "You have friends, family; I have neither."

"You have us."

"Not hardly. You have me. I don't have anything, but I am working toward it."

Dexter sighed. "We came when you called."

"You came when Jerry called." She stroked his cheek.

His growl was pure frustration. "I would have come if you had called."

"No room for my cell phone in these leather pants. Speaking of which, I had better get them back to wardrobe. Someone probably wants to auction them off or sniff them or something."

"You are really cynical."

"Practical. I know what omegas are in the world. Pets for the alphas. I want more, and I am trying to get it."

Dexter smiled. "Independence. I think I might be starting to understand. We wanted to be feline alphas with a shared omega, but it never occurred to us that her independent streak would have to be as big as ours."

She grinned. "At least you are getting it. I know you live together but separately. I want that for me as well. Ford is an excellent gateway."

"As long as the toll isn't too heavy."

"It's pretty light, actually." She chuckled. "He doesn't ask for more than what I am ready to give and gives me parameters and options for my own direction. It's actually refreshing. I know there is no pain waiting with him behind a bad mood."

He sighed. "He wouldn't hurt you."

"He *said* he wanted to. I have to believe it when folks say they want to hurt me. It has kept me alive." She looked at him. "Until he tells me otherwise, I have to believe he knew what he was saying."

"Wait. All he has to do is tell you that he won't hurt you?"

She shrugged. "Basically. If someone punched you in the face for walking into a room, you would stop going there. If you had been punched in the past and someone told you that if you walked in that room, it would happen again, you would not go in there."

Dexter grimaced. "I get it."

"I don't court pain. That sums it up. If he wants to do that

190

with others, he's welcome to do it. Just leave me out of it."

Dexter sighed. "I want to rub myself all over you, but you need to get that body paint off first, or I would just make a mess."

"I think Ford is taking me out for dinner. I have never actually been out for dinner."

Dexter looked stricken. "You haven't?"

"Nope. He's helping me collect experiences, and he thinks of stuff, so I don't have to crunch my brain to do an assessment on something I have no frame of reference for."

Dexter sighed. "Are you going to go paintballing with Argus?"

"That sounds like it should be dirty, but it isn't." She chuckled. "I am. Dating isn't something I thought I could do."

"I am so sorry. I thought we would have time."

She stroked his neck. "So did I, but we didn't, and this is what we are stuck with. Are you heading back to wardrobe?"

"Yeah. It was fun playing with you for the video."

"Thanks. The more money for the animal rescue, the better."

Dexter blinked. "You are donating the money to the rescue?"

"Ford had to donate something to Argus to use the boys. How is Hector feeling, by the way?"

He blushed. "She has Caesar whipped."

They linked arms, and he walked her back to makeup.

When she finished getting cleaned up and was back in her normal clothing, her guys were gone. She sighed.

Ford wasn't anywhere to be seen, so she shrugged and walked back to his place. The crew was there, setting up for a barbeque and having fun. She smiled at a few familiar faces and headed up to the guestroom she had been assigned. She closed the door and crawled into the closet with a blanket and a pillow. She had dozed off, and her phone started vibrating.

She answered. "Hello?"

"Honey? Where are you?" Ford's voice was concerned.

"I went to rest."

His voice got husky and sweet. "Back at home with the guys?"

"No. In the guestroom you said I could stay in."

He paused. "I was just in there. Where were you?"

She sighed. "In the closet."

She heard his footsteps outside the door, and she squinted at him when he stood looking at her.

She hung up the phone. "Hey."

He crouched in the doorway. "Hey. Sorry, we aren't going out for dinner. Where were you?"

"I talked to Dexter, and then, I walked back here when I couldn't find you."

"Damn it. He was supposed to walk you back."

"Maybe he got trapped in his leather pants." She shrugged.

"We are watching the footage and a rough cut tonight. You should come see it." Ford smiled. "Let me rephrase that. Your coming downstairs is mandatory. Come on, honey."

She cringed back. "I don't want to."

"The fun part about being part of the world is that you sometimes have to do things that you don't want to, even if you think it will bore you."

He held out his hand, and she sighed and put her hand in his. He pulled her to her feet and held her against his body. "I am sorry that your pride is such a bunch of dumbasses."

"Me, too."

He smiled. "Argus is downstairs with the boys."

She blinked and started to quiver. "He is? Did he ask to see me?"

"Of course he did, honey. That is when I realized that you hadn't come back with us. Where were you?"

"Stuck in makeup, getting my spots off."

Ford chuckled. "He's going to enjoy the video clips."

"Uh, how much could you have cut together?"

He grinned. "The digital age is a wonderful thing."

"How long did you work on it?"

"Of and on, two hours. We added your footage as it came in, and then, we rendered it all and added the soundtrack."

She bit her lip. "Do I look okay?"

"Honey, you could be covered in mud, and he would still want to take you to his bed."

She smiled, and they left her guestroom.

"Honey, if you need comfort, go to my nest. I would rather you are there than be lost in the house while the party goes on."

"There is a party starting?"

"Yes, honey, there is a party started."

She smiled. "I have never been to a proper party."

"I will take you out for dinner another day; just make sure you fall asleep in my nest tonight. I don't think anywhere else is safe." He chuckled, and they headed downstairs.

The makeup artists were fawning over Argus, and the boys were watching the grill area with intense focus and lashing tails. Argus saw her coming down, and he smiled, holding out his hand.

She saw the irritation in the eyes of the makeup artists when Argus pulled her in, but he held up her hand and kissed his mark on her wrist. "Ah, kitten. You finally look like you."

She curled against his chest and whined. He held her tight and purred for her.

The women who had been ogling him stared with wide eyes as he held her to his chest. He ran a hand into her hair, and he murmured, "It's okay, kitten. We will sort it out. We just have to set back to one and start courting you. You want to go play paintball on Friday?"

She nodded against his chest. "Yes. Are you sure you want to go out and play?"

He chuckled. "I am sure. You need to learn how to play,

Olivia. It is my pleasure to show you some of that. Now, do you want to curl up on a couch and watch the crew go crazy in Ford's place?"

"Yes. You'll stay with me?"

"Of course, kitten." He grinned. "It is going to become my favourite way to spend an evening."

"How long can you keep the purr going? I really like the purr."

He laughed. "As long as you need it."

They found a couch, and he pulled her onto his lap, and he purred for her. Olivia started off tense, but she rapidly lost focus on what was going on around her, and she existed in the slow rhythm of his purr.

Ambrose and Dexter walked in and headed straight to their partner and their mate. Ambrose sat, and he took her, purring when Argus needed to go and get something to eat and drink. Dexter ate a kebab and brought one for Olivia. Ambrose chuckled and said, "See if you can get her to eat."

Dexter nodded and took a seat. Olivia ended up in his lap, and he purred in a slow burst that woke her.

He stroked her cheek. "Olly, I have a kebab for you. Not a euphemism. They are really good."

He held out the stick, and she reached for it. "Ah, ah. Teeth only."

She blinked sleepily and reached out, taking the first chunk in her teeth and chewing.

Ambrose stared in surprise. "That easy?"

Ford was watching from nearby. "She likes orders. They give her something to follow. To tell someone who has lived their life in a closet that the world is wide open and you will support what they want to do is just so fucking cruel. She has no idea where to start."

"Is that what you are doing?"

"I am giving her starting points and familiar faces who

aren't threats ... well, most of the time. You should have seen her outrun the pack of alphas today. It was epic, and I got it all on film."

Ambrose went cold. "What?"

"Yeah, she started to perfume during a chase sequence on a motorcycle, and the alphas behind her lost all focus. She has a helluva pull." Ford grinned.

He was ill at the magnitude of that threat. "How ... how did she get away?"

"It's in the video. Come on, we are ready to show today's clips."

Dexter crooned to her, and she kept eating. "Open your eyes. It's time to watch the video."

Ambrose looked around. The betas looked jealous, and the alphas had a mix of lust and wistfulness. *Huh.*

The giant screen rose up, and Ford used his computer to start the video. The song played, and a sad-looking Olivia in the jaguar makeup filled the screen while the song was wistful. The song continued, and she was standing in an arena, and motorcycles with alphas circled her. Ambrose watched the bola flying and taking the alpha down and then her obvious skill with the motorcycle as she revved up the motor and took off with a bright grin on her face. Romantic visions of her and Dexter were misty and projected above her head and then came her looking behind her and the gathering of alphas glazed with lust and chasing her down. She ditched the bike and climbed to the roof, waiting. There was a billow of smoke, and then, she was running through the field with the boys, and then, Hector and Caesar came bounding up, the cats keeping pace with her.

Scenes of her dancing with Dexter were interspersed, and when the song was over, she was sitting with the jaguars and staring into space before she stood up and walked away, Dexter's shadow rising on the bluff behind her.

The video ended.

The crew went wild.

Chapter Twenty-Two

Olivia snuggled against Dexter and opened her mouth for the next part of the kebab.

Ford was grinning. "So, I have a few days of edits ahead of me, but I think it looks really good."

Olivia smiled. "I enjoyed the motorcycle."

Ambrose asked, "Did you actually ride that bike?"

She nodded. "I like them. I started riding dirt bikes as a kid."

Argus was sitting on the edge of the sofa. "Country stuff." He smiled.

She nodded. "Yeah. I grew up doing all kinds of sketchy stuff. Climbing trees, catfish noodling, riding bikes, trikes, fixing trucks at neighbour's houses, and I was on the scholastic swim team. I won a few awards before I manifested. After that, I was locked to my home property, but I still climbed and kept myself fit. To counteract the other issue, I took up yoga and light gymnastics. One of the guests at the B&B got me into it, and regulars brought me DVDs so I could practice and watch stuff."

Dexter chuckled. "So, you have had a bit of a life."

"Yeah, but I am in the same situation as a lot of folks coming from the countryside, but I have a distinct lag in the knowledge of modern contemporary society. I have been cramming like hell, but I need a practical application for what I have read."

Ambrose blinked. "Right. If we gave you a list, would you tell us things you haven't done?"

"Sure. Just email it to me. *That* I have gotten the hang of."

Dexter nuzzled her neck. "If we ask you, would you do

those with us?"

"Um, probably. I am not going to say for sure because it is plausible that I make some friends by the time you figure out what you want our relationship to be."

Ford chuckled. "I want in on that list."

The guys frowned at him. Ford grinned. "Guys, I am trying to make sure that she keeps a connection to you. She could have run back to the Omega Centre, and they would have been happy to find her a new group of alphas while surgically removing your marks. They have done it before. They can do it."

Her guys were shocked.

Ford leaned in, "Now, honey, how did you like the video?"

"It was good. I can hardly wait to see it with Leora's face on it."

He looked at her in surprise, and then, he cackled. "Olivia, it is going to be your face on the video, and enough snapshots of you in action have been shared that my assistant has had to start fielding calls to have you appear in videos, short films, and designers are throwing clothing at you."

She blinked. "What the fuck?"

"You are all over the net, honey. Images of you reclining on Hector are everywhere, not to mention you riding Caesar or cuddling with the boys." He grinned. "Then, there is the payoff to Ambrose. That is getting a lot of play, but Vera is dismissing those calls."

Dexter chuckled. "I can imagine."

Ambrose raised his brows. "Well, that explains why my voicemail is full. I hope it isn't my parents."

Dexter snorted. "Mine already called. My grandma got a shot of Olivia and me in our costumes. My parents didn't tell her we have a mate."

Leora was slowly approaching their group. She grinned, and her bodyguard was looking wary. "Um, I had a question for all of you guys?"

Ford glanced back. "Ask them."

"Uh, you too. I have a song that I would release as a single because it doesn't match anything on the album, but I think you five would be perfect for the video. I am self-releasing this one, so I have a small budget, but I always imagined it as a sword and sorcery thing."

Ford grinned. "You want me in there?"

"You are kinda striking." She blushed. "And your body language with Olivia is super sweet and slightly predatory. I think it's perfect for making you the villain."

He laughed, and Olivia tilted her head. "Can I hear the song?"

Leora blinked. "I don't want to play it here."

"Come on. We will go to someplace private. We can talk there."

Olivia got off Dexter's lap and headed upstairs, with Leora walking behind. The bodyguard trailed after. Ford yelled, "Not the nest."

"Yes, Ford."

She took Leora to the guestroom and pulled her into the large closet. "Okay. Here is safe, and I wouldn't know how to record on my phone if I tried."

The singer laughed. "Yeah, normally, folks try and convince me that no one is recording in a crowd."

"If it comes out, and it doesn't sound like it has been recorded through a door, it was me."

"Could I sue you?"

"You could try. I don't have anything, though." Olivia shrugged.

Leora looked at her. "You are kidding, right? Your mates are some of the most successful alphas in the city."

"They are? Huh. It must have been why the centre didn't have a problem handing me over. Okay. Do you want to make with the song?" Olivia looked at her curiously.

The phone came out, and they stood as the music and lyrics filled the small space. It was a song with longing and softness and desperation and determination.

Olivia sighed. "That is really pretty."

Leora grinned. "Thank you. I like the harder stuff, but every now and then, I want to bust out and just sing something sweet."

"Well, I would be happy to go and play for this. Just tell me what you want me to do, and I will try and do it."

Leora hugged her. "Thank you. I hope your guys will be as easy to work with."

"They won't be. Ford might taunt them into it."

Leora stroke her skin. "You are so soft."

Olivia smiled. "Yup. Designation hazard. Shall we exit the closet? You go first."

Leora blinked. "Why?"

"Because four people are in that room aside from your bodyguard, and if they have cameras, I don't want the internet to get all weird about you and me in a photo."

"Ah. Right. Okay." Leora smiled. "Thanks."

Olivia nodded and receded into the shadows as the door opened. Leora left and closed the door behind her.

The group stayed in there and talked for a minute, and then, the outer door opened and closed.

Olivia could still feel people in the outer room, and she peeped out to see Ford and the guys. She stepped out, and she looked at them. "I didn't commit you to anything. I just told her I could see her vision for it."

Ford sighed. "Did you negotiate a price for your time?"

She scowled. "No. I go places, and I do stuff. That is my new thing."

Dexter snorted. "We will come out and play with you. Even Ambrose."

Ford crossed his arms. "Even me."

She held up her hand. "I told Leora she would have to negotiate for your time."

Ford nodded. "She told us. I got fifty percent rights after production costs. All funds going to the big cat rescue."

She blinked. "Why? I mean, I know why for me, but you

guys have other stuff to do."

Argus smiled. "If we can do a few things that will embarrass our kids, I think it is worth it."

Ambrose's expression got soft. "Yeah, what he said."

She blushed.

Dexter grinned. "I just think it's cool."

Ford smiled. "And I just want to see you smile and in some hot and elaborate costumes."

"Leora said she has a small budget."

Ford grinned. "And I said that the designers are beating down your door to cover that body of yours in something sparkly and formfitting. I think a costume isn't too far out of the range."

Dexter asked, "Is Yemeen one of the designers?"

"Yeah. How did you know?"

"I have done jewellery for the award shows. We have worked together a few times. He can definitely do something elaborate but flattering. It will just cost me, my soul."

Ford grinned. "The idea is to get them to offer it."

"Yeah, but his work is so good I will have to make some jewellery to match the video. I hate letting him upstage me." Dexter's eyes narrowed.

Ford shrugged. "I will put my request for costumes to them and get sketches, then we all get together and decide. Dexter, if you want to do accessories, you are welcome to do it."

Dexter grinned. "I have a few ideas that I have been toying with, just for some of the award things and donor events we have to go to for the rescue."

Ambrose was smiling wryly.

She knotted her fingers together. "I don't know how to thank you."

Dexter grinned. "I know how. Group hug."

Her eyes widened as they started to surround her. "No. Oh, no."

Ambrose slid his feet between hers and cupped her sex.

"Oh, yes." He started to purr, and it hummed up higher until she had shrieked and collapsed between them.

Ford was laughing, and he caught her when her guys made room, kissing her and stroking her slightly sweaty body.

They all kissed her good night, and she leaned against Ford. Her heart was lighter, and she smiled. They were going to join her on a project. They were coming to her. She crawled into the nest after the party, and she turned to Ford, running her hands over him, but he pushed her down and went down on her again.

He lifted his head and sighed. "If you feel that way tomorrow, I will definitely agree, but I think your emotions are high right now."

She looked at him. "I thought you were supposed to be an oversexed-omega. You are making the rest of us look slutty."

He grinned and slid three fingers into her before devoting his tongue to licking up the slick and honey that she started creating. She moaned, twisted, and under the ferocity of his mouth, she screeched.

He kept pumping his fingers while he lapped at her clit, and her slow pulses of release continued for long, torturous minutes. She moaned softly, and he continued until her body was finished.

He slurped his hand and cuddled her again. "You are lovely, honey."

She sighed. "So people keep telling me."

He pressed his lips to her temple. "Don't stop changing. You are willing to put yourself out there. This is good. I might not be able to be in your ear when the filming happens. Or at least when I am in a moment with you."

"It will be fine. Pretty sure. Thanks, Ford. Even if you turn out to be an ass, today was good."

He chuckled. "You need more good days."

She sighed. "Thanks. I think so too."

He held her until she slept.

Olivia woke in dark silence. Ford was next to her, but she felt weird. There was a sore ache in her bones that she hadn't experienced before. Her side throbbed, and her eyes went wide. Dexter.

She eased out of Ford's nest, and she grabbed a robe. She crept out of the house and ran at full tilt to the house next door. Dexter was hurting, and she didn't know why.

She crept into the house and climbed up to Dexter's room. The room was empty. A look at the other rooms made her check hers, and he was in her nest, curled in a ball.

She sat next to him and stroked his back, soothing him as he shivered and twitched. "Hey, Dex. I am here, babe."

He rolled and wrapped his arms around her, pulling her down to him. She brushed her lips against his. He growled and pushed her back, sliding his hand between her thighs. The growl caused a surge of slick, and she parted her legs and invited him in. He thrust into her suddenly, and she inhaled sharply before she let out a low moan.

His eyes had been glazed, and they focused on her suddenly. "Olivia! Did I hurt you?"

She stroked his cheek. "Just surprised. Are you okay? I felt pain."

"Growing pains. I started my final growth spurt. It isn't comfortable."

She kissed him softly and rubbed her cheek across his. "Is this helping?"

He grinned. "If I say yes, will you stay?"

"As long as you need me."

"Then, yes."

She smiled. "Then, I will be with you until you don't need me, and then, I will go."

He nodded, and his hips started to move. "You will come back?"

"As long as you need me."

"Good enough." He nuzzled her, kissed her, and started to

thrust. He had rocked into her for a few minutes when he withdrew, turned her so that her back was to him, and he cupped her breasts while kissing her neck. He held her breasts, licked the base of her neck, and ran his hands over her arms.

"You sneaky bastard."

He nipped her shoulder with a grin. "We agreed that if you came for one, we would alert the others."

The door opened, and the other two joined her in her nest. She moaned, rolled her hips against them, and then whined when Dexter locked inside.

Argus trailed his fingers over where she was joined to Dexter and rubbed her clit. She started to rock helplessly, and her release made her squeeze tighter.

Argus kissed her as she panted. "We are going to have to explain to Dexter that if he doesn't knot in you every time, we have more time to play."

Dexter blinked. "I don't have to?"

Ambrose treated him to a lecture about holding back and having some self-control. The lecture continued so long that Olivia had uncoupled from Dexter, and Argus was sneaking her away to another corner of the nest.

She laughed and wrapped her arms around his neck as he slid into her. "I came because Dex was in distress."

"You stepped into our trap. Now you pay the price." He draped her over his arm and kissed her neck as he slowly and leisurely thrust into her and lazily retreated.

"Trap?"

He chuckled. "We knew Dexter was going to start his final growth. His parents warned us a few weeks ago. He stopped taking his pain killers tonight to draw you over."

She gasped as he kissed her wrist and tongued the mark. "You could have just invited me."

He smiled. "Where would the fun be in that?"

Olivia shuddered in his arms, her breath catching as another orgasm swept through her. She felt her body bathing him in slick, and he grunted as he spilled into her. They clung together until Ambrose asked with soft touches and strokes along her body.

She looked at him, and he met her gaze.

Ambrose was sincere. "I will never raise a hand to you that you didn't expressly permit before we get into bed or commence any sexual interaction. Frankly, while it is something I am generally very interested in because it brings you to fear, it has no place between us."

She swallowed. "As long as you are sure. If you want that other stuff, I don't mind you seeking it elsewhere. Honestly, I am just a new toy. The interest will wear off."

Argus laughed, Dexter snorted, and Ambrose gave her a slow grin.

"When that day comes, precious, I will let you know."

Argus slipped out of her and kissed her softly, leaving the decision up to her.

She looked into Ambrose's eyes, and she reached for him. Being covered in the scents of her mates was soothing to the riot inside her. When his deft touches and slow exploration of her body brought them both to a joyful completion, she stroked his cheek and smiled. "I am going to have to learn your last names eventually."

They all looked at her in shock. She smiled and got to her feet, putting on her robe and leaving her nest. It was fine. They were still hers. She was still theirs, and she would come when they needed her. Now, they had to figure out how to bring up their names decorously.

She returned to Ford and crawled into the nest near but not touching him. He pulled her in close. "Hmm. Smells like you had some fun."

"Dexter needed me, so he acted as bait and called the others once I was there."

"What's wrong with Dexter?"

"Growing pains, apparently. He's having his final growth spurt."

Ford squeezed her. "How big is he gonna be?"

"Six-six. Six-eight. No idea. I don't even know how old he is. He won't tell me."

Ford chuckled wickedly. "He's twenty-one. He's been designing jewels for select clients for years, but two years ago, he met the other two, and since there aren't many feline alphas, he moved in immediately."

"Oh, god. I'm a cougar." She covered her face.

Ford kissed her shoulder and stroked a hand between her thighs.

She hissed. "Don't. I'm a mess."

He chuckled. "And yet, you are still delightful, but this makes you so slippery."

She squeaked, and he started trying to see how many fingers he could get inside her. She squirmed and panted, "Ford?"

"Yes, honey?"

"Can you be inside me now? I am a little desperate, and the fingers are just a tease. Please, Ford?"

She looked at him over her shoulder. "Please?"

He rolled her over, and he narrowed his eyes. "Are you playing me?"

She held up her fingers about a centimetre from each other. "Just a little."

He grinned, and his eyes were bright. "Maybe I will get inside you, just a little."

She kissed him softly, and their tongues tangled together, sliding against each other until he pinned her down and took charge. His tongue's slow thrust started to make her whimper and raise her hips to him.

"Oh, no, honey. You want me, so you are going to have me on my terms." He nuzzled her cheek and slowly made his way down her body. She moaned, yelped, and giggled twice before he smiled and moved over her, sliding inside her.

She blinked. He was producing the same style of slick that she was. His cock felt nearly yielding but really tense at the same time. She arched back as he thrust into her, and the heavy waves of satisfaction rippled through her and had nothing to do with an imminent orgasm. He just felt so . . . good.

The slow roll of his hips pushed him deep, and there was no knot to deal with. She was surprised at how smooth it was, and she clenched around him. He paused and shuddered. "Gods. Do that again."

She clenched, and he groaned, his throat vibrating. She clenched, and she purred. His eyes went wide, and he shoved deep. "Honey!"

Olivia felt every spasm and every twitch as he came. She held him when he collapsed on her. She calmly wrapped her arms and legs around him, giving him a smacking kiss to the jaw.

He groaned, and she purred.

"How are you doing that, honey?"

"I don't know. I used to do it for pain control. To keep me calm. Don't other omega's do it?"

"None of the women I know do it. I can, but it took practice. I was referring to the death grip you have on my cock. Alpha females have a lock like that, but it isn't something I expected."

She sighed. "I can stop."

His head lifted. "No!"

She laughed and slowly rolled her hips against him.

His erection recovered, and he gave her a smug look. "I have a quick recovery time."

"I am suitably impressed."

"I also cum a lot, so if you thought you were messy after your three, you haven't seen anything yet." He kissed her. He moved his fingers between them and stroked her clit as he moved up her body and moved inside her at a different angle.

He pushed up against her g-spot, and she whined and began to tremble against him as he stroked inside her.

"Oh, I like that sound, do that again."

She glared at him, but he struck that spot again, and the whine came out. She shuddered, and he played her body, eliciting the sounds he wanted in the order he wanted them. She came twice during his exploration and only managed to squeeze him tight once.

He shuddered and kissed her neck. "Oh, honey. I could drown in you happily."

She blushed. "You keep cumming, and I will be drowning from the inside out."

He nuzzled her and slid free, moving down her body to lie with his head between her breast. "There, that should let you drain, and then, I can fill you up again."

She blushed and held his head as he rubbed his face between her breasts. "Don't you need to get some sleep?"

"Ah, honey, this is better than sleep any day."

Her face remained warm, but she was pretty happy with the evening's events. She had her guys, and Ford was really good at sex, so she had folks who could make her feel good, which meant that she was ahead of the game from two weeks prior, if she was counting score . . . and she was.

Chapter Twenty-Three

Yawning in the editing suite was distracting for Ford, so he sent her off to the pool for a swim to clear her head.

She was finishing a lap when she saw feet next to the pool. She pulled up and leaned against the tiled edge, and looked up.

A handsome alpha stood there, his clothing was impeccable, and his appearance was Indian.

She smiled. "Hello."

He crouched next to her. "Hello, pretty. Is Ford in?"

"Yeah. He's editing."

"He left you alone?"

She grinned and pointed to the shadows where Rick was waiting. "No."

"Ah. Very wise. I was fighting the urge to sweep you away, little pretty."

"Please, fight it. I don't want you hurt." She glanced behind him and smiled.

She waved at the figure behind him. "Hey, Dex."

He growled at the man and said, "Hey, Olivia. Is he bothering you?"

"No. But he is between me and my towel, so things are about to escalate one way or another."

"Yemeen, stand aside."

She looked at him with understanding. "Oh, I get it now."

She touched the bottom of the pool and lunged upward and out of the water. Dex muttered, "Oh, for fuck's sake."

Yemeen stared as she walked to the towel and wrapped herself up. Dex walked up to her and took another towel, drying off her hair. "You have to swim naked?"

"The suits don't fit, and the tops come off when I swim anyway. I am just skipping an unnecessary step." She beamed.

"And the bottoms?"

"I don't want to clash."

He pressed his forehead to hers and kissed her. "Very sensible."

Yemeen looked at her and Dexter. "She's your mate?"

"She's our omega." He rubbed his nose against hers.

Yemeen stared. "She's an omega."

Olivia looked at him. "Yes. Don't worry about the scent thing. There is an explanation, but you don't need to hear it."

Yemeen blinked. "But, you are an omega compatible with feline alphas?"

"Yeah."

Dexter wrapped his arms around her. "She's part of our pride. You have made your opinion of our little gathering quite clear, so you can just stuff it."

Yemeen was staring at them in shock, "But, she's an omega with a feline affinity."

Olivia gave him a thumbs-up. "I am also screwed up as hell. So, it is a lot of giving and take."

Yemeen looked at her, at Dexter's protective grip, and then Ford came out, and he said, "Yemeen. You made it. I see you have met Olivia. Olivia Haven, this is Yemeen Basu. He's one of the designers I mentioned yesterday. Yemeen, come inside. Olivia promised to act as a housekeeper when I have solitary guests, and since I need to talk to Dexter as well, it is best that you both come inside together."

Olivia blinked at the thought of Dexter and Yemeen coming inside together. Her perfume started up, and Dexter chuckled. Yemeen physically jerked in surprise. He smelled like sweet almonds. She could catch his scent from ten feet away.

She rinsed off under the outdoor shower when they had gone inside and towelled off her hair. She had never considered herself an exhibitionist, but pulling on her bra, panties, and jeans, she realized that she didn't give a fuck who was looking. Her crop top slid into place, and she pulled her hair into a loose tail. She dropped the towels into the hamper and headed inside.

She smiled brightly. "So, what's everyone in the mood for?"

Three pairs of intense eyes locked on her, and she blinked. "Oh. That isn't on the breakfast menu. How about waffles?"

Ford grinned. "Spoilsport. And coffee."

She nodded and set about the coffee, gathering ingredients on the way. The guys were talking earnestly at the table, and she brought the carafe and supplies out with cups while the waffle iron was heating.

Dexter wrapped an arm around her waist. She looped an arm over his shoulder and pressed a kiss to his temple and then his lips when he lifted his head.

Yemeen rapped his knuckles on the table. "I get it. Look at what I am missing. Subtle."

Dexter laughed. "No. She doesn't know about that. She's just super tactile when she knows she can touch and be touched."

"Stop bragging. My apologies, Mr. Basu."

"So, you don't know that I turned down membership in the pride two months ago?"

She blinked and shrugged. "I just joined the pride six weeks ago tentatively, and a week and a half officially. No one mentioned you until yesterday. And only then in reference to costume design or dress design. I forget which."

The waffle iron chirped, and she headed over to make waffles.

Yemeen blinked and asked Dexter, "You really didn't invite me over here to taunt me?"

Ford sipped at his coffee. "I did. I spent a very sleep-depriving night in the arms of Miss Haven, and I must say, she has stamina that I find gratifyingly endless. She also gives herself with no reservations and thrives at every touch."

She threw a strawberry at his head, and it landed with a satisfying thwack. He stared at her in shock. "You threw a strawberry at me."

"No, Ford, I *hit* you with a strawberry. I don't miss." She smiled sweetly and made the next waffle while she dusted the first with icing sugar, a fanned strawberry, and a blob of whipped cream.

She brought it to the table. "Mr. Basu? Waffle?"

"Uh . . . yeah, please. Thank you. Call me Yemeen."

She slid the waffle in front of him with a smile, and then she stroked Dexter's cheek as she passed. He was suddenly more smug and less pouty.

The next waffle went to Dexter, and Ford got the third. She set it down in front of him and then hugged him from behind, rubbing her breasts gently against his shoulders. "Let me know if you want more . . . waffles."

Dexter held his plate out eagerly.

She came around, took his plate, and kissed his forehead, ruffling her fingers through his hair.

He tilted up his head for a proper kiss, and she administered one, tasting the strawberries and cream.

Yemeen was breathing heavily. "Now you *are* taunting me."

"Yeah. I am." She winked and looked at his plate. "Are waffles not to your liking?"

He looked down, and his cheeks darkened. "I forgot I had it. It does look good."

"If you want a fresh one, let me know, but if you don't like it, I can make you an omelette or something."

He paused. "May I have a kiss?"

Dexter growled.

Olivia looked at the tiny nod from Ford. "Only a kiss?"

Yemeen nodded. "Yes, I just want to know how badly I fucked up."

She shrugged and walked over to him, leaning in when he

got to his feet. She blinked and leaned back. "You are a pretty big fella, aren't you?"

He grinned and leaned down, touching her neck, the other hand at her waist. She was going to warn him, but he pulled her tight to his body, and his mouth moved carefully across hers as if he was worried she would break. He reminded her of Dexter in his approach. He gained her full cooperation, and then, his tongue teased her lips. She opened her lips, and he started purring. That started a reaction in her, and his hands tightened, pulling her flush against him as her scent filled the air around them.

His scent thickened the air, and she rolled her hips against his erection. She whined, and his hands clenched on her, activating Dexter's mark. He groaned and was on his feet, pressing against her back and sliding a hand up and under her shirt. She whined again and broke the kiss with Yemeen. He growled and leaned in, but she hissed.

He jerked his head back.

She pulled Dexter's hand out of her shirt. "Easy, Dex."

He leaned his head toward her shoulder and licked at her neck. He whined.

She could feel his tension, and she turned to him. "What do you need, Dex?"

He looked at her and whined.

Ford murmured, "Take him upstairs if you like. Or bang him on the counter. I don't mind."

"Since I don't want to rub Yemeen's nose in it, I will take him to the guestroom. We'll be down in a few minutes."

Dexter picked her up and tossed her over his shoulder, striding up to the second floor and right to her guestroom. He dropped her on the bed and removed her jeans, cut her panties off with the claws he rarely used, and then, he pushed up her shirt, pulled down her bra, and sucked hard while fumbling with his own clothes. He was inside her a few moments later, and she was slick and welcoming as he drove home.

She screamed. He roared, and then, they had to wait.

He sighed. "I really have to learn to stop knotting you. Well, when there are other things to be done."

She giggled. "I don't mind. My therapist appointment isn't until two anyway. I have plenty of time."

He sighed. "Is Ford taking you?"

"Um, no. I didn't ask him. He offered one of his bodyguards, but I am going to try to figure out how to take a cab."

"So, you didn't remind him."

"Nope."

Dexter sighed.

"So, what is the deal with Yemeen anyway?"

"Well, his aura is like mine. Tiger affinity. When Ambrose ran into him at a fundraiser, he offered him an association with our pride. Yemeen was . . . not complimentary about our pride. When he was told we were registered with the Omega Centre, he laughed in Ambrose's face."

She blinked. "Oh. Now that makes sense."

She undulated to check his status and contracted hard around him. He jerked and fell forward with a grunt. "Damn, Olivia."

She threaded her fingers through his hair. "I just had to check. You have about a minute before you come loose."

"You can tell that?"

Olivia smiled. "I am building a mental catalogue of your reactions, how deep you go, and how hard your knot is." She frowned. "It shouldn't be that engorged."

He ducked his head. "I think I am close to my first proper rut."

"Oh, geez. Well, at least it only lasts for a day or two. Wait, do the others go through it as well?"

"Only once a year or so. Argus and Ambrose are older; it doesn't hit as often as it does for me."

She blinked. "What did you do before I came along?"

"Jerked off . . . a lot."

She giggled.

He came loose, and she exhaled as the cool air met wet flesh. "That is so disconcerting."

He kissed her and said, "Wait a moment."

He left her and disappeared into the bathroom. He returned and pressed a warm washcloth to her. "Ambrose has been impressing the importance of aftercare on me."

She hissed as he tidied up after himself and herself. "Nice, but remember that a few seconds ago, your barbs were joining the knot in me to lock you in place. Gently."

"Does it really hurt?"

"No. It is like . . . you know that super tense feeling right before you cum?"

"Yeah."

"It is like that but sharper. It feels good, but it is a dangerous kind of good. Like when I get bitten during sex. Same kind of thing."

She put her breasts back into their proper configuration and pulled her shirt down.

Dexter sighed. "I can bite you at other times?"

"Yeah, just not a bonding bite. More pressure, less puncturing the skin."

"You know I am going to have to try that."

"I have to be really high to enjoy that, so keep that in mind, or I will punch you."

Dexter grinned. "I will keep it in mind. Are you up to put your jeans on?"

"Yeah, but that was my last pair of panties. You jerk. I am going to have to head to your house to get more."

"Oh, I don't think so. There's an order coming in later today, along with some swimwear that will fit. You don't have to wear it, but it is an option." Ford grinned from the open doorway.

She smelled sweet almond. "Don't tell me he was watching."

"Okay, I won't tell you, but he is grovelling to Ambrose

right now."

Dexter chuckled.

"Ford, what are you up to?"

"Olivia, I collect the best and the brightest in my orbit, and you are definitely the brightest."

She got to her feet and slithered into her jeans. The seam was a little abrasive against her groin, but she had felt worse.

Ford grinned. "He's ready to take your measurements for the costume. He's willing to take us on as a client where your clothing is concerned and has recommended someone else for our costumes."

"So, he's that into viewing sex lives? That is an expensive kink."

She ran her hands over her hips, and Dexter straightened. When she passed Ford, he spun her and pinned her to the wall while he inhaled deeply. "Mmm. You smell like pie."

"Uh-huh. I have to go clean up."

"Already done. In case you wonder, Ambrose is telling Yemeen that he has to court you to gain entrance into the pride. Since the others are doing the same, it shouldn't take long."

"What shouldn't take long?"

"Ambrose is working on a redesign for this place so that we can all fit comfortably. A few more small nests and hideaways, large rooms for them, a super plush nest for us. You can work with me or find other options over time. Finish your book."

She blinked. "Oh, right. I haven't finished it. Damn it. I need to bring it with me to the therapist today."

He blinked. "That's today?"

"Yup. In four hours."

He sighed. "I will send you with Rick."

"You don't have to. I was going to call a cab."

He leaned back. "You have no clue, do you? I am not going to let you put yourself in the deep end just because you haven't seen the sharks."

She looked at him. "Are you worried for me?"

Ford exhaled. "Yes."

She cupped his cheeks. "Then, I will go with whomever you choose."

He looked relieved. "Good. Your perfume is coming out more frequently, and without an alpha near you, you are going to look like fair game. Remember the motorcycles?"

She shivered. "Right. I had forgotten."

He nuzzled her head. "It's okay, baby omega. We will get you to understand what you are."

"I am not a baby." She mumbled it against his neck.

"Yeah, you are. You are less than two months into knowing what it feels like to just be free."

She mumbled, "I will remember that I am a baby and can't possibly understand when you are in heat."

He whined suddenly, and she giggled. He licked softly at her neck and gnawed lightly. She gasped, and her toes curled. "Stop that."

"I am just following your instructions to Dexter. You really like it, huh?"

"My toes just curled into the ankles. What do you think?"

Dexter came out, and he had his phone in his hand. "Ambrose is really smug right about now."

She sighed. "I don't like being used as a pawn."

Ford shook his head. "Honey, you are the board; we all just want our turn to get on you."

She punched him in the arm. "Not funny."

He grinned. "Not kidding. I have never met a female omega who wasn't a total bitch to me until you. You, sweetness, are currently my favourite person in the world."

She ducked her head. "You are a nice person. It is easy to be nice to you."

"I am not a nice person, but you see that in me, and for that, I am grateful."

Olivia bit her lip. "I am still ticked at you using me as bait to provide your favourite flavour of alpha."

He laughed. "I like the felines. They aren't clingy, and if they are all bonded to you, they won't try to bond me, which means I get the benefits without being covered with triggers."

"Nice."

"Hey, I like my lifestyle a lot. I don't want to be tied down to one or more alphas."

"So, during your heats, do you use protection?"

"Yeah, and because I don't have any alphas, I can take care of any complications immediately."

"You don't want kids?"

He shrugged. "Not on my own. Maybe if you have some for the alphas, you will be inclined to offer me a pity baby, so I don't need to carry one."

She snorted. "It wouldn't be pity. I am planning on keeping my birth control for one more heat, and then, I am going to throw caution to the wind, so to speak."

His eyes lit with delight. "I don't suppose I can call dibs?"

"Can two omegas even get pregnant? They really don't cover that at the centre."

He grinned. "I don't know, but I want to try. How long do you think it will be before you cycle again?"

She blushed. "Uh . . ."

She looked, and Dexter had gone downstairs.

Her silence was enough for Ford. "You have a fast cycle?"

"That is what they told me at the centre. Six to eight weeks. It has already been one."

"Oh, I wanna be there for that. Seeing you after was good, but I imagine that you are completely wild when it has you." His eyes lit up. "How fabulous would it be if we synched up?"

"Oh, god." Her body loved that idea. "Can we go check on Yemeen?"

"With you smelling like that? Oh yeah."

She punched him again and then realized that if hitting was against her rules for Ambrose, she should practice restraint. *Fuck.*

Chapter Twenty-Four

Her eyes were puffy, her chest felt cold, and her lips were numb when she left the new therapist's office. The woman was very encouraging, very calm, and she supported Olivia's efforts to document her life to date. She was to continue her writing until she felt comfortable with her situation and the people around her.

When she stumbled into the lobby, she looked for Rick and didn't see him. Panic ensued, and she retreated to a corner. She picked up her phone and sent a text to Ford.

Where is Rick?

He asked if he could go for coffee. Why?

I am alone, and I don't feel particularly calm.

Shit. Okay, he's on his way.

Thank you.

Stay where you are.

Rick showed up with his coffee and saw her in the corner. He eased up on her and said, "Okay, Olivia. We can go home now."

She nodded. "Okay. Thank you."

She uncurled and walked with him to the car, silent and messed up.

She got back to Ford's place, grabbed her laptop, and went out into the yard, climbing a tree to get herself up to where it was safe. She made herself comfortable with her legs braced in the branches, and she started writing.

It was about two hours before she felt tugs on her marks. She put her hand on them one at a time to notify them that she was okay.

Ford came out to the yard, and he called, "Olivia!"

She sighed and closed her computer. She climbed down from the tree, and he stared at her when she stood on the ground. "Hiya, Ford."

He walked up to her. "Honey. Have you been up there since you got back?"

She nodded. "I needed to get some writing done."

"You could have used my office."

"I don't know where that is, and you were busy."

"I was talking with Yemeen. We were designing your outfit for the video."

"Don't let me stop you."

Ford looked at her warily. "Are you all right?"

"I am still a little freaked out. I haven't felt like that for a long time, and I had forgotten how bugged out it makes me."

Ambrose was walking toward them across the grass. He picked her up and held her the moment he was close enough to grab her.

Ford blinked. "Why do you look so serious, Ambrose? She said she's fine."

"She isn't fine. Her emotions are a raw riot. She's scrambling around in there trying to find a way to escape."

She let the big fat tears fall and held onto Ambrose with one hand. He took her computer and handed it to Ford, and then Olivia held onto him with both arms and legs.

Ambrose murmured, "Do you want to go cuddle in your nest, precious?"

She nodded.

Ford murmured, "Use mine. She's comfortable there."

Ambrose nodded and walked inside with her, stroking her hair and murmuring to her.

Yemeen looked at her. "What happened?"

Ford put the computer on the table, and Olivia heard as Ambrose walked up the steps. "I forgot that therapy sessions ended ten minutes early, and I sent her bodyguard away, so when she came out, there wasn't anyone, and she was in a particularly raw state. So, she's in a strange city with a new therapist, and she's newly omega, and there were alphas in the area starting to watch her. Apparently, she perfumes when she is upset, which is progress. Fear used to shut her down."

She didn't want to discuss it, she just held onto Ambrose until they were in the nest, and he stripped her down to her underwear, did the same for himself, and then, he cuddled her under a furry throw. She blinked and relaxed against him; the scent of cinnamon buns and vanilla icing was right. It was her mate.

He traced her lips with his finger, and she licked it then sucked on it. He purred, and she lifted her gaze to his. "Ah, so precious. Stubborn, determined, independent. And very beautiful. I have been trying to treat you like a standard omega when you were born to be with off-standard alphas."

She bit down on his finger gently, and he chuckled and stroked his fingertip along her tongue. "Aw, you don't like it when I don't say you have the best alphas ever? You had a trying day, huh?"

She nodded.

"Therapy is scary?"

She nodded again. She stopped sucking his finger, and he pulled it out from between her lips.

She burrowed her face against his neck. "So many things I don't want to think about, and I have to, so they echo in my head for the rest of the day. Which is why they space it out. So, you don't end up insane, but you do go there for a while when you talk to the therapist."

"So, why do you do it?"

She knew he knew the answer, but she told him anyway. "Because someone I had to trust because they had the duty to care for and protect me denied me that care and protection. They hurt me, and when that couldn't stop the manifestation, they had someone else hurt me. Then, it was endless rounds of beatings and verbal abuse."

"How did he die?"

Olivia let out a throaty chuckle. "Like a man filled with rage should die. He had a heart attack while he was beating me. He told me to call for help, but I couldn't move, and I didn't know how to use his cell phone. So, I lay there, and he died next to me. Lara called for an ambulance, but it was far too late."

"Good god." Ambrose held her tight. "What did the authorities say?"

"What authorities? I was dragged into the screaming shed and locked there until the first responders were gone. When she let me out two days later, he had been buried, and Lara was in charge. She couldn't hit as hard."

"What about your injuries?"

"They healed. They always heal with no trace. There were other experiments that Lara tried, locking me down, so I am sorry that I can't be the tied-up submissive that you long for who needs to take punishment to please you." She started to cry big, fat tears.

"Aw, precious. My preferences were a toy to play with. They are my past. If my precious doesn't want to play, we won't play. Having you in my arms is all the blind trust I need."

She smiled weakly. "And the occasional fucking."

His arms tightened. "More than the occasional. It is a need now, through the link. When you brush against it while combing your hair, I ache. When your body throbs because someone arouses you, I feel it. All that feedback was dumped into me, and you weren't here to hold. It hurt."

She was going to apologize, but he pressed his finger to her lips again. "Don't apologize. I was too smug, and I knew what I had asked of women before. But you aren't the others. You are my mate and deserve my respect and my attention. I knew a portion of what you had experienced, and I still tried to control our interactions instead of just enjoying your presence. I tried to put you in a category that you didn't belong in, and I am sorry."

"Why are you apologizing?"

He chuckled. "It's therapy day."

She smiled and kissed his chest. "Therapy can have benefits." Her hands started to move over his skin and the taut muscles underneath.

"Really? I don't think your psychologist would approve. Sleeping with a patient and all."

She chuckled. "Good thing that you were just sharing and that I am *not* your therapist."

He smiled slowly, his golden features glowing happily.

"What do you think if we can do if we keep some clothing on?"

He chuckled. "Something I haven't done since I was a teen."

"Well, I never got that chance, so let's take something off my list."

Ambrose kissed her and muttered, "One torturous teen make-out session with dry humping coming up."

She giggled. "Oh, I doubt it will be dry, but do the best you can."

He rolled her to her back, and with his mouth above hers, he murmured, "Challenge accepted."

She laughed until the kiss got serious, and then, she let his caresses burn out the last bit of pain and fear to just leave heat.

Ford watched Yemeen. "You look concerned."

"She is so delicate, and she's in therapy? What kind of omega is that?"

"A strong one. You don't have to court the pride, you know. You can just let things be." Ford watched Yemeen stiffen at his words.

The designer looked grim. "You are kidding, right? I can't get the taste of her out of my head. She's so clean and sweet with heavy overtones of sex."

Ford laughed. "That is a good description. Don't tell her about the overtones, though. She thinks she just smells like peaches."

Yemeen looked at him and chuckled. "What is your CG budget for the video?"

"Non-existent. This is all on Leora. Ambrose is providing the locations. Argus is building any sets that we need, and Dexter is doing the accessories. If you help with the costumes and I provide the filming crew and editing, we are set."

"Hmm. I had a thought about getting Olivia into as many costume changes as possible then putting the costumes up for auction or, at least, keep them to play with later." Yemeen showed him the tablet.

Ford stared, and he looked back at Yemeen. "You had these waiting?"

"I drew them while we were talking. The moment I met her, my mind started filling with designs for *her*. I am going to start the courtship, but you had better brace for me to be here. I am going to be pursuing her between dates as well."

Ford nodded and put the elegant and highly erotic images down. "I am sure the guys will be accepting . . . or you will have to head to the gym and wrestle out rights to time with her."

Yemeen blinked. "They still do that?"

"It is the best way, given what they are. No teeth and hand to hand."

"What are you getting out of this?" Yemeen asked him curiously.

"Ah, it is my chance to get an omega of my own and alphas that I want and trust. They have her, so I won't push for a bond, and she is what I want. So, to have her, I need them. It is a trade I am willing to make."

"I thought all male omegas were alpha crazy, male or female?"

He chuckled. "I want a woman that I can be the protector for. Olivia is tough, but she is also vulnerable as hell. It is quite the mix."

"What about when she steadies herself?"

"Then, she is going to be spectacular. She has been out of her situation and community for less than two months, and she has already shed a lot of societal norms. I wouldn't have guessed that she would have lost the urge for concealment. It means she's feeling secure. That is definitely new."

"Oh, you mean when she shot out of the water, and my cock exploded? Yeah, she's pretty body confident. I mean, she has a right to, but it will be fun to design for natural breasts again." He grinned. "Or any breasts, for that matter."

Ford got a text from Ambrose, and he chuckled at the image of Olivia sweaty and spent across Ambrose's chest. The attachment was what he had been waiting for. The pride was expanding, and they wanted kids. The house needed an expansion, and Ambrose had one ready to go.

Yemeen looked over at the screen. "What's that?"

Ford projected it onto the screen that rose up from the counter. "That one there next to Dexter's? That's your room."

Yemeen glanced over his shoulder. "A little presumptuous."

Ford brought up the image of Olivia, sweaty and sleepy, with a slight smile on her face and her skin flushed. "Really?"

Yemeen started a growl that ended on a whine of need. "Fine."

The expansion would provide quiet spots for Ford and Olivia, as well as some hidden spots that only they could access. Little cuddle spots where no alpha was allowed.

The upper floor was full of bedrooms. The central floor was full of family entertainment spaces, and the main floor was for public access. Ford still had to party, after all. The hidden nest in the basement was for heats. It would have supplies, a communication centre, and a few grosses of condoms. It also would have the ability to lock down the house when they were distracted and vulnerable. That was important. Ford had been caught unawares once, and once was enough.

Olivia walked into the kitchen with Ambrose, and she blinked to see the guys and Yemeen sitting around the table with Ford. "Uh, what's going on? I am not defiling another countertop."

Yemeen's eyebrows hiked. "That sounds interesting."

Dexter chuckled. "You have to be tall."

Yemeen nodded. "I am tall."

Argus brought Olivia a lemonade and kissed her forehead. "You okay, kitten?"

She drank it happily, "Yes. More please."

He kissed her cheek and then pressed his lips to hers. "Hmm. You did drink it all. Good girl, kitten."

She blushed, and Ambrose chuckled.

Yemeen got a curious look on his face, and he reached out to touch her chin, steering her face toward his. She saw his parted lips and winced as he kissed her gently, breathing in the scents from her mouth. He pulled back. "Hmm . . . you did drink it all."

She blushed hot and put her head down on the table, covering her head with her arms. She could still taste Ambrose's cum on her tongue, so she knew they could.

Dexter rubbed her back. "Don't be upset. We are glad that you and Ambrose made up. Will you come home now?"

Ambrose smiled. "She is home. She has come further with a few days with Ford than with weeks at the Omega Centre. They gave her guidance and let her go. When it comes to dealing with Olivia, the pamphlets are useless."

She sighed and mumbled toward the table, "The counselling helped. The writing helped. Being able to learn how to use the tech that everyone took for granted helped. Even getting a bullshit job from Ford helped."

"Uh, honey. That job was real. You are really in the video, and I was even able to put in some of the real alpha chase to get the sense of deadly urgency. Leora is pissing herself with excitement, and so is her label. The twelve seconds I have sent them is having them slobbering with glee."

She looked up. "You are kidding."

Ford shook his head. "I am not kidding. I am the furthest thing from kidding. You were in a video, and there is a lineup of people who want you to do it again. It might not be what you wanted, but it is an actual job, honey. You actually got paid."

She frowned and pulled her phone out of her jeans pocket. She pulled up her account and blinked. "What the actual fuck."

Yemeen appeared stunned at her expression. "That is quite the change."

She glanced at him. "Sex apparently makes me meek and pliable for a while. When something else distracts me, I get back to my practical self."

He met her gaze with eyes so brown they were black. "I like the pliable, cuddly you."

She laughed. "Then, you will have to earn it."

The guys laughed, Ford laughed, and Yemeen looked around, and a slow grin split his features. Dexter nodded and said, "Don't worry. If you need her compliant, we can help."

Argus blinked. "I am out of that. I will take care of her however she comes and with whomever."

She blushed and gave him a glance. "Thanks, Argus. My hero."

"Ah, speaking of, I have an invitation to Paul's engagement party. They issued the invitation to the pride, so everyone here is invited."

Olivia froze. "You are kidding, right? They . . . are not going to like my presence there."

"If they offer insult, we drive back."

"Are you going to tell them I am coming?"

"Paul and Emily and maybe Uncle Derek. No one else."

She nodded. "When is it?"

"Next weekend. If you want to skip it, we can."

"Can I video chat with Emily?"

Argus smiled. "Sure."

"If she is okay with it, I will go." She pulled a lock of her hair around. "I am gonna need a trim, though. My split ends have split ends."

Yemeen smiled. "I may be of assistance there. Before I was a designer, I was a hairstylist. Anyone has any scissors, a spray bottle, and a comb?"

Ford nodded. "Sure." Ford got up and collected the items and a few other things that he thought might be needed.

The other three looked at each other, but they didn't say anything. They were serious about allowing Yemeen in. Physical care of the omega was reserved for the pride. They could do it or arrange it, but the omega was in their hands.

She shivered, and when she was seated away from the kitchen table with a smooth towel around her shoulders, she laughed. "My aunt did this once. My mom had to hold me down."

Argus chuckled. "I volunteer to hold you if you get squirmy."

"The order is usually reversed. I get squirmy when you are holding me."

Yemeen brushed, combed, and then started trimming her hair, one piece at a time. She breathed deep, surrounded by sweet almonds.

"When was the last time you had your hair trimmed? There is a weird pattern here."

"Oh, six months ago. I did it with a kitchen knife." She snorted. "For some reason, she thought scissors would be too dangerous."

Argus lifted his head. "How is that going, by the way?"

"She has been charged with unlawful confinement, abuse, negligence, financial abuse, fraud, profiting from human trafficking, and hate crimes. Her lawyer is having seizures to avoid going into court to arraignment. The second that it is formal, the press is going to go insane." She sighed.

Yemeen frowned. "How did she incur those charges?"

"Me. The way she treated me. She was just following a pattern, so you can guess how much fun my father was. So, this is why the therapy."

Dexter shuddered. "When I heard about the damage, I puked. So did several of the med team."

Ambrose growled, and Dexter winced. "Sorry."

"It's fine, Dex."

Yemeen continued working and asked casually, "What damage?"

Ambrose sighed. "It healed, but . . ."

As he explained, Yemeen kept working until he had to stop and take a break. When he finished, he nodded and got back on his feet, finishing the cut and then massaging her scalp.

She started her heavy purr, and he paused before he chuckled. "I have never heard a woman with a purr so developed."

She shrugged. "I have had a lot of practice." She stopped her purr.

He frowned. "Did I do something wrong?"

"I thought you didn't like it. I know it is primarily a masculine trait."

"It just startled me. I like it. I like it a lot." He purred to her while he kept massaging her scalp.

Her purr returned and blended with his. His pitch was different than her other guys.

When he finished rubbing her head, she was limp, and the air smelled like peach nectar.

He tilted her head back and gave her a kiss upside-down, his lips taking her lower lip between them and plucking it gently. She exhaled a whine of need as her sex clenched hard. Nothing turned her on more than careful handling, except rough handling and any handling, really.

She smiled up at him, and her purr still thrummed along. His upside-down grin showed her something that she hadn't thought was possible. He wants to come to her not out of pity but just because of who and what she was.

At this moment, with her guys, Ford, and now Yemeen around her . . . she was enough.

Author's Note

So, this is the first of a series of books about the omegas that are found in places no one has bothered to look. Olivia was my Cinderella. She needed a better ending than her start . . . so I hope I wrote it.

I expected this book to be over and done in one shot . . . but that didn't happen. So, stay tuned for the second instalment, the third book is already written (I wrote them out of order). Hah.

About the Author

Viola Grace (aka Zenina Masters) is a Canadian sci-fi/paranormal romance writer with ambitions to keep writing for the rest of her life. She specializes in short stories because the thrill of discovery, of all those firsts, is what keeps her writing.

An artist who enjoys a story that catches you up, whirls you around, and sets you down with a smile on your face is all she endeavours to be. She prefers to leave the drama to those who are better suited to it, she always goes for the cheap laugh.

In real life, she is now engaged in beekeeping, and her adventures can be found on the YouTube channel, Mystery Bees Apiary. Just look for the cartoon kittens.